FALSE START

an
Assignment: Romance
novel

Barbara Valentin

To my husband, who taught me that running down a dream is a marathon, not a sprint.

PROLOGUE

———

"My weaknesses have always been food and men—in that order."
– Dolly Parton

Of all the things to say to a bride-to-be on her wedding day, "You have no business wearing that skinny minidress with your full figure and in a church!" isn't one of them.

But Mattie had other things to worry about besides her Aunt Viv's chiding. The ceremony was scheduled to start in two minutes, and the church, overflowing with three shades of fragrant peonies and more than a hundred well-adorned guests, was missing just one thing. The groom.

"I'm sure he'll be here any minute," Claudia, the matron of honor, promised with all of the sincerity of a used-car salesman.

Claudia never did like Eddie. When she learned the object of her baby sister's lifelong, one-sided crush had finally balled up and proposed, she made every attempt to hide her disdain. Almost.

"All people can be divided into two groups, Mattie—givers and takers. You are a giver. Eddie is a taker." Claudia said this so frequently, Mattie expected to see it cross-stitched on a pillow as a wedding gift.

Maybe she was right. Against Eddie's smoldering good looks and irresistible charm Mattie's better judgment abandoned her. Even now, with her stomach in knots, she still made excuses for him.

"Maybe he overslept and had a flat tire on his way to the church. And he forgot to charge his cell phone. And he's having another one of his migraines. And, and, and…"

Claudia rolled her eyes. "Whatever."

The dimly lit storage closet-turned-bridal-room at St. Matthias church felt claustrophobic even in the best of circumstances. Unable to pace back and forth to ease her anxiety, Mattie snuck a frantic peek into the church. Her wide-set eyes swept the pews like a pair of heat-guided missiles seeking their target, scanning the area in front of the altar where Father Bennet stood waiting. At his side was the one element of the wedding to which Mattie did not agree. In fact, she vehemently protested but to no avail.

Nick DeRosa. Why Eddie chose his estranged twin brother over any of his esteemed colleagues at his LaSalle Street investment firm, she had no idea. The awkwardness of their greeting the night before was matched only by its impropriety. Mistaking him for Eddie, Mattie had pulled his face down to hers and, with all of the exuberance of a jubilant bride-to-be, planted a passionate kiss on his surprised lips.

That he had the same chiseled Mediterranean features and wore his chestnut-colored locks in the same style as his brother's was hardly her fault.

That he kissed her back was his.

Hours later, as she was leaving the rehearsal dinner, Nick managed to confirm, if not worsen, the bride-to-be's opinion of him when she overheard him ask Eddie, "Why do you want to marry somebody like Mattie?"

Somebody like Mattie.

Taken out of context, that question could be twisted any number of malicious ways, and twist it Mattie did. But, given that she was less than a day away from becoming Mrs. Eduardo DeRosa, co-owner of a custom-built Gold Coast penthouse and a cherry red Ferrari, she simply added the insult to the already long list of offenses Nick had incurred against her over the years and filed it away for future reference.

Squinting at the spot in which the groom was supposed to be standing, Mattie discovered her veil did little to obscure the obvious. Eddie was indeed missing. She stared so long and so hard, hoping to will him into existence, that Nick frowned at her, glanced behind him, and delivered an awkward wave.

Oh, puh-leeze. How he could possibly share the same DNA as his brother was beyond Mattie's comprehension.

"It's 2:15." Claudia's voice slapped her back to the present.

"I'm sure he'll be here any minute," Mattie heard herself say. But this time, even she didn't believe it.

She turned her gaze to the window, panic welling up inside of her. Seeing the black limousine parked at the curb decked out with ribbons, more flowers, and a professionally hand-painted "Just Married" sign affixed to the back bumper, she whispered, "I don't understand."

She was so thrilled when Eddie proposed that she offered to take care of everything, right down to the color of the bowties he and the groomsmen would wear. Figuring her bills would become their bills post-nuptials, she adopted Eddie's own mantra of "only the best" when selecting the flowers, the photographer, and the Drake Hotel for their reception.

Curiously, the honeymoon was the only thing Eddie insisted on handling. He wouldn't even tell her where they were going.

Claudia gripped Mattie by her bare shoulders. "Nobody can get hold of him. He's not coming, honey. I'll go tell Father Bennet. Wait here." Before leaving, she took her sister's chin in her hand and asked, "You OK?"

Mattie nodded. When she heard the door click shut behind her, she turned and faced her reflection in the full-length mirror. She had starved herself for weeks to fit into the Vera Wang gown she had dreamed of wearing before Eddie even slipped the two-carat diamond on her finger. Despite the weeks of deprivation, it took only a few seconds to convince herself that her Aunt Viv was right—she looked like a sausage stuffed into a casing of silk taffeta and hand-sewn mother-of-pearl beading. The singsong rhythm of cruel childhood taunting echoed in her ears.

Fatty Mattie, Fatty Mattie, Fatty Mattie...

The more she stared, the more her chin and lower lip started to quiver. She closed her eyes and tried to make the nightmare disappear.

It was 2:33. She stood there frozen, waiting for Claudia. In the stillness of the unventilated room, filled with hymnals, vestments, and choir robes, there was nothing left for her to do but let the truth sink in. Eddie didn't oversleep, get the time wrong, or have a flat tire on his way to the church.

He had stood her up.

An uncharacteristic darkness settled over her as she envisioned him writhing in pain from one of his debilitating migraines. She was surprised and somewhat disturbed by how much the image lifted her spirits.

As Mattie stood transfixed, the corset underneath her gown started constricting around her midsection like a lace-covered python. Her head began to swirl. Questions started racing through her mind. How could she have misread the cues? Was she that desperate? A combustible mix of despair and fury began to well up inside of her.

Where's Claudia?

She needed her help to get out of her gown, out of the church, and out of this nightmare.

Almost on cue, Mattie heard the door open behind her, but it was a male voice that spoke her name in a low, apologetic tone. "Mat-"

As she delivered a two-carat-weighted left hook to his perfect chin, she felt the fifteen silk-covered buttons holding her bodice together pop with the force of champagne corks.

"Take that you son of a —"

She took a step back. With buttons ricocheting off the walls, the windows, and the mirror, she wondered aloud, "Why aren't you wearing the white bowtie?"

CHAPTER ONE

———

"One cannot think well, love well, sleep well, if one has not dined well."
– Virginia Woolf

"Come on you hunk of junk. I'm on deadline."

When she worked at the *Wall Street Journal*, Mattie Ross, investigative reporter extraordinaire, took for granted that she had the latest technology at her disposal. But here, under the flickering lights of the *Chicago Gazette's* newsroom, she sat waiting for her dated laptop to show signs of life. As she glared at the screen, the fingers of her left hand undressed a large bar of imported Swiss chocolate. To her right, a small vat of coffee emitted wisps of caffeinated steam. She blew over the rim and took a sip just as the future museum exhibit prompted her to log on. It was Monday morning, and *The Plate Spinner,* one of the *Gazette's* most popular features, was on the clock.

Letting the hot liquid warm her mouth before it slid down her throat, she opened her pseudonym's inbox. At least a dozen emails had arrived overnight. Some were from fans of the seemingly perfect working parent and multi-tasking guru. Some were from harried working parents, asking for advice. Some were from loyal readers either complaining about or complimenting her on advice given in previous columns.

Mattie loathed them all.

Unlike Carlotta Crenshaw, the original author of *The Plate Spinner* column, she was not married, did not have kids and couldn't multi-task her way out of a paper bag. On the contrary. She had sworn off men, was drowning in debt, and routinely tested the limits of the American Heart Association's guidelines on red wine and dark chocolate consumption.

If only Eddie DeRosa hadn't re-entered her life when he did. She was on the cusp of fulfilling her dream to become one of the top journalists at the iconic financial news publication. When the Chicago bureau chief assigned her the task of flushing out allegations of shady transactions at Chicago's oldest investment firm, she could almost feel the Pulitzer Prize gold medal in her hands.

But that all changed the minute she stepped foot in the firm's swanky offices high atop the corner of LaSalle and Monroe to begin her investigation. Eddie greeted her personally with a warm hug. Having not heard from him since college, he was the last person she expected to see. What didn't surprise her was that he still had the power to melt her steely resolve faster than a stick of butter in a hot frying pan.

While writing a searing expose on Eddie's well-calculated crimes would have gone a long way towards exacting revenge on the man who left her at the altar after six of the happiest months of her life, by the time she had come to her senses, he was long gone, and she was out of a job.

Never again.

Mattie snapped off a hunk of the exquisitely smooth chocolate and shoved it in her mouth.

Stuck with a mountain of wedding-induced debt, she knew she was lucky to find another job so quickly. Even if it meant filling someone else's place on the lowest rung of the journalism ladder—an advice column. Turns out, her decision to keep her two-carat Tiffany wedding set wasn't such a bad one after all.

Mattie sat back in her chair and stared at her faux marriage prop, watching the prism of colors dance off of it before giving it a quick buff against her pant leg.

Narrowing her eyes, she mulled which email to open first.

Only two piqued her interest. One was a request for the chicken recipe that she mentioned in last week's column. The other was a plea for advice from "Stressed in Sycamore."

Since she had left her mother's delectable chicken recipe at home, she decided to go with Stressed—a wise choice since the guilt-ridden, corporate-ladder-climbing mommy's letter proved to be far more entertaining.

Mattie hammered out what she thought was a fitting response.

"Dear Stressed—It is not for me to judge whether you are a bad mother for missing your daughter's third grade poetry recital. Who could blame you for prioritizing your contribution to a high-profile corporate merger over sitting in a tiny chair next to other grinning parents, knees tucked under their chins while their little ones recited rhymes that took them days, if not weeks, to memorize? Truth be told, you have effectively taught her a valuable lesson: in life, we all experience rejection at one point or another. Better that she learn to get over the sting of it while she's young. If hurt feelings persist, perhaps you can parlay some of that handsome bonus you received into a new American Girl doll."

"Boy are we gonna hear about that one."

Startled, Mattie turned to see her editor, Dianne Devane, peering over her shoulder.

While she dished out the advice, Dianne had the pleasure of fielding the inevitable rebuttals from parenting organizations, the American Pediatric Association, and high-ranking school district officials.

And this response would be no exception.

"That's the goal, isn't it?" Mattie quipped. Looking back at her laptop, she asked, "Any openings in Metro yet?"

The transplanted Manhattanite leaned against the edge of Mattie's desk careful not to knock over more props—several framed pictures of smiling children and a ruggedly handsome man.

Ignoring her question, Dianne asked, "Is everything all right, Sweetie? You seem out of sorts."

Dianne called everyone "Sweetie" unless she didn't like them, and then it was "Putz."

"I've been writing this column for almost two years, Dianne. When you hired me, you said it would be temporary."

She lowered her voice and added, "Until you could find someone who was really married and had kids."

"Has it been two years already? Time flies when your circulation just keeps growing."

Mattie sat up in her chair. "Dianne, I'm serious. I'll be the first to admit that I needed a place to hide out for a while after, well, you know. And I'm grateful you hired me. I am. But I'm ready to come out of hiding. You know, with my own byline. My own life…"

She studied Mattie and gave her back a quick rub. "Sorry. No can do, sweetie. Your problem is that you're too good at what you do."

Standing up, Dianne announced, "Come on. Let's celebrate your success at the spa this Saturday. My treat. We can spend the whole day there. Massages, hair, nails. What do you say? Blake and the kids are going to visit his parents in the Hamptons this weekend. This would give me the perfect excuse not to join them."

Mattie mulled the veiled bribe while she twirled a strand of her untamed curls. She knew she could definitely use some pampering, but with the added weight she'd put on since her rather traumatic humiliation, the thought of letting a stranger knead her bare skin made her shudder.

Through an apologetic smile, Mattie said, "Thanks, but you know what would really help me?"

"Name it."

"A raise." Plastering a big cheesy grin across her face, she clasped her hands in front of her and added, "Please, please, please."

Dianne chuckled. "Sorry, sweetie. I don't hold the purse strings. You want a raise, you're going to have to take it up with the big guy." She pointed her finger towards the ceiling.

"God?" Mattie teased.

"Close enough," Dianne laughed. "You know I mean Lester Crenshaw. Although, if you ask me, he's more devil than deity."

A shiver went down Mattie's spine at the mere mention of the publisher's name. While she had never met him, she did not relish the thought of confronting such a powerful figure.

"And heaven help you finding an open slot on his calendar," Dianne continued. "That man has more appointments than the Pope."

She had just turned to leave the already cramped cubicle when a slight delivery boy blocked her exit. Fumbling with a large box and a clipboard, he asked, "Plate Spinner?"

Dianne looked down on him and said, "No, not even close. Here's your girl."

Mattie stood up, took the parcel from him, jiggled it slightly, and then set it on her desk. "Oh goodie. Another slow cooker."

Mystified, Dianne asked, "How can you be so sure? Judging by the size of the box, it could be a Smart Car."

"Because it's the fourth one I've gotten since I wrote that column on how my life would be so much easier if I could just get my hands on a programmable slow cooker."

"What was it last month? Blenders?"

"Smoothie makers," Mattie corrected. "My apartment is starting to look like an appliance store. And I hate carrying these things home on the train."

"Donate them," Dianne laughed. "Or, better yet, sell them on eBay."

And just like that, she turned and left, reminding Mattie of the Cheshire Cat in *Alice in Wonderland*.

* * *

Arriving at her train stop that evening, Mattie hoisted the slow cooker box into her arms and apologized to everyone she bumped into on her way down the steps that deposited her at the corner of Fullerton and Sheffield.

Her cheeks burned in the cool fall air that carried with it the tantalizing aroma of basil-laced tomato sauce, covered with imported mozzarella on a crispy bed of butter and cornmeal crust.

Her inner food slut moaned, "Melvin's."

Ducking into the purveyor of the best deep-dish pizza in the city, she set the box on the counter with a huff.

A perky blonde greeted her with a sugary smack of enthusiasm, "Hey Mattie. What can I get you today?"

"Hi Trish. The usual. Only this time, make it a large and could you ask one of the guys to bring it by?" Patting the box, she stated the obvious. "I've got my hands full tonight."

Handing over her credit card, she added, "And throw in a pint of gelato too, please."

Holding the card in midair, Trish asked. "Chocolate or pistachio?"

Mattie gave her a knowing look.

"What was I thinking?" Trish laughed. "Chocolate, it is."

She handed back the credit card and sent Mattie on her way with the promise of a dinner she shouldn't eat to an apartment she couldn't afford, and carrying a slow cooker she didn't want, all the while thinking of a marriage that could have been.

* * *

Nick DeRosa planted his feet on the edge of the red spray-painted line that served as the first mile marker at the Illinois High School Association's boys' cross-country state meet. Peering down the trail that wound through Peoria's Detwieler Park, he checked the stopwatch cupped in the palm of his hand. The bright green numbers flashed "4:20."

"Where are they?" he whispered.

Standing within earshot, a trim man, fiftyish with a casual, but well-appointed air about him edged closer and replied, "Must be the mud, Coach."

Nick glanced at his unofficial assistant Lester Crenshaw, publisher of the Griffin Media Group's *Chicago Gazette*. Like Nick, he was a former all-American runner, but Lester was also the proud father of the team's number seven man.

Before he could respond, Nick felt the ground begin to rumble as two hundred high school boys charged toward them.

Backing away, he handed his stopwatch to Lester, pulled a pen out from behind his ear, lifted his clipboard from under his arm, and shouted, "Give me the times."

Lester didn't miss a beat.

"5:05, 5:15, 5:26, 5:45, 5:48, 6:10, 6:40."

When the last Knollwood Knight flew past them, the two men started marching across a manicured field toward the second mile marker. The sky had cleared after the early morning shower but neither took notice of the brilliant fall colors surrounding them.

"Think we'll place?" Lester ventured as he hurried after Nick whose strides were nearly double in length to his own.

Nick stopped and turned to face him. "Like I tell my guys, it's not about winning. It's about doing their best. If they place, they place. If they don't, they don't."

He watched Lester's eyes rove from his worn shoes to his frayed cap, noting the disappointment he had in his "hometown hero" almost as clearly as if Lester had spoken it out loud. "You know, Coach, some parents seem to think you're too soft on the guys. I think they miss Burt's ironfisted approach."

"Is that right? I'd like to see them survive the workouts I put these guys through."

He left Lester in his wake as he continued his stomp across the field, trying to shake off the ghost of his former coach, even if he did give him a job when no one else would.

By the time he reached the two-mile marker, Nick had calmed down enough to realize that Lester was right. Their coaching methods were not the same. Where Burt Stoltz, an iconic figure in the field of high school boys' cross-country, had focused on punishing workouts to build up his runners' physical strength, Nick believed the greater reward came from building up their emotional strength.

Catching up to Nick well before the hoards of other parents, coaches, and well-wishers, Lester checked the time on the stopwatch against the numbers flashing on the big digital timer on the opposite side of the trail.

Turning to Nick he said, "I hope you know I don't share in their opinion. I'll never be able to thank you enough for all that you've done for Bobby. For us."

Nick frowned at him. "What are ya talkin' about? Bobby's a great kid."

Lester slapped him on the back. "Yes, but you are an amazing coach. You are. I don't care what anybody else thinks.

When his mother and I divorced, that was really hard on him. Just a couple of months ago, he was frail, bullied, and starting to self-destruct. But look at him now. He's a varsity cross-country runner. Never thought I'd see the day. They ought to call you 'The Transformer.'"

Nick shook his head and thought about Bobby. He first met the boy when he caught him trying to swipe a stack of hall passes from the teachers' lounge. There was something about his manner that reminded Nick of his own twin brother. Like Bobby, Eddie didn't feel that the rules applied to him, so he broke them. Often. And, like Eddie, who bought his popularity by selling exam answer sheets that he had stolen after hacking into the school district's database, Bobby thought the only way he could get people to like him was by selling them a hall pass.

Like so many high school underdogs, all they needed was the right combination of discipline and positive feedback. So, instead of regretting for the thousandth time that he didn't do more to get Eddie to join the cross-country team with him their freshman year in high school, Nick gave Bobby an ultimatum—join the team or face disciplinary action. Thankfully, Bobby chose the former.

Lester's voice sliced through the brisk autumn air like half-inch spikes through a hard-packed dirt course. "You have a tremendous gift for bringing out the very best in people, you know that?"

"Yeah, well tell that to the school board for me, will ya?"

Leaning closer, Lester asked, "Why? What happened?"

Nick lowered his voice. "If we don't finish in the top three today, they're gonna pull my contract."

Lester winced and drew a deep breath. He was well aware of the hard road Nick had to travel to get where he was. "How can they expect that after just one season?"

"Well, they hired me when no one else would, didn't they? But I know a lot of board members aren't willing to leave the past in the past."

Patting him on the shoulder, Lester did his best to sound encouraging. "Ah, screw them. Hell, you're the Comeback Kid, remember?"

Taking in a deep sigh, Nick said, "Not yet, I'm not."

Lester chuckled. "Are you kidding? Look at what you've been through. Your own twin steals your identity, you're accused of a crime you didn't commit, you lose everything, you exonerate yourself, and you manage to convince your old high school coach to let you take over when he announces his retirement. You've been to hell and back, kid."

Nick looked down at his mud-covered shoes and thought of his tiny Bucktown apartment and the fact that he still had to borrow his mother's old Buick sedan whenever he had to drive anywhere.

"No. I'm not back yet. I'm not even at the door."

Remembering the days when, as team captain, he led the same team to first place three years in a row, he mumbled, "I just need one good win."

Staring toward the spot in the woods out of which the runners would soon burst, he stood tall among the crowd of spectators surrounding him. A curious mix, to be sure. For each skinny teenage runner with a number pinned to his chest, there appeared to be at least two middle-aged adults who evidently hadn't broken a good sweat on a regular basis, on purpose for quite some time.

He heard Lester chuckle beside him. "Man, oh man. If you could do for some of these folks what you've done for the guys on the team—and charge them for the privilege—you'd have enough cash to wipe out the national debt. Why, I bet-"

"No offense, but I've had my fill of adults bent on making stupid decisions."

The image of a particular auburn-haired woman with a fierce left hook emerged from a remote corner in his mind.

Before Lester could reply, Nick announced, "Here they come."

After recording the boys' splits, they made their way to the finish line. There, amid all of the screaming bystanders, Lester yelled, "Care to make a wager?"

Nick's eyes widened. "You know that's against the rules."

Lester laughed. "No, not on the meet. On you."

Narrowing his eyes, Nick replied, "I'm listening."

Looking as if he was about to sell black market plutonium to a third world arms dealer, Lester checked to make sure no one was eavesdropping on their conversation. When he was satisfied, he motioned for Nick to lean down, and spoke into his ear. "You take an unfit adult, of my choosing, and train them to run in the Chicago Marathon next October. If they finish, I'll cut you a check that will be more than enough to get you back on your feet again.

Nick stood up straight and frowned. "I don't follow."

Lester smiled, spread his hands out before him like a game show host and announced, "Nick DeRosa, personal running coach."

Nick narrowed his eyes and asked, "What's the catch?"

"No catch. Just lots of free publicity." Under his breath, Lester murmured, "And a boost in revenue for the paper."

As the boys started appearing over the last rise before the final approach, Nick, still not entirely convinced, mulled the proposal. He himself had run a number of marathons, but training someone to do it? It was all he could do to get high school boys to train for three-mile races.

The crowd's excitement grew in intensity as the boys began to appear in the distance. The slow rise of the last stretch was always the most demanding. If one teammate ran out of steam now, the whole team would suffer. When Nick was in their spiked and muddied shoes, this was his favorite part of the race. Adrenaline would start pulsing through his veins, and he'd surge through the crowd of weary runners, crossing the finish line on a hidden reserve of power known as "the kick."

It was hard to teach this concept to other runners. Either you had it or you didn't. Some races you had it, others you didn't. But, no matter how far back Nick had gotten during the course of the race, he always managed to come back from behind and carry his team to victory.

The Gazette was the first to dub him the "Comeback Kid" when he carried his team to the State finals for the first of three consecutive championships. It was the best time of his life. Nick knew the Gazette followed his every move. His mother had collected scrapbooks full of clippings to prove it. But the last time he made the papers, the Gazette used his unofficial title to magnify his disgrace: "Comeback Kid Jailed."

God, I hate reporters.

After the team roared across the finish line with times good enough to garner fifth place, Lester pressed a business card into Nick's hand and said, "Think it over then come see me.

* * *

Where's Claudia?

Mattie expected her sensible, happily wedded sister to stop by any minute. Ten years older with an "I told you so" always at the ready, Claudia was the last person she wanted to see on her day off. Still, Mattie knew she was her only trusted source for all things married and maternal. Besides, her column on gift ideas for kids' athletic coaches was not going to write itself.

While she waited, she read the label of a rather large chocolate bar from Benziger's, a local chocolate maker. A glowing endorsement from Mattie in column on holiday gift ideas had saved the struggling company from bankruptcy. To show their appreciation, they enrolled her in their bar-of-the-month club.

This is so much better than a slow cooker.

"Deliciously smooth chocolate flavor that melts into the crunch of sweet caramel highlighted by bursts of savory sea salt."

She picked it up and inhaled. A small groan escaped her lips. Then, in a practiced move, she flipped it over and read the calorie count. Four hundred and twelve.

Hello, dinner.

She closed her eyes and held the bar to her forehead, but the tick of the clock invaded her senses. The plain round wall-mounted fixture was identical to the one in the bridal room at St. Matthias. Both clocks moved unnervingly slow and emitted an annoying tick-tock.

Mattie sat frozen in her chair, defenseless, as the Technicolor images came flashing back. The beautiful blue sky, the deep green leaves on the mature trees in front of the church unfurled in the afternoon sun. Claudia, in a periwinkle taffeta tea-length dress, was followed by Mattie's nephew, itching to get out of his size six-X black ring bearer's tuxedo. Her own gown making her feel like a movie star.

She had eaten nothing but radishes and hummus for weeks, but it was so worth it. For the first time in her life, she felt beautiful. It was unfortunate that her satisfaction was so short-lived.

Putting the chocolate bar down with a resolute slam, she pressed her fingers to her temples and gritted her teeth, but the memories kept coming.

"Such an idiot," she whispered, feeling the same panic and self-loathing that set in as the big hand on the clock kept ticking off the minutes despite the groom's absence. With each tick that tocked by, she felt the same nagging doubt that used to wash over her whenever Eddie cancelled a date at the last minute or forgot to make a promised phone call.

A loud buzz brought her back to the present.

Mattie sprang up, pushed the button on her intercom, and, with as much enthusiasm as she could muster, sang out, "Who is it?"

"It's a little early for martinis, isn't it?"

Mattie checked her watch and said, "Um, no Claud, not really. It's four o'clock. Come on up."

She assessed the condition of her apartment. Situated on the top floor of a two-story house, she knew she only had a few harried moments to pick up. After stacking the cookbooks she had left scattered on her living room floor and hiding her Michael Bolton CDs, she darted into the tiny kitchen. The garbage can, overstuffed with a pizza box, an empty bottle of cheap Merlot, and used tissues, had to go. Deciding that she didn't have enough time to run it down the back stairwell to the dumpster, she zipped into her bedroom, shoved it into her walk-in closet and closed the door just in time to hear her sister's knock.

"Come on in."

Claudia burst into the living room, pulled off her scarf and gave her sister a quick hug. "What did I tell you about leaving your door unlocked?"

"Please. I knew you were coming," Mattie explained. "And I always keep the outside entrance locked. That's why I gave you a key, remember? Besides, with Mrs. Driscoll downstairs, nobody's gonna mess with me. I think she's a retired warden from Stateville penitentiary."

"Well, if you ask me, she looks like Mrs. Claus."

"Yeah, Mrs. Claus packing heat," Mattie retorted.

Laughing, Claudia surveyed the bar of chocolate on the kitchen table.

"Tell me that's not your dinner. When are you going to learn that all the chocolate in the world is not going to make what Eddie did—"

Mattie pointed a finger at her. "Let's not say *that* name again."

"Sorry. I forgot."

"Whatever."

Mattie loved her sister despite her occasional verbal lapses and the fact that, even after giving birth to three children in four years, she was still thin as a rail.

Settling onto the floral-print overstuffed couch, Claudia leaned back, closed her eyes and asked, "Okay, what is the Plate Spinner covering this time? Getting a gift for your kid's coach?"

"Yep. Hang on a sec." Mattie sat back down at her table and, hands poised over her laptop keyboard, said, "OK, shoot."

"Well for starters, plan ahead. Don't wait until the last minute like I did. Today was the last day of the fall soccer season, and, since no one else volunteered to take up a collection for the coach, Tom and I had to ask all of the other parents if they wanted to contribute. Then during half time, I flew over to Malcolm's—you know that new steak place on Walnut—to get him a gift card. Only they don't open until 11, so I decided to zip over to the sporting goods store on the other side of the street, and who did I see but…"

Eyes bright, Claudia sat up before she continued. "Come on. Ask me. You'll never guess."

Mattie looked up from her laptop and shook her head. "I have no idea."

Claudia started giving her hints. "Tall, good-looking, dark hair, wearing a—oh what do you call those things?" She started pantomiming as if she had something dangling from her neck.

Mattie stared at her, shrugged her shoulders, and said, "Necktie, police whistle…really, I have no idea."

Undeterred, Claudia continued, "I still say he was sweet on you."

Mattie forced a nervous laugh. "Oh, like that narrows it down."

Pulling out all the stops, Claudia leaned toward her and delivered her final clue. "You can barely see the scar anymore."

Slapping on her best poker face, Mattie felt her heart drop into her stomach and her throat begin to tighten.

Pity.

She started twirling her married-with-kids costume accessory under the table.

Claudia let out an exasperated sigh and sank back into the couch. "Forget it. I don't know why I even bother."

"Can we keep going, please? You left off at the sporting goods store. Did you get the kids' coach a gift card there? What happened next? Did the team give it to him or the parents?"

But Claudia wasn't ready to move on. "It wasn't Nick's fault you-know-who did what he did. He was just the messenger. And you decked him for it."

Mattie bit her lip. She could still hear the sound of her buttons ricocheting off of the walls, the windows, and mirror in the bridal room at St. Matthias's when her fist made contact with his chin.

Hell hath no fury…

"He was just in the wrong place at the wrong time," she replied with a shrug.

Narrowing her eyes, Claudia studied her sister. "I still think you're pinning the blame on the wrong DeRosa."

"Claud, I am not going through this with you again." But she couldn't help herself. "I'm not saying Eddie—well, you know what?" Mattie held up both hands in the air before continuing, "I've wasted enough breath on that man."

"Halleluiah," Claudia sang out.

"But Nick?" Mattie continued, "I'm not letting him off so easy. I mean, the night before our wedding, I overheard him ask Eddie 'what do you want to marry a girl like that for?'"

She looked at her sister with both eyebrows raised. "Who does that? I don't care if the guy made it to the Olympics. He had no right to put me down like that. He doesn't even know me. Our whole lives, he always looked right through me like I wasn't even there."

Taking a deep breath, she continued. "Then when Eddie didn't show up for the wedding—I can only assume he had second thoughts. Why else would Nick, of all people, go out of his way to deliver the news to me personally? Talk about smug. He's lucky I just punched him in the face."

Claudia leaned forward. "I'm sorry, kiddo. You never heard from either of them again, did you?"

Do you mean besides the message Nick left, asking that I vouch for him with the Cook County Sheriff's department?

"No. And to hell with them both." Mattie tried focusing on the draft of her column before mumbling, "I can fix this up later."

Eager for a change of subject, she continued, "Hey, how are the kids? Sorry I missed trick-or-treating with them. Their costumes looked great, though. That picture was a big hit with my readers."

"They're fine. You're the one I'm worried about."

Mattie waved her off.

"I just want you to be happy."

"I'm fine."

"Right. Let's see. You live alone, if you ask me, you drink too much and the only vegetables you ever eat are on the top of a pizza. Yet, at work, you're passing yourself off as this successful career woman who is happily married with kids. This isn't healthy. You're hiding behind the column. And that ring." She pointed to Mattie's hand in disgust.

"I'm happy. I am. Deliriously. I love my job, where I live…"

Claudia ignored her. "It's been almost two years, Mat. It's time to move on. You're still young. You've got to start living your own life on your terms. There's plenty of fish in the sea."

Considering her sister's uncanny ability to channel their deceased mother, Mattie almost expected her to add, "Why a pretty girl like you, you could have any man you wanted if you just slimmed down a bit."

In response, Mattie shut her laptop with a little more force than she intended. Unfazed, Claudia continued with her rant.

"Besides, what do you think is going to happen if the paper gets wind of the fact that their latest 'Plate Spinner' is just a fabrication? I'm not sure, but I think what you've been doing for the past couple of years here, Mat, is fraud."

Mattie waved her off. "You worry too much. No one's going to find out that I'm not married, and that I don't have kids. Dianne's got my back at work. I've got all my bases covered. She promised to find a replacement, and, when she does, I'll get my own column and that will be that.

She neglected to tell Claudia that her desk was cluttered with pictures of her husband, Tom Bragassi, a paramedic, and all of the little Bragassis, ranging in age from six years to six months.

Picking up a pile of bills, Claudia started rifling through them. "And what about these?" Maybe it's about time you sold that rock and took care of your debts."

Mattie snatched them away before Claudia saw the envelope from First Midwestern Bank that contained yet another overdraft notice.

"No way. I have to wear it at work. Besides, it helps me ward off the wrong sort."

Claudia pounced. "Yes, but it wards off all sorts, Mat— even the good kind."

Softening her tone she added, "You know you always have a home with us, right?"

"Thanks, sis. I appreciate it, but I've got everything under control."

Skepticism oozed from Claudia's expression.

Mattie stood and pulled what used to be an oversized sweatshirt down over her hips. "I do, really. As a matter of fact, I have a meeting first thing Monday morning with the publisher, and I'm going to demand a raise."

And, I know just what to wear. If it still fits.

* * *

What Mattie knew of Lester Crenshaw she did not like. A middle-aged man, he rose quickly through the ranks at the *Gazette*. Once he became publisher, rumor had it, he ditched his wife, a long-time lifestyle columnist at the paper, then had the gall to fire her before marrying a young blond hotshot from accounting.

Talk about a schmuck.

She had thought long and hard about her plan of attack and decided to stoop to his level. It was the only reason she found herself standing outside of his office, in full view of the media company's executive assistant staff, wearing a skin-tight, fire engine red, long-sleeved, high-necked sweater dress and punishing four inch heels.

Nearly immobilized by the amount of spandex that was keeping her curves in check, she leaned back against the wall and checked her watch. It was seven fifty-nine in the morning. Despite their eight o'clock appointment, his office was empty, and the lights were off.

"He should be here any minute," his assistant, Natalie Foster, offered.

After waiting for twenty minutes, Mattie hobbled her way back to her desk and initiated a computer search on how to file for bankruptcy.

By noon, she had resigned herself to the idea of throwing in the towel and moving in with her sister and her family. The bag of potato chips she had for lunch offered little in the way of consolation. By 1:00, she had abandoned her shoes and was finishing a brief, albeit succinct reply to a reader in search of a healthy holiday-coping strategy.

"Dear Wiped, I find the best way to keep my energy high throughout the busy holiday season is to consume copious amounts of caffeine and refined sugar."

"Now I know you're kidding. You are kidding, aren't you?" The gravely edge to Dianne's voice was unmistakable. She peered at Mattie over her reading glasses, waiting for a response.

Mattie stuck out her index finger and pressed the backspace key on her keyboard until it was gone. "Of course."

She made no effort to sound anything other than defeated.

"Well if it means that much to you, leave it in. Go ahead. I can handle the sugar cops at the American Diabetic Association."

Mattie let out a chuckle and turned around. Her eyes were bloodshot and she assumed what was left of her mascara was smudged underneath her lower eyelashes like the paw prints of tiny puppies that had been running through the mud.

Dianne hoisted herself onto her usual perch on the desk and whispered, "Oh, this can't be good. How did the meeting with Les go?"

"I waited for twenty minutes. He blew me off."

"Oh, sweetie. He's a busy man." Dianne handed her a tissue.

Mattie pressed it to her eyes. "Yes, and I'm an insecure mess with major rejection issues. First Dad, then Eddie, now Les."

Dianne twirled Mattie's chair around so she was facing her. "Stop it. You're better than this. You're the *Plate Spinner,* for Pete's sake. You should be angry. You had an appointment with him, and he didn't even have the courtesy of letting you know he couldn't make it? You know what I'd do to him if it were me?"

Mattie shook her head.

"I'd called him on it, and I wouldn't drop it until he apologized. Now clean yourself up, march right up to his office, and demand that raise."

"You're right." Taking a deep breath, Mattie stood up, and fluffed her hair. Twirling her ring with her right hand, she nodded at Dianne and said, "I'm not coming back until I have that raise."

Dianne looked skeptical. "Nice try, doll. Now say it like you mean it."

Narrowing her eyes, Mattie clenched her jaw, and tried seething, "I am *not* coming back until I have that raise."

She poked Dianne in the shoulder for good measure.

"Ow. Better, but don't poke."

"Really?"

As Mattie plopped back into her chair to put her shoes back on, a grin started to spread across her face. She clenched her fists in front of her as she broke into a sad attempt at a moonwalk from the comfort of her ergonomically correct office chair.

"Hello, solvency."

"Focus," Dianne scolded. "Demand first. Dance later."

CHAPTER TWO

————

"If you wish to make an apple pie truly from scratch, you must first invent the universe."
– Carl Sagan

Nick, wearing khakis and a tie instead of sweats and a stopwatch, was finding it hard to breathe in the opulent office overlooking Michigan Avenue. A desk big enough to land a plane on. Expensive leather chairs. Built-in book shelves. Dark paneling. The last time he was in an office this stuffy it was to meet with the judge and an official from the Securities and Exchange Commission to defend himself against accusations that he willfully participated in Eddie's pyramid scheme.

The metallic *clink* of the handcuffs the uniformed police officer clasped behind his back echoed in his ears as he stood at the window, watching city workers string holiday lights on the building facades of Chicago's Magnificent Mile. He shook his head as he remembered being in the emergency room after Mattie knocked him out. The doctor had just finished stitching up his chin when the police arrived. His mother never was able to get the bloodstains out of the tuxedo shirt. It cost him fifty bucks to replace it.

I got a bad feeling about this.

After spending the last two weeks contacting old teammates and trainers, trying to sniff out openings for a coaching position at another school, all Nick had to show for it were a lot of empty promises to follow up with him if they heard of anything. Lester's wager seemed like the only game in town.

He sat down on the edge of a chair, knee bouncing, and checked his watch one more time before deciding to make a break for it.

Just as he was about to leave, Lester burst through the door with his hand extended.

"Hey there, Coach. Sorry I'm late. Budget meeting."

Shaking Lester's hand Nick smiled and said, "That's all right. And, as of two weeks ago, it's just Nick."

Lester sat down and clasped his hands behind his head, smiling. "So. Are you in? I'd like to kick this off as a big New Year's Resolution feature right after Christmas." He waved toward his door and added, "We've got a whole media campaign planned."

Nick pulled his chair closer to the desk and let out a short cough. "Um, yeah, but can we go over a few of the details first? I'd like to get this all down on paper so nothing comes back to bite me." He lowered his eyes and added, "I'm sure you understand."

"Sure, sure. Absolutely."

Nick hesitated. This was too easy. "Um, I brought a couple of forms." He handed Lester two sheets of paper. "One's the physical examination form," he explained, "and the other is the waiver we used at the school. I'm sure you've seen them before. The guys have to fill these out before they join the team, so you should have whomever you've picked fill out something like that too, releasing me and the paper from liability should anything happen." He ran his hand through his overgrown wavy hair. "And I think we should draw up a contract."

Lester beamed. "I'm a step ahead of you. I just got this from Legal." He handed a document to Nick with a pen and kept talking while he skimmed it. "You'll be paid the standard consultant rate for the duration. Not a lot, mind you, but enough to keep your head above water. Then, after the marathon, I'll get you that bonus we talked about."

Looking up, Nick replied, "Bonus. Great." He bent his head again to scan the document before signing it.

He handed it back to Lester who winked and said, "I'll have them mail a copy for your files. If you can come back tomorrow, I'll have Finance send up the rest of the forms you'll need to complete."

Nick settled back in his chair. "Sure, I can come back. So, all we need now is a victim. Who'd you have in mind?"

Lester squirmed in his chair. "I've got a few folks in mind."

"Sounds good." At that, Nick stood up and said, "Remember, the clock's ticking. It's almost December. That only gives me about ten months to get somebody marathon ready. That's cutting it close even for a healthy person."

"No worries. I'll have someone for you in a day or two."

Slipping his jacket on, Nick reached over and shook Lester's hand. As he held it, he said, "There's just one more thing."

"Sure. What is it?"

"What if I fail? What if the person you pick out doesn't win? We never talked about that part of the wager."

A warm smile spread over Lester's face. "I never said anything about winning." He pointed his finger at Nick and in a sterner tone added, "But they have to finish."

Feeling as if a weight had been lifted, Nick agreed to return the next day to sign the rest of the paperwork and left feeling much better about the arrangement than when he had arrived.

When he reached the elevators, he pushed the down button and stood with his hands stuffed into the pockets of his weathered bomber jacket. He caught his reflection in the mirrored door, barely recognizing the face that grinned back at him. He hadn't seen that guy in a long, long time. Maybe Lester was right. Maybe he was in the final stretch of his comeback. Maybe the win he so desperately wanted was in sight after all.

The elevator dinged, and he bounced right in front of the doors, waiting for them to open. His mind was filled with the possibilities that lay before him. He had heard of accomplished runners becoming celebrity coaches, holding clinics for wannabe athletes, and making a mint in the process.

Just as he was envisioning a book signing at a running shoe store jammed with fans and potential clients, the elevator doors began to part. He lifted his foot to step in, but before it had the chance to make landfall, a woman burst out and laid his six–foot two-inch frame flat on the carpeted floor, knocking the wind out of him.

For a nanosecond, Nick took in the not unpleasant feel of a woman's warm body pressed against his and the flowery scent of her hair that tickled the spot just under his chin. As she tried to push off of him, he instinctively lifted his knees and attempted to sit up but couldn't move.

"Oh my gosh. I'm so sorry," he heard her gasp. "I seem to be stuck to your zipper."

Nick looked down and saw that the clasp of his zipper had indeed attached itself to the most prominent point of her red sweater dress.

Speaking to the top of her head, he sighed, "That's all right."

At the sound of his voice, the woman's head snapped up, and he found himself face-to-face with, of all people, Mattie Ross.

"What the hell are you doing here?" she gasped.

Nick couldn't help but notice her distress. "Relax."

He let his head drop back against the floor and added, "I'm not my brother. You tagged me yourself, remember?" He pointed to his chin and let his hand drop to his side.

Mattie glanced at the scar that cut a jagged path through the dark stubble.

"Sorry."

What her apology lacked in sincerity it made up for in brevity.

Pinned to the spot, Nick placed his hands under his head and stared at the ceiling as Mattie mounted a furious attempt to extract herself from his jacket with one hand, while propping herself up with the other. When that proved unsuccessful, she tried switching hands, wiggling on top of him, and growing exceedingly frustrated.

It wasn't long before Nick's body began reacting to the onslaught of perfume and pressure, much against his will.

Worse, Mattie noticed.

"What is that?" she huffed. Her voice was thick with disgust.

Mortified, Nick grabbed both of her wrists. With her full weight pressed against him, he grunted her name with all of the breath he could muster. "Mattie."

She whipped her head up, her face just a few inches from his. "What?"

"Calm down. I got it."

He released her wrists and, pressing one hand against her lower back and the other behind her neck, rolled with all his might until he was straddled on top of her. With a quick flick of his fingers, he extracted the latch of his jacket from the intertwined yarn of her dress, leaned back on his heels, and pulled himself up.

Mattie, in the meantime, rolled to her side, propped her four-inch heels in position, and stood while Nick looked on. As she righted herself, his eyes fixed on a strand of yarn dangling haplessly next to the gaping nickel-size hole where his zipper had just been. It provided a generous peek at her ample cleavage, and it was everything he could do not to reach over and tug it.

Following his stare, she let out a small groan before snarling, "Nice. You tore my dress. Thanks a lot."

"You should be more careful getting out of elevators," he advised as he gave his chin a quick rub with the back of his hand. When he turned his back to her to press the down button, he heard her emit a quick growl before stomping off.

On his way down to the lobby, Nick inspected his zipper. The flowery scent that lingered on his coat collar infiltrated his nose. He closed his eyes, inhaled deeply, and whispered to no one in particular, "What the hell are you doing here?"

* * *

The restrooms at the Gazette with their art deco design, dark marble floors, soft lighting, and private stalls still bore the luxurious touches of the newspaper's golden days. Ducking into one situated down the hall from the elevators, Mattie yanked open a stall door, stepped inside, locked it, and took in several deep breaths. Resting her forehead against the cool chrome, she grasped the coat hook affixed to the door just above her head and whispered, "What the hell are you doing here?"

Beads of sweat moistened her forehead. Her cheeks were flushed, and she felt hives beginning to break out under the wool

blend material stretched tightly across her skin. The urge to peel
it off and splash herself with cool water was overwhelming.

The calm she longed for was not coming without a fight.
The too-close-for-comfort encounter with her former fiancé's
body double threatened to stir up a hornet's nest of emotions.

Nick DeRosa.

She tried taking several deep breaths but just felt more
light-headed than she already was.

"Well, at least no one else saw it happen," she thought to
herself. The last thing she needed was another public
humiliation.

When her breathing finally returned to normal, she
forced the image of Nick from her mind and unlocked the door.
After checking to make sure she was alone, she stepped in front
of the mirror.

Holy crap.

Her hair, which she had spent over an hour that morning
trying to smooth, was coiling back into ringlets before her very
eyes. After combing through it with her fingers, she dabbed cold
water on her face, cleared the mascara from under her eyelashes,
and inspected the hole in her dress before tucking the errant
thread back into it.

Looking long and hard at her reflection, she announced
with as much determination as she could muster, "I am not
coming back without a raise."

* * *

For the second time that day, Mattie took the long walk
down the hall leading to the office of the *Gazette's* publisher. She
knocked as loudly as she dared on his door and from within,
heard his voice boom, "Yes?"

Pushing it open, she stepped in, doing her best not to be
intimidated by the man or his office. When she noticed his eyes
zero in on the hole in her dress, she folded her arms high across
her chest and said, "Mr. Crenshaw, I believe we had a meeting,"
and braced herself for his reply.

Lester bounced up like a spring and nearly sprinted around his desk to greet her. "Mattie, is it? I do apologize. How's the, uh, family?"

He looked at her like a lion eyeing a raw steak.

Holding her left hand mid-air, she gave the ring on her finger a twirl and replied, "I'm not here to talk about my family. I'm here to talk about a raise."

In response, Lester sat on the edge of his desk. "Sure, sure. Listen. I have a new, high profile assignment for you. Your readers are going to love it. If you pull it off, I can promise you a very nice bonus, and I'll see what I can do about syndicating that column of yours."

"What?" Caught off guard, Mattie struggled to take a breath, but was prevented from doing so by the ultra-restrictive spandex undergarments. She dropped into the chair that was closest to Lester's desk.

Settling into its warmth, she relaxed, smiled, and said, "I'm listening."

Mattie was well aware of Lester's power to persuade. As Dianne had warned her, "Think of the best chocolate mousse you've ever had. He's that smooth. No. *Smoother*."

Lester didn't disappoint.

He tried complimenting her. "You always had a keen eye for a great story."

If that were true, I wouldn't be here, talking to you now.

He tried commending her. "Think of the example you'll be setting for your readers."

I couldn't care less.

He tried enticing her. "Think of how victorious you'll feel once the new, fit you crosses that finish line."

Possibly.

He kept slinging his pitch until Mattie felt her resolve crumble faster than a warm chocolate chip cookie dunked in cold milk. By the time Lester had finished, she was mesmerized.

Barely aware that the words were coming from her own mouth, she heard herself say, "So all I have to do to get a raise is train for the Chicago Marathon and chronicle my experience?"

Lester nodded, smiling. "All that's standing between you and your dreams is twenty-six point two miles."

Mattie blinked. The spell was broken. "Tell me that's not the tagline for the feature." While he denied it, she could see from his expression that he was seriously considering it. He turned his back to her, looked up, and muttered to the ceiling. "Running down a dream…the long road from buxom to buff…"

Stunned, she cried, "Hey. I'm sitting right here."

Lester turned to face her, looking like a die-hard vegetarian who just got caught scarfing down a cheeseburger. "What?"

Taking a deep breath, Mattie shook her head and said, "You know what? I can see where this is going. Before and after pictures. Publicizing my weight and measurements. Let's turn the fat girl into someone more socially acceptable. I'll pass, thanks."

Standing up, she added, "I need—I *deserve* a raise right now. Not ten months from now."

As she turned her back on him, Lester shot out a rapid-fire reply, barely pausing to take a breath. "I don't see why you would pass on this outstanding opportunity. We'll set you up with your very own trainer, a world class running expert, who will work with you every step of the way. Quite literally. Of course, we're going to advertise it all over the city, but think of the exposure. If this takes off—which I'm sure it will—it'll run in all of our affiliates. You'll be famous. Now, I think that family of yours can do without you for a few hours a day, can't they? All you have to do is put yourself in Coach's hands, and he'll make a new woman out of you."

Mattie was flummoxed. "I think I'm fine just the way I am, thank you very much."

At that, Lester stood up and started ushering her to the door. "Think it over. I want to see your first piece by Thursday." He handed her the sheets of paper Nick had left behind and added, "In the meantime, find some place where you can get a quickie physical, and sign this waiver, all right?"

Just as he placed his hand on the doorknob Mattie stopped him and said, "Hang on. What do you mean a couple of hours a day? And who's 'Coach'?"

* * *

Nick stepped out onto the sidewalk and pulled his jacket collar up against the cold wind that was whistling down Michigan Avenue. He stalked toward the train station as fast as he could manage given the swell of commuters following suit. His mind was swimming with a future he couldn't see, a dream that eluded him, and a woman who had a long track record of driving him absolutely crazy.

He was halfway across the bridge spanning the Chicago River when he stopped cold in his tracks, causing other pedestrians to brush by on either side of him, annoyed at the obstacle he had become.

"There's no way," was all he said before turning and jogging back to the Gazette's building.

By the time he made it to the lobby, he had compiled a list of excuses to back out of the deal if it turned out his hunch was correct. Topping the list was "I can't help people who refuse to help themselves."

Next was, "I'd rather get a job bagging groceries."

Last was, "I've been in love with her since the third grade."

By the time he made it to Lester's office, Nick knew that he would talk him out of the first two. The third, he had no intention of sharing.

He lifted his hand to knock on the door, but paused when he heard Lester's voice boom from the other side, "I think that family of yours can do without you for a few hours a day, can't they?"

That family of yours?

A rush of relief washed over Nick. He let his hand fall to his side and was turning to leave when the person in there with Lester replied, "I think I'm fine just the way I am, thank you very much."

A cold chill ran down his spine. *Mattie? Has a family?*

Nick took a deep breath and was trying to process what he had just heard when the door yanked open from the other side, and she stood before him for the second time in an hour. But this time, she didn't look defiant and flustered. She looked confused and somewhat defeated.

He had seen that look before. If it weren't for Lester beaming behind her, he would've thought he'd walked through a portal in time that dumped him back into the bridal room at St. Matthias.

His eyes swept over her left hand to confirm what he thought he had overheard. There it was. A wedding ring.

Well, I'll be damned...

Taking a step back to let her pass, he heard Lester exclaim, "Nick. Perfect timing. I just found your victim."

Well over a minute went by before anyone spoke. All they could do was stare. Mattie and Nick at each other and Lester at the two of them. Each bore different expressions that somehow managed to convey the same unspoken thought: *This just keeps getting better.*

Lester was the first to break the silence when he burst forth with, "Don't tell me you two know each other."

With no small amount of effort, Mattie pulled her gaze from the same long-lashed hazel eyes that had reeled her in so many times before. Only this time, they were in someone else's body. Someone who didn't think she was good enough to marry his brother.

Why, just the other day, she told the new cashier at the little bakery down the street. The sturdy elderly woman with an eastern European accent sympathized completely.

"He actually zed that to your fiancé? What a *yerk*. And on the eve of your vedding? You poor ting." Handing Mattie a freshly-baked Napoleon, she added, "Dis one's on da house, OK?"

It wasn't the first time Mattie had played the jilted bride card to her benefit. Had she known it would be the last time, she likely would've opted for something bigger. Like a whole cheesecake.

Giving her head a quick shake, she glanced at Lester and tilted her face towards Nick before responding. "Don't tell me this is 'Coach.'"

When he grinned and nodded in response, Mattie thought she could actually hear the sound of the cash register that was Lester's brain make a "cha-ching" sound.

"Oh, please. How does he qualify as 'world class?'" She made quotation marks with her fingers as she said it.

Lester passed the buck to Nick. "Sorry to put you on the spot, Coach, but do you mind filling Mattie in on your credentials?"

Nick looked at her, eyes narrowed, with an expression that read, "You know damn well what my credentials are," but he listed them anyway.

"In high school, I broke every record on the books. As team captain, I led my team to the state championships three years in a row. After that, I got a full ride to Oregon State, where I was captain of the men's cross-country and track teams and broke a bunch more records. Before graduating, I tried out for, and got a spot on, the Olympic track and field team—"

Unimpressed, Mattie interrupted, "As an alternate. That hardly counts."

Nick chuckled and shook his head in disbelief. "I've been trained by some of the best coaches in the world. You don't think I can coach a—"

He held his hand out, as he searched for the words to describe her.

Somehow, Mattie knew those words wouldn't be "successful female journalist."

Before he could deliver his description, she arched an eyebrow and whispered, "My fan base is over a half a million strong. Screw with me and you're toast."

Smirking down at her, he replied, "Better start you on a low-carb diet then."

Mattie sneered, "Thanksgiving is next week."

"Is that an invitation?"

Undeterred, Mattie addressed Lester and delivered the best punch to Nick she could without actually making any physical contact. "Since when does the *Gazette* hire ex-cons? Or is this part of some twisted work-release program?"

Except for a flicker of disappointment that extinguished the glint in his eyes, Nick didn't flinch.

He gave a quick nod to Lester and said, "Catch you tomorrow."

Mattie glanced at the all-powerful publisher. His eyes were closed, but his lips were moving, which only meant one thing—he was seeing headlines, flicking them across the blank front page that was his brain.

She heard him mumble, "From Sedentary to Sensational…"

"Lester!"

He looked at her over his reading glasses and then waved her away, saying, "You kids work this out. I have a newspaper to run."

Before she could get away, Nick wrapped his fingers around Mattie's upper arm. Like a blood pressure cuff, he slowly strengthened his squeeze as he closed Lester's door behind them. Just as he was about to cut off the circulation in her arm, he pulled her close and spoke into her ear. "We gotta talk. Now."

Mattie surveyed their surroundings. In front of them was a bright, wide-open office space with lots of prying eyes and cell phone cameras at the ready.

Her eyes fell on the stairwell door through which she planned to escape, alone, when Nick whispered, "Any place we can find some privacy around here?"

Mattie yanked her arm from his firm grasp and turned on him, ready to issue a condemnation so scathing, he'd leave the building and never look back. Damn the assignment, damn the raise, damn her career.

But then she noticed his face.

No longer a mirror image of Eddie, Nick's countenance had become leaner and harder since the wedding-that-wasn't, reflecting a wound she couldn't see and a scar for which she could not take credit. Not entirely.

Suspecting that the arrogant, smug, carefree Olympian she mistook for her fiancé the day before her ill-fated wedding was long gone, she stashed her verbal daggers and softened her tone, just a touch.

"Come with me."

The two walked to the elevators with all of the solemnity of school children facing a detention after a visit to the principal's office. They descended in brooding silence as they made their way to the lifestyle section floor that held a steadily shrinking staff and one reluctant advice columnist—all of whom were under Dianne's domain.

When they reached Mattie's desk, she pointed to an extra chair.

"Have a seat."

Within the confines of her cubicle walls, she watched as he studied the pre-school artwork pinned to them. He seemed to fixate on the drawing of a Thanksgiving turkey with blue and orange feathers glued to it that her nephew had made for her.

After a very long minute, his gaze drifted to the framed photographs of her faux family.

Emitting a short laugh, Nick bit his lip, shook his head and said, "I can't believe you're married."

Mattie started twirling her ring with her left thumb. She arched her eyebrow so high it nearly touched her hairline. "Why? Because you can't imagine anyone ever falling in love with someone like me?"

Nick stared at her and pursed his lips. Pointing to a picture on her desk, he asked, "Is that the lucky guy?"

Mattie frowned at the picture of her brother-in-law, Tom, grinning like he was indeed the luckiest guy on the planet. She had taken the shot in the bleachers at Wrigley Field on opening day twelve years before, just seconds after Claudia had agreed to marry him.

When she didn't respond, Nick prodded, "Does he have a name?"

Cool as a cucumber, Mattie suggested, "How 'bout we keep this strictly business. You coach. I write. Nothing more. Okay?"

Narrowing his eyes, Nick thought for a moment, then said, "Sure."

Eager to change the subject, she asked, "What did you want to talk about?"

Something in the pit of her stomach told her it wouldn't be complimentary.

Nick clenched his jaw and scooted his chair closer to hers. "Listen, I can't change what happened, you know, *before*."

He spoke in a voice so low, Mattie found herself leaning closer just so she could hear him, oblivious to the fact that it afforded him a generous view of her newly-exposed cleavage.

Pointing to Tom's beaming smile, Nick continued, "You've clearly moved on with your life, and I'd like to do the same. I'm willing to keep the past in the past if you are."

When he locked his eyes on hers, she felt as if he were trying to erase every memory she ever had of him always getting in the way of her quest to win Eddie's heart, all the way back to the third grade.

But there was one memory that even his smoldering gaze couldn't melt away.

As if it had just happened yesterday, she could picture herself searching the playground for Eddie, hoping for a response to a homemade Valentine's Day card she had snuck in his desk, but Nick spotted her first. Dressed as usual in a blue shirt as opposed to the red shirts Eddie always wore, Nick approached and handed her a note.

"It's from Eddie. I didn't read it. I swear."

When she tore it from his hand and unfolded it, she saw the words, "There once was a girl named Mattie who looked like a great big fatty" scrawled in pencil across the page.

Luckily for Nick, he was the only boy who could outrun her; otherwise, she would've socked him. As fate would have it, she finally got her chance twenty years later.

While Mattie was reliving the past, Nick had moved onto a different subject.

"I didn't realize you worked here. In fact, I haven't seen your byline anywhere since, well, you know."

That he had actually looked for her byline caught her quite by surprise. Just as she made up her mind to take it as a compliment, he added, "I assumed you went into hiding or something. For a while there, I assumed the worst. I mean, why else wouldn't you have returned my calls? Especially when you knew you were the only thing standing between me and a stint in jail."

He stared hard at her, but still Mattie didn't react.

So much for keeping the past in the past.

Nick leaned forward, rested his elbows on his knees, clasped his hands together, and continued, "Now I don't know what you're getting out of this little arrangement, but whatever it is, neither one of us is gonna get what we want if we don't play nice."

With his face dangerously close to hers, he raised an eyebrow and asked, "Got it?"

Mattie raised her own eyebrow. "That depends. Define 'play nice.'"

"It means you gotta trust me. Completely."

His breath smelled of cinnamon and felt warm against her parted lips.

Like hell I do.

She met his gaze. "Don't hold your breath."

At that, Nick leaned back in the chair and shrugged. "Suit yourself. We can do this the hard way."

Standing up, he continued, "Meet me at our old field house at six tomorrow morning. We have a lot to go over, and," his gaze dropped to the hole in her dress, "I'm gonna have to assess you, so don't be late."

With a quick wink, he turned and left Mattie alone in her cubicle, pondering the directive.

Whatever you say, Coach.

CHAPTER THREE

———

"Ice cream is exquisite. What a pity it isn't illegal."
– Voltaire

Later that evening, Mattie rushed to an urgent care facility located just off of Chicago's Magnificent Mile for a fast physical. The doctor's parting words rang in her ears all the way home.

The funny little man with a curious, indiscernible accent looked at her over his reading glasses when he told her, "Your BMI should not exceed your age. I can recommend a good nutritionist."

"Just sign the form," she retorted.

He begrudgingly pulled a pen from the pocket in his white lab coat and made an undecipherable scribble. "Take better care of yourself, Mathilde, and you'll live a nice long life."

As soon as his pen left the paper, she grabbed the form from him and headed for the door. At Dianne's urging, she stepped into an upscale sporting goods store down the block. Her eyes widened as she stepped through the doors. Bright lights, lots of chrome, and every color of the rainbow on the racks of clothes and shoes.

She stood agape, wondering where to start when a middle-aged man, looking like he could bench press a semitrailer truck, approached her.

"Can I help you?"

Mattie stared at him, waiting for the words to form in her brain. "Running clothes."

The man looked amused. "Yeah?"

Her eyes scanned his nametag. "Tell me, *Roy*. Do you work on commission at this store?"

A cautious grin spread across his pockmarked face. "You betcha."

"Oh good. I'll be sure to find someone else to help me then." She slipped away, leaving the clueless Roy in her wake.

Unable to tell the men's section from the women's, she instead went in search of hot pink pieces of clothing and found a rack of long-sleeved shirts. After an exhaustive search for an extra large, she realized she was in over her head and decided, against her better judgment, to call Claudia.

She worked her way to a less populated area of the store and dialed her number. As soon as her sister picked up, Mattie regretted her decision.

"What? I can barely hear you. Why in the world are you shopping for running clothes?"

"I got a new assignment, Claud."

"Uh-huh. And what about a raise? Did you ask about that?"

Mattie let out an exasperated sigh before responding, "Yes, I did. I'll get it when I complete the assignment."

"Which is…?" Claudia pried.

Standing up straight, Mattie took another deep breath and announced louder than she intended so as to be heard over the store's booming stereo system, "I'm going to run the Chicago Marathon."

She held the phone away from her ear and waited for her sister to stop laughing.

"Are you finished?" she asked as she began accosting a stack of running tights.

Ignoring her question, Claudia instead asked one of her own. "This is a joke, right? Do you remember when you tried out for track in high school?"

Mattie turned to a display of running shoes. Inspecting a purple pair, she looked at the price tag and dropped them like they were hot coals.

"Vaguely," she lied. She had no intention of indulging Claudia who, on occasion, could be somewhat sadistic to her only sibling.

This prompted another bout of giggles from the other end of the line. Firing out phrases between gasps for air, Claudia did her best to recapture the pivotal moment in Mattie's brief affair with sustained aerobic activity.

"You barely finished the workout. Next day, you couldn't move, couldn't climb stairs, and couldn't get out of your chair."

Mattie's hamstrings ached at the memory.

"Oh, Claud," she growled into the phone. "Be serious. What choice do I have? I royally screwed over my career. If this is my only shot at redemption, I have to go through with it, and I don't think I can if you're not in my corner."

Not wanting to add gasoline to the fire, she carefully avoided any mention of her coach's name. Instead, she listened as her sister took in several deep breaths.

"All right, Mat, but are you really sure this is a good idea?"

"Claud, please. I need advice, not doubt. I need proper running clothes and haven't a clue what to get."

"Okay, okay," Claudia relented. Then, with resignation, added, "Don't wear black. I know everyone says it's slimming, but with your coloring, it'll just wash you out."

Not finding even a simple sweatband in her price range, Mattie left the store two hours later, empty-handed and beyond discouraged. Her train ride home did little to lift her spirits.

She watched as a young family boarded—a husband and wife with a little boy whose snowflake-patterned mittens were so big they looked like oven mitts. His mother snuggled him close, and his father sat with his arm protectively around them both. She pulled her eyes away from the familial cocoon and looked out the window.

It used to be enough that she was the favorite aunt to her sister's kids. It used to be enough to dole out parenting advice to entitled parents who took their blessings completely for granted. Looking at her reflection in the frost-edged glass, she realized that, at the tender age of twenty-eight, it wasn't enough. Not anymore.

When she got home, she made a box of macaroni and cheese, ate it all in one sitting, and washed it down with the remnants of a room temperature bottle of Pinot Grigio.

She had just started diving into her mess of a closet, looking for anything that would pass for workout clothes, when her phone rang.

Holding it to her ear with one hand, she rifled through her clothes with the other. "I still can't believe it, Dianne. I went in for a raise and I came out with a," she contorted her face before spewing, "coach."

She stopped accosting the hangers and put her hand on her forehead. "And it's Nick DeRosa, of all people," she moaned. "How did this happen?"

"Nick DeRosa? Why does that name sound familiar?"

Not wanting to go into too much detail, Mattie replied, "I may have mentioned his name. He's the identical twin of a guy I was engaged to. A long time ago."

Dianne was quiet for an unnerving moment. "No, that's not it."

Mattie pulled a sweatshirt down from her closet shelf. "Oh, then you might know him as the Comeback Kid. Remember? About two or three years ago?"

"Yep. That's it. Whatever happened to him? Didn't he go to jail for something?"

Inspecting the sweatshirt, Mattie tossed it on her bed and lied, "I don't remember what it was for, but he was cleared of all charges." Her Aunt Vivienne, who still lived down the street from the DeRosas, actually went to the party they threw for Nick when he got out. Mattie never opened her invitation.

"Well, they say the world just keeps getting smaller, don't they?" Dianne replied, sounding rather distracted.

Mattie inspected a pair of sweat pants she found that were tucked between two old pairs of jeans that no longer fit and asked, "Is everything OK? You sound funny."

"Me? No. It's just—well, never mind."

"It's just what?" Mattie pressed.

"Well, I know it won't be easy having to look at a clone of your 'ex' everyday for the next ten months, but you need to think this through. There's a lot at stake. Like our jobs."

"I have to do a lot more than just look at him, Dianne. I have to *submit* to his will," Mattie exclaimed, "and that's so much worse."

"Calm down," Dianne sang out. "Just look at it as a business partnership. Nothing more."

Regaining her composure, Mattie continued. "I just wish they weren't so damn good-looking."

Dianne paused before coaxing, "Well, good thing you're a quote-unquote married woman, right?"

"Yes, I am, and quite happily, too. Thanks for reminding me."

"Anytime, doll," Dianne replied. "Now is not the time to blow your cover. The paper is treading water, and this would be just the kind of ammo the *Gazette* could use to fire us both."

God forbid you lose funding for your shoe fetish.

Mattie held her hand up to admire her ring, sparkling under the closet light bulb. If push came to shove, she could pawn it for one month's rent, tops.

"Just focus on that fat bonus Lester promised, and this assignment will be behind you in no time."

Goosebumps spread across Mattie's forearms—a sure sign that her internalized radar system had intercepted an unidentified lying object.

She held the phone away from her ear and stared at it a moment. "Did I tell you he promised me a *fat* bonus? Because I'm pretty sure I would've used a better word to describe it."

Not skipping a beat, Dianne answered her question with another. "Why else would you do it, sweetie? Now, tell me. When do you start?"

Appeased for the moment, Mattie's goose bumps subsided. "We officially start tomorrow. I'm meeting him at six so he can assess me. Whatever that means."

"In the morning? Good lord. Are you even out of bed at that hour?"

"No, never." Feeling panic rise up and grip her by the throat, Mattie gurgled, "Do you think this is a bad idea?"

Dianne shot back, "Remember when Oprah went on her fitness binge?"

"Which one?"

"Don't diss Oprah," Dianne scolded. "She ran the Marine Corps Marathon, for God's sake. You can do this."

In a somber tone, Mattie replied, "I suppose. But what if I can't? What if I just end up making a fool of myself again? Except this time it will be at the hands of a different DeRosa and in front of the entire subscription base of the *Chicago Gazette*." She shuddered at the thought.

Dianne laughed. "You'll be fine. Just remember, what doesn't destroy us makes us smarter."

"Stronger," Mattie corrected. "It makes us stronger."

"Same difference," Dianne chuckled.

Mattie stepped out of her closet dressed in a pair of too-tight sweat pants and an old sports bra that had lost it supportive properties several wash loads back.

As she assessed herself in the mirror, she gripped her phone like it held the last supply of oxygen on the planet. "Dianne. There's no way I can run a marathon next October. I jiggle like Jell-O."

"So don't jiggle."

Mattie watched herself as she hopped up and down. "Right. I don't think you can run without at least jiggling a little. Or, in my case, a lot."

"As I told you this afternoon, go get some running tights and a compression jacket. I see women jogging along the lakefront all the time in those. Not a jiggle in sight. Now get to bed. You'll want to be well rested for your assessment. And make sure you have something better for breakfast than a Twinkie. Good night and good luck, doll."

The phone clicked, and Dianne was gone.

Mattie went to the kitchen and dug into a tub of premium, slow-churned chocolate ice cream, searching for the empathy her editor did not provide.

* * *

Nick turned the key in the dead bolt on the door of his parents' bungalow. He could smell his mother's legendary pasta sauce as soon as he reached the top step on their back porch.

"Hey, Ma. How ya doing?"

Lucy DeRosa waved at him from across the warm, cozy kitchen, then pointed to the phone receiver and mouthed, "Your father."

Nick nodded his acknowledgement, hung up his coat in the foyer closet, and sauntered over to the refrigerator as he loosened his tie. He flung open the door and stood staring at its contents.

"If you're hot, go outside," his mother scolded after she hung up the phone. "But if you're hungry," she continued, "sit down. Dinner's ready. Your pop should be home in about an hour, but he said not to wait for him."

Nick, still guilt-ridden after his parents drained their retirement fund to cover his legal expenses, did as instructed.

"Aren't you eating?" he asked.

"Nah, I'll wait." Instead, Lucy joined him at the table.

On the day Nick was exonerated, she threw a party for him, inviting no less than fifty friends and family from their Ravenswood neighborhood. She forbade all of them to speak Eddie's name from that day forward, declaring, "He is dead to me."

It was Nick, of all people, who counseled her to forgive and forget.

Still, when his parents insisted that he move back in with them, he did so reluctantly. With no job, no car, no income, and no prospects, he knew he didn't have a choice. It wasn't long afterwards that he remembered the healing powers of his mother's manicotti. That they didn't charge him a dime in rent helped, too.

"Just 'til you get back on your feet," they cooed as he unpacked his belongings in his old room.

It took him a year to find a place of his own that he could afford, but it didn't stop him from accepting his mother's invitations to dinner.

She waited until he shoveled a forkful of hot spaghetti into his mouth before asking, "So how did it go at the *Gazette*?"

Nick looked at her, incredulous. Chewing quickly, he tried to manage, "Fine," without spewing food.

"Don't talk with your mouth full. Did they offer you a job? I'd be leery. Make sure you get everything in writing.

Newspapers are going under just like everything else these days."

Nick finished chewing and responded. "Yeah, they sort of offered me a job. And yeah, they'll put it all in writing."

His mother arched her penciled-in eyebrows. "What do you mean 'sort of'?"

"Well, it's not a regular nine-to-five job. I'm going to be a consultant."

This did not appease Mrs. DeRosa. "What kind of consultant?"

Nick, with his fork in mid-air, gave up all hope of being able to finish his food. "I'll be coaching someone on their staff to run for the Chicago Marathon."

"Oh yeah? Who? That doesn't sound like much of a job, training just one person. And what does that have to do with the newspaper business anyway?"

"You wouldn't know her, Ma."

"Her? Is she a reporter? Hey, it's not that gal that writes that column, is it? What is her name? The one who gives those snooty working mothers their what-for."

Lucy stood and started rifling through a stack of papers destined for the recycling bin. Pointing a finger at Nick, she added, "But she definitely knows her way around a kitchen."

Nick thought of Mattie. Stubborn. Impulsive. Undisciplined. "No, Ma. I can safely say it's not her."

At this, he stood and set his plate on the counter, hoping to stop her line of questioning.

It didn't work.

"Aw, that's too bad. I'd like to meet her someday. So who is she, huh? This one you'll be coaching? Does she have a name?"

Nick narrowed his eyes, mulling whether to respond. His mother, a top-notch seamstress, never missed a chance to remind anyone willing to listen that, after she tailored her off-the-rack Mother-of-the-Groom dress, as well as the gowns of all her sisters, none could be returned when Eddie's wedding fell through.

Divulging Mattie's name would most certainly dredge it all up again, and, after the day he had, Nick just wasn't up for it. Not on a partially empty stomach.

Stepping toward his mother, he took her by the shoulders and planted a kiss on her upturned cheek. "Mind if I spend the night? I've got to be at the track pretty early tomorrow."

Even after being away at college and running in races all over the world, Nick still relished the comfort and security of his childhood bedroom. As sparsely furnished as it was, it seemed luxurious compared to the minimum-security jail cell in which he was housed for one very long month.

His mother maintained it like a museum exhibit. The light-up globe that fascinated him as a kid still sat on his desk. The room didn't have a phone or television. Just a simple clock radio and a reading lamp on his night stand. On the walls hung posters of his heroes—running greats Steve Prefontaine and Frank Shorter.

His mother had already converted Eddie's into her sewing room that was, for all intents and purposes, a monument to Nick. The shelves were lined with his trophies, and the bookcase was stuffed with scrapbooks and newspaper clippings.

Pulling a pair of neatly folded pajama bottoms from his duffle bag, Nick tossed them on his bed and looped his tie on a hook in his closet. Slipping the brown leather belt out of the loops on his khakis with one yank, he slung it over the back of the plain wooden desk chair. Easing his pants off, he slid them carefully onto a hanger, careful not to wrinkle the creases. On top of that he draped the same pale blue button-down dress shirt he was wearing when the federal judge threw out the case against him a year earlier.

What should have been a day of great celebration was tempered only by the solemn resignation that his own brother had indeed framed him for embezzling millions of dollars from investors before vanishing without a trace.

* * *

Sleep didn't come easily to Mattie that night. When it finally did, she tossed and turned through a bad dream. In it, she was struggling to run as fast as she could through the marathon course, but her legs seemed to be filled with wet sand. Fit runners blew past her on either side. The route was lined with onlookers who all seemed to be yelling at her to hurry up. When the finish line finally appeared, Nick and Eddie were there, waiting side-by-side, pointing at her, laughing so hard they were wiping tears from their eyes. Mattie woke up shaking.

Tucked into a fetal position while her comforter sat in a pile at the foot of her bed, she was cold, groggy, and disoriented. She reached over, clutched her cell phone and squinted at it for several seconds before making out the time—4:55.

Throwing back her flannel sheets, she felt around under her bed for her flashlight, always at the ready and always right next to her trusty baseball bat. There was no time to shower and, worse, no coffee to drink. She yanked on the faded black too-tight sweat pants she had found the night before and an oversized sweatshirt bearing the logo of her alma mater. Taming her curls into a haphazard ponytail, she swiped on some mascara, inhaled a cold Pop Tart, slipped her ring on her finger, yanked her down coat around her shoulders, and headed for the train that would take her north to Nick. Doing her best to dodge the puddles in the dark, her shoes still managed to become waterlogged by the time she made it to the platform at the station.

The entire way there, she tried to imagine how he would assess her level of fitness. Would he count the number of jumping jacks she could do in a minute, or would his weapon of choice be push-ups? Crunches?

I swear to God, if he pulls out a measuring tape, I'm outta there.

She looked at her reflection in the window as the train flew past dark, wet building facades. Couldn't he tell just by looking at her that she hadn't intentionally broken a sweat before? Ever?

As hard as it was for her to discern Nick's methods, she couldn't even begin to fathom his motives. What a former Olympian was doing as a personal running coach payrolled by the *Gazette*, she had no idea. At the moment, all she cared about was getting this assessment over with as quickly as possible.

Mattie arrived at her old high school's field house with five minutes to spare. As soon as she stepped onto the property, she felt her face start to break out and her hair begin to frizz. The all-too-familiar urge to duck into the nearest bathroom and hide threatened to overtake her.

Standing at the entrance of the indoor track, the same debilitating unease that accompanied her every day before gym class began to wash over her. She scanned the cavernous space for any sign of Nick, but didn't see him. Instead, she spied a dozen or so senior citizens shuffling along on the inside lanes of the track and women wearing nothing but sport bras and matching shorts jogging past them in the outer lanes. Not a jiggle in sight.

The Pop Tart Mattie had for breakfast sat like a hard, indigestible lump in her stomach. She was cold, wet, and ready to sell her soul for a cup of hot coffee.

Before long, she heard footsteps approach behind her.

"Did you bring the forms?"

Startled by the sound of Nick's voice, Mattie turned to face him.

Like his brother, he had a commanding presence. He looked sharp, dressed in a charcoal gray workout suit and a slightly frayed, royal blue Cubs hat. And, like his brother, he had the annoying ability to look as drop-dead gorgeous first thing in the morning as he did when he was dressed to the nines for dinner at a five-star restaurant.

Mattie brushed an errant curl off her forehead and retrieved the folded sheets of paper from her pocket. "I trust it's ok that I didn't get my parents' signature?"

Nick inspected the forms before tucking them under other papers already affixed to his clipboard. Pointing at her feet, he asked, "What are those?"

She looked down at her plaid Keds, gushing with water every time she took a step, and replied, "Gee, Nick. I thought you of all people would know. These are called *shoes*."

In reply, he scrawled something on the clipboard he was carrying then led her to the center of the track. Hurrying after him, Mattie whispered as loudly as she dared, "Why is it so crowded in here? These aren't all teachers, are they? I thought we'd have some privacy."

Nick stared straight over the top of her head and said, "The track is open to the public from five to seven every morning. Anybody can use it. It's co-sponsored by the park district."

Nodding at his explanation, she hoped whatever he was going to make her do wouldn't take an hour and a half. She stood in front of him, arms folded, and braced herself.

"So, let's get this over with. Assess me."

From under the brim of his hat, Nick's eyes locked onto hers. "Excuse me?"

Mattie stared back at him for a second too long, feeling as if she had just been zapped by the tiniest of electric charges. She shifted from one waterlogged shoe to the other, wishing she could make herself invisible.

"Assess me," she repeated. "Isn't that what you said you were going to do this morning?"

He lowered his eyes to his clipboard. "When I'm good and ready."

Mattie rolled her eyes and shot back, "Fine."

Nick frowned at her. "Fine yourself. Give me a lap."

"What?" Mattie cried a little too loudly, drawing attention from the early morning fitness fanatics running circles around them.

"You heard me. One lap. No stopping." When she didn't move, he pointed to the track, clicked his stopwatch, and added, "Lane one. Move it."

I'm in hell...

She slipped off her jacket and let it fall in a puffy pile at Nick's feet.

As if she was testing for quick sand, she took a tentative step onto the black rubbery surface of the track. Once she was certain it would not swallow her whole, she began shuffling along in the same direction as everyone else, doing her best to minimize the jiggling. But, it was no use. Each time her foot hit the track, every cell in her body seemed to shout, "Jell-O City!"

Her pride abandoned her.

By the time she rounded the first corner, her lungs felt like they were about to burst into flames. She wondered if Nick knew CPR and began praying that she didn't have to find out.

Shuffling into the second turn, she felt blisters erupting on the back of both ankles as her damp feet rubbed against their wet canvas confines. Determined not to let him get the upper hand, she kept chugging along, panting hard.

When she heard him yell, "Pick it up, Ross," she started chanting to herself, "I hate you, I hate you, I hate you, I hate you."

After what seemed like an eternity, she steered herself through the third corner. By this time, her thighs felt as heavy as cement blocks. An old couple, walking slowly enough to hold hands, passed by on her right, looking concerned.

She wiped the sweat from her brow with her sleeve. Her right side, just below her rib cage, felt as if she'd been stabbed with a thousand knives. Her parched mouth seemed to be coated with glue.

Kill me. Kill me now.

"Almost done," she heard him shout. That's when she heard a different voice, a friendlier voice, say, "Don't give up now. You can do it."

Mattie looked around, but didn't see anyone close by.

I'm hallucinating.

She pushed up the sleeves on her sweatshirt and ran a hand across her eyes. The salt in her sweat caused them to sting. Her mascara clumped, making her eyelashes stick together. Her ponytail felt like it had a large rock tied to the end of it.

If I could just stop to catch my breath.

Then she saw him.

Nick had moved from the center of the track to her lane and stood several yards in front of her. He had tucked his clipboard under his arm. In one hand, he was holding his stopwatch and was waving her toward him with the other.

"Come on, Mattie. Let's go."

Was he a mirage? She gave her head a shake and decided to aim for him, wishing she had the power to run right over him and keep going, all the way home to a nice cool shower.

When she finally finished, she barely had enough force in her to knock him off step, let alone keep going.

Nick caught her by the arm, clicked his stopwatch, and announced just loud enough for her to hear, "4:13."

In response, Mattie bent over, grabbed her knees, and threw up on lane one.

I'm never eating Pop Tarts again.

After a minute, she felt a hand on her back and saw a paper towel come into view.

"Here. Clean yourself up."

Mattie watched as he waved over a janitor to clean up the mess before he ushered her back to the center of the track.

It was clear to her that his brand of torture had elicited this type of response before.

"You ok?" he asked.

Making a face that told him she wasn't, he pointed to the water fountain near the entrance. "Go rinse your mouth out and splash some water on your face. You'll be fine."

He spoke with all the compassion of an IRS agent conducting an audit.

Still, Mattie did as she was told. On her way back to Nick, a jolt of pride began to work its way up from her blistered heels. By the time she reached him, she was fighting back the urge to squeal, "I did it."

Instead, she asked, "What now? Are you going to hang me by my thumbs for a couple of hours?"

Nick smirked at her. "No, upper body workouts come later. Thought I'd give you something to look forward to." Nodding toward the track, he added, "Three more of those and you have a mile. Twenty-six point two of *those* and you have yourself a marathon."

""Don't remind me," Mattie muttered under her so-not-minty breath.

Nick lifted his hat off, ran a hand through his wavy hair, and looked at her.

"Listen, Mattie. I'm not gonna lie to you. Training for a marathon takes hard work, discipline, and guts."

Mattie grimaced. "Bad choice of words."

He stood staring at her with a pained expression on his face. After a minute, he nodded towards the entrance. "How about we go grab some breakfast. We've got a lot to go over if we're gonna do this."

Mattie stayed planted to the spot. "You want me to go to breakfast. With you."

Nick glanced at his watch. "In about four minutes, first period PE is gonna start. I'd rather detail the plan you're going to follow for the next ten months over a stack of pancakes. But if you insist, I can do it right here in front of a bunch of gawking teenagers, too. It's your call."

"What makes you so sure I'm going to follow your plan?"

"Oh, you'll follow it." His eyes glinted under the shadow cast by his cap. "'Cause I won't get my win if you don't."

As her caffeine-free brain scrambled for a sharp retort to his veiled threat, he continued, "And neither will you."

CHAPTER FOUR

———

"Hell is other people at breakfast."
– Franz Kafka

The Cozy Cup, a greasy spoon down the street from their old high school was nearly empty. When Nick opened the door to the narrow storefront establishment, he addressed a buoyant waitress who was busying herself with wiping down the long Formica counter.

"Hey Peg. How are ya?"

"Hey Nick. How ya doin'?"

She flashed a pink-frosted smile at him and pointed to a booth in the back before pouring coffee for a construction worker who was sitting on a bar stool, hunched over the sports page.

Nick slid into the seat, pulled two plastic-coated menus from a holder on the table, and handed one to Mattie. She looked around. With its big black-and-white tile floors and dark red sparkly vinyl covering the seats, the restaurant looked exactly as it had when she used to dive in there after class to pick up an order of cheese fries to go. Still, it was a far cry from the establishments Eddie had taken her to. A very far cry.

Before she had a chance to study the menu, Peg appeared at their table, holding a little pad of paper. Mattie was fascinated by the waitress's hairdo, expertly styled, shellacked, and void of any natural color.

Addressing Nick, she asked, "So how are ya? You look good. How're your folks?"

Nick let out a short cough. "I'm fine. Folks are fine."

Peg pulled out a pencil that was tucked over her ear.

"Glad to hear it. Tell your Mom I still have her cake pan from the potluck at the church, would ya? If I knew you were coming, I woulda brought it."

Mattie watched as Nick unfurled the trademark DeRosa grin, shiny white teeth gleaming between deep dimples on each cheek.

"No worries, Peg. I'll let her know." He delivered his reply with a wink.

While the waitress-slash-family friend seemed unfazed by his brazen onslaught of charm, Mattie felt her pulse race and her heart do a gallop in her chest. She held the menu in front of her face, certain it was turning as red as cherry pie filling.

Damn that Pavlov...

"Now, what can I get you kids?"

Nick started, "I'll take the usual."

"How 'bout you, honey?"

After giving her menu a quick look, Mattie listed her breakfast demands. "Coffee, blueberry pancakes, bacon, and a large OJ."

Nick put his hand on Peg's arm and shook his head. "No. Make that a veggie omelet, egg white's only, turkey bacon, and a fresh fruit cup. Oh, and a water."

When he saw Mattie scowling at him, he asked, "Or would you rather have plain oatmeal?"

"You said we were going to go over the details of your plan over a stack of pancakes."

"I intend to."

Mattie stared at him for a moment. When he did nothing more than look through the notes on his ever-present clipboard, she folded her arms and sat back in her seat watching as Peg disappeared through the kitchen doors.

"Look, I've got to get to work. Can we get on with this?"

Nick handed her a piece of paper with "The Rules" typed across the top. "Like it or not, from now until October, you are my work."

Ignoring him, Mattie laid the paper on the table in front of her and studied it. "Running every day? Seriously? Isn't that a little excessive?"

When she looked up, she was surprised to see him watching her with an expression that, if she hadn't known better, could be mistaken as fondness.

But she did know better. At least she thought she did.

She slapped on a frown as he explained, "We've gotta get a lot of miles on your legs. You're going from not running at all to running over twenty-six miles in one shot."

"Again, don't remind me."

She looked longingly at the picture of a scrumptious, over-sized blueberry muffin on her placemat.

"If you don't think you can do it, you won't," he continued. "Besides, you won't be running every day. Some days, we'll cross-train. Swim or bike. I might even throw in some yoga."

It was a little past eight in the morning. Without her usual caffeine fix, Mattie's wit evaded her. "Whatever," was all she could come up with, so she kept it to herself.

Instead, she turned her attention back to Nick's list and began reading each rule aloud with increasing alarm. "No late nights. No junk food. No coffee? Are you insane? How do you expect me to function?"

"You just gotta replace those bad habits with some new ones."

"You know, that line might work with your sixteen-year-old protégés, but I'm a grown woman. A successful working woman."

"Yeah. So I see."

Feeling his eyes comb over her sweaty mass of curls, frumpy sweatshirt and almost makeup free face, she turned her attention to the omelet Peg slid in front of her. The clumps of vegetables on the otherwise stark white plate did little to stir her appetite. It's not that she minded the green peppers, mushrooms and onions, but she preferred them sitting on a cornmeal pizza crust, smothered in melted mozzarella cheese, and dripping with basil-laced tomato sauce.

After filling her mouth with a forkful of hot food, her face contorted into a pained expression.

Nick nodded, "I know, right? It's good stuff."

Mattie groped for her water and guzzled it. When she had distinguished the fire in her mouth, she gave him a weak smile. "So good."

Nick swallowed a mouthful of buttermilk pancakes saturated with melted butter and syrup, and nodded at her plate. "From here on out, no more rich food. Not while you're in training, got it?"

While Mattie tried to discern his use of the word "rich," the memory of Eddie taking her to brunch at the Hotel Intercontinental on Michigan Avenue came to mind. She had never seen such a sumptuous display of her least favorite meal in all of her life.

It was the first and, unfortunately, last time she ever had Eggs Benedict. She savored every single bite, not minding in the least that the dish consumed her entire recommended daily calorie allotment. Salivating at the memory of the silky sauce, she sighed.

While she still fantasized about Eddie returning from wherever slimeballs go just so he could grovel at her feet and beg forgiveness, there was still no denying the fact that he had impeccable taste. He was what her mother would have described as a cad. Her absentee father, she could only imagine, would have admired his audacity.

She could still hear her ex-fiancé saying through mouthfuls of foie gras, "Everything tastes better when you wash it down with champagne."

Yes, especially when you don't have to pay for it, you low-life scumbag.

Mattie looked across the table at Nick. He sat frozen, fork in hand, waiting for her reply. His expression was a collage of pride, vulnerability, and hurt, but Mattie noticed something else in those long-lashed eyes. Hope?

Forcing an expressionless smile, she admitted, "I'm just not much of a breakfast person."

First, she noticed his shoulders relax, then his entire countenance. "Well, you're gonna have to become one. You're in training now. What you eat and when you eat it fuels your body and has a direct impact on your performance."

"Easy, big guy. I didn't say I was going on a hunger strike. I know I may not look like it, but I've been dieting on and off my entire life, so please, don't lecture me about proper nutrition."

She was relieved that Peg appeared before Nick could respond. With check in hand, she stared at Mattie's plate and asked, "How was everything? Want a doggie bag?"

Mattie nodded and Nick handed her a twenty. "Great, Peg, as usual. Keep the change."

She stashed the cash in a pocket of her apron and sashayed towards the cash register, humming an unrecognizable tune.

After she returned with a box, Mattie filled it with her leftover food, pulled on her jacket, and grabbed the list of rules Nick had given her. "So, are we done?"

She waited for his reply with the patience of a teenager begging to be excused from the most excruciating dining experience ever.

Nick, using the tone of a parent admonishing an ill-mannered teenager, responded, "You're welcome."

Mattie rolled her head back. "I'm sorry. It's just—I've got to get going. Really."

Nick stood and nodded toward the entrance. "Yep, we're finished."

As they made their way to the door, Mattie's conscience threatened to get the better of her. It was obvious that Nick's finances were not as robust. Why else would he need to take a job coaching someone like her? From her perspective, his plight reeked of desperation. What happened to the Nick who, on more than one occasion, used to strut through the halls of Knollwood High with at least three members of the cheer squad drooling in his wake? Eddie always used to grumble about how Nick would steal the limelight when they were kids, rubbing Eddie's nose in his athletic achievements.

Having grown up in the shadow of a pretty, popular, and petite older sister, Mattie had always sympathized completely. Thing was, he sure didn't seem to be rubbing anyone's nose in anything now.

Feeling compelled to thank Nick properly, she stopped and turned to do just that when her nose pressed against his chest, and her words got lost in the soft synthetic fabric of his jacket.

He sprang away from her like she had just spritzed him with cold water. "What's the matter?"

Mattie looked away, embarrassed. Her benevolent mood had passed.

"Geez. Forget it. I was just thanking you for breakfast."

Nick looked down at her with the faintest hint of a smile tugging at the corners of his mouth. "Forget it yourself."

She took in the sight of him standing before her, all spiffed up and authoritative. When she spotted his smirk, the reporter in her suddenly felt compelled to interrogate him.

"Listen, if we're gonna do this I have to ask you a question."

No longer smiling, he pulled himself up tall and nodded.

Mattie fired away. "Why are you doing this?"

"I lost my job. Why are *you* doing this?"

"I need a raise. What was your job?"

He titled his head in the direction of the high school, a crease forming between his eyebrows. "Coaching boys' cross-country at Knollwood."

"How'd you lose it?"

"We didn't win."

"Do you miss it?"

Nick's entire forehead crinkled while he contemplated his response. "I miss the guys. I miss helping them get over stuff."

"What stuff?"

"Stuff. You know, high school stuff. Demanding parents. The pressure to be perfect. The bullying. High school can really suck."

Mattie let out a laugh. "You say that like it's news to you."

Nick folded his arms and narrowed his eyes. When he said nothing in reply, Mattie muttered to herself, "Oh, that's right. How could I forget? He *was* perfect in high school."

"Excuse me?"

After waiting for a woman pushing a baby stroller to pass by on the cracked, narrow sidewalk, she explained, "I used to see you all the time in the halls with groupie cheerleaders following you like you were a rock star."

Man, oh man, she had hated the jocks at her high school. They swaggered around like they owned the place, objectifying the more than willing cheer squad, and passing all of their classes without so much as picking up a book.

He scowled down at her. "I think you're confusing me with my brother. Again."

Feeling as if he had just shoved her backwards a few feet, she said, "I don't think so," and turned to walk away.

"Hey," he called after her. "High school was just as hard for me as it was for everybody else."

There was an edge to his voice that made her turn around. Marching right up to him, she asked, "Oh, really? Tell me, did anybody ever leave a dirty diaper in your locker?"

A look of disgust swept over Nick's face. "No."

"Anybody ever loosen the bolts in the chair they knew you'd be sitting in so when you did, it would break?"

Nick shifted his weight to his other foot and stuffed his hands in his jacket pockets. "No."

Her eyes welling up, she leaned closer, lowered her voice, and asked him one last question. "Anybody ever make you feel like you don't deserve to be loved? Ever? By anybody?"

Titling his head to one side, Nick looked at her, his eyes filled with compassion.

Mattie pressed her lips together and whispered, "I didn't think so."

She turned her back and walked several paces away from him before calling over her shoulder, "Thanks again for breakfast."

* * *

Two hours, one hot shower, and three cups of strong black coffee later, Mattie had put her outburst with Nick behind her and stormed into Dianne's office. She was barely able to contain herself.

"I ran a whole lap without stopping."

But, Dianne wasn't there. Looking around, she noticed that the entire lifestyle department seemed to be missing.

What in the world...?

On her way back to her desk, she heard the sound of laughter spilling from a conference room. As she approached, she noticed the door was slightly ajar.

"Over four minutes to run a quarter mile? My grandmother can do better than that," said a voice belonging to Troy Baker, the new intern who made up for his lack of experience by inflating his own accomplishments at every turn.

"Is that the same grandmother who taught Martha Stewart how to use a glue gun?" retorted the unmistakable drone of Hugh Fink from classifieds, already tired of hearing Troy's tall tales.

"Check this out," said a man whose voice she didn't recognize. "This is the best part of the whole thing."

The room erupted with sounds of disgust. The intern exclaimed, "Hey, do you mind—I'm eating?"

"All right. That's enough." It was Dianne. She was in there with them.

Goosebumps crept over the surface of Mattie's arms, and the nausea threatened to return. She racked her brain trying to recall if she saw someone with a cell phone recording her every move.

As much as she wanted to slink away and hide in her cubicle, she felt compelled to stay and listen.

Dianne shot out, "We need a name for this feature and fast. What've you got so far?"

"Fat to fantastic?" one voice offered.

"Forget it. First, she's not fat. Not by my definition anyway. Second, this isn't about losing weight. It's about training for a marathon. Focus."

"Rubenesque to ripped," offered another.

"Did you even hear what I just said? What else?" Dianne fired back.

"Plump to perfection?" This one actually got booed.

"Buxom to buff."

"Tubby to Terrif—"

Mattie laid her head against the corridor wall. Aside from Dianne, she associated with no one, fearful of exposing her charade. That, however, did not make her co-workers' jabs any less painful.

"All right. That's it. This is a feature title, people. It will be plastered on billboards across the Chicago metro area and slapped on the side of CTA buses. Use your brains. I'm sure you can come up with something at least a little clever and far less insulting. Think of a working mother who's too busy to exercise, committing to train for this marathon. Think 'A Cinderella Story,' but with runners."

Mattie closed her eyes and pictured herself crossing the finish line, skinny and fit, waving to a mob of her adoring fans before accepting a giant bonus check from Lester.

Running down a dream...

An unrecognizable female voice asked, "So if she doesn't want to lose weight, why is she doing it?"

Dianne's heels click-clacked on the hardwood floor as she circled her team. "Excellent question, Nancy. For starters, she's doing it to inspire her readers, mostly working parents who don't make the time to take care of themselves. And, since they make up the majority of our subscription base these days, we're standing behind her a hundred percent."

Troy spoke up, his voice inappropriately bold. "It didn't look to me like this was her idea."

The click-clacking stopped and Dianne spoke. "I'm only going to say this once. If I see that video making the rounds, make no mistake—I'll fire the lot of you. Now get back to work."

Mattie had never heard Dianne threaten anyone before. She could picture her taking Troy by the ear as she led him out of the room sneering at him the entire time. Not wanting to find out if her vision was spot on, Mattie rushed back to her cubicle. It was the one place she could pretend she was someone else, someone better than everyone else, herself included, and get away with it.

She set Nick's list of rules to the right of her keyboard and got busy doing just that. Soon, her hands were flying, cranking out her very first "Running Down a Dream" column.

Dear Readers—I have often extolled the virtues of well-crafted to-do lists. They have the power to turn us from stressed, harried, unproductive working parents to efficient, productive, nurturing working parents. Often the goal of many a New Year's resolution, these lists are task-based and short-term. But ask yourself, what do you have to show for using them except a fleeting sense of accomplishment? Is your life better because you scratched off each item at the end of any given day? Does it make the next day's list any shorter? This year, why not create a list that will leave you better for having followed it? Or, should I say, better for not having followed it? I'd like to introduce you to the To-Don't list. Generated by an expert in his field, I intend to use this list to help me accomplish a long-held, though seemingly impossible goal—running the Chicago Marathon, and I invite you to follow along.

As she reread it, she felt like she was reading someone else's copy.

"Because I'm lying through my teeth," she muttered to herself as she saved the file.

"So, tell me. How'd it go, sweetie?"

Startled, Mattie spun around to face her only ally. She fought the urge to cover her earlobes.

"Fine. It went perfectly fine, thanks for asking."

Looking surprised, Dianne cocked her head and let out an awkward laugh. "I'm glad to hear it. Like I said, it's a simple business arrangement."

"Speaking of which, what's the publicity plan? No photos of me, right?"

Dianne folded her arms and looked down at her brand new Manolo Blahnik pumps.

When she didn't reply, Mattie repeated, "No pictures of me, right?"

Dianne took off her reading glasses and smiled. "Sweetie, what kind of piece would it be without photos?"

Mattie sat up straight and gripped the arms of her chair. "Dianne, the only saving grace to writing this column is the anonymity. If you take that away, everyone will know I'm a fraud. We'll both be out of a job."

With her heart thumping, she thought of the potential whistle blowers in her life—the cashiers at all of her favorite fast food places and grocery stores, and all of the pizza delivery guys. She saw them so often, she was on a first name basis with most of them. Then she thought about all of the readers she had ever riled. She imagined them organizing into a vigilante group bent on revenge, hunting her down like a third world dictator in a well-orchestrated working parent coup.

Dianne picked up the picture of Tom and said, "Maybe it's time you take your sister up on her offer to move in with them."

A sickening feeling washed over Mattie. "Why?"

"So the illusion is complete."

"With who? Nick?"

"No. With you."

Before she could reply, a clerk from the mailroom appeared, holding a package.

"Mattie Ross?"

The two women exchanged glances. Packages never came addressed to her by name.

"See who it's from before you open it," Dianne cautioned. She held her hand to her chest as she peered at it. "It's too big to be from Benziger's. And I call dibs if they send truffles at Christmas again this year."

"Deal," Mattie laughed. "I'll need all the help I can get staying away from chocolate for the next ten months.

Turning the package over in her hands, she announced, "No return address," and after giving it a quick shake, added, "And it's not ticking."

Tearing away the plain brown paper, she exposed a shoebox emblazoned with an athletic manufacturer's name on the side and a note taped to the lid.

Mattie plucked off the piece of paper. In hard-pressed print, it read, "Tomorrow morning. Same time, same place—N."

After sneering at the note, she slowly lifted the lid, afraid of what she might find.

"Oh my."

She pulled out a pair of silver running shoes with hot pink trim by its laces. Dangling them in front of her like puppets, she examined them from all angles.

"Oh my, indeed. Do you know how much those things cost?" Dianne exclaimed to Mattie who was already easing them onto her blistered feet.

After jogging in place a bit, she announced with no small measure of curiosity, "They fit perfectly. And they're so bouncy."

Dianne was intrigued. "Why did he buy you new running shoes? And how did he know your shoe size?"

Assuming her plaid gym shoes were not the focal point of her first and already-banned workout video, Mattie thought it best to retain the last shreds of her dignity. Instead, she shrugged and said, "I have no idea, but I can't accept these. It would be like I'm signing a deal with the devil."

Dianne laughed, "Trust me. If the devil looked anything like Nick DeRosa, I'd sign a deal with him in a heart beat."

And, with that, she was gone.

Mattie took off the shoes and hugged them close to her chest. Nick's gift couldn't have come at a better time, providing just the shot of encouragement she needed.

Whether she planned on letting him know that, though, was another matter entirely.

After morphing Nick's list of rules into a palatable New Year's resolution column for her readers, Mattie headed home. She taped the list to her refrigerator door, making sure it was at eye level. The words leapt off the page like a nightmarish, post-apocalyptic rationing mandate.

> *No junk food.*
> *No coffee.*
> *No refined sugar.*
> *No processed foods.*
> *No carbonated drinks.*

Disgusted, she flung open her refrigerator door and took out the only item not on the list—a half-gallon of whole milk that she had purchased to wash down a package of Oreos a few days before. When she slammed the door closed, the list of rules, secured in one corner by a "World's Best Aunt" magnet, wafted upwards, revealing a second list on the back.

Mattie set the milk on the counter and flipped the list. The first thing that caught her eye was, "No selling yourself short."

She stared at the words, letting them sink in.

"If I had a dime for every time I sold myself short, I'd be a wealthy woman," she mused.

Her whole life, she made excuses for people. By all accounts, she was a seasoned enabler.

Dad left because we were too much responsibility. Mom let herself go because she was too busy supporting me to take care of herself. Eddie used me because—

Feeling as if a bolt of lightning had just taken aim at her chest, she took a deep breath and whispered, "Because I let him."

She took the list with her into the living room and curled up in a chair. Her lips moved as she held the paper in front of her face and read the rest.

"No disrespecting yourself, physically or mentally. No underestimating your awesomeness. No negativity. No thinking that you're in this alone."

A strange sensation, starting at the top of her head and working its way down to her toes, gave her the distinct feeling that she had just been hugged.

She closed her eyes and let the piece of paper fall into her lap.

Holy crap.

"There is no way Nick DeRosa could've written this," she tried convincing herself. The Nick DeRosa she knew, the one who was idolized by his teammates, canonized by his mother, and adored by nearly every female in the school, students and staff alike. Yet, whenever she'd walk by, he managed to look right through her like she wasn't even there. Never so much as a "hey," or "sup?"

But that was then, and this was now, right?

* * *

"You're late."

Nick stood at the edge of the track with his arms folded, watching Mattie like a hawk as she winced with each step that brought her closer to him.

"You're lucky I made it here at all."

"What's the matter? Shoes too tight?" he asked, sounding a little too flip for Mattie's liking.

So as not to draw the attention of any camera phone-carrying bystanders, Mattie waited until she was directly in front of him before whispering, "No, Nick. It's not the shoes. It's my legs. I'm in serious pain."

His face brightened. "You're welcome."

Unzipping her coat to reveal the same dreadful sweats she wore the previous day, she glanced up at him. "For what?"

"The shoes. I'm glad they fit. I took a guess on the size."

"Do tell," Mattie replied, making sure he knew how little his shoe-size-guessing skills impressed her.

Before letting her coat fall to the ground, she pulled the rules list from her pocket and demanded, "Who wrote this?"

Nick frowned. "I did. Why?"

Mattie was not convinced. "Where did you get it from?"

"My notebook," Nick replied, putting his hands on his hips.

"Seriously?"

"Seriously."

Mattie studied him like he was an oddity on display at a kitschy country fair before emitting a quiet, self-directed, "What do you know?"

"What's with the inquisition?" he asked as she slowly squatted down to return the list to her pocket.

Before responding, she groped for his hand so she could pull herself back up. When he didn't offer it, she grabbed at the cuffs of his jacket and pulled.

Once upright, she explained, "If I reference it in my column, I'd need to confirm the source. That's all."

As soon as the words left her mouth, she grimaced, having exposed more about her role at the paper than she intended.

Nick made no attempt to hide his surprise. "You have your own column? At the *Gazette*? Seriously?" He sounded impressed. And he was staring at her.

Not wanting to share more than she already had, Mattie glanced at her watch. "So what's the game plan for today, huh?"

In reply, he pointed to her legs. "We're not doing anything 'til you stretch those out."

He waved her over to the center of the track. As Mattie hobbled after him, she scanned the crowed of joggers and walkers for any sign of pedestrian paparazzi.

"Do what I do."

Nick turned to face her, spread his feet apart, and put his hands back on his hips. She watched as he bent his knees and started easing his lower body from right to left.

Chuckling, she pointed towards him and said, "I am not doing that."

Nick stood straight up. "Do it. Now."

After glancing quickly over her shoulders, Mattie tried mimicking his movements.

"You should feel the pull in your hips."

What I feel is completely embarrassed.

"Yep, I'm feelin' it."

She resumed her normal stance and asked, "What's next?"

"This." Nick crossed one foot in front of the other and leaned forward at the waist, resting his hands on his kneecap.

When Mattie followed suit, she stifled a grown. Her face crunched in pain.

"Now, just hold it for a minute, but don't forget to breathe."

She shut her eyes, trying to block out the feel of razor blades slicing up the backs of her legs. "Is this supposed to be helping, because if it is, it's not."

"Okay, now switch legs."

Oh, good lord.

"It'll get better. I promise," she heard him say.

"Why don't I believe you?" Mattie asked as she followed him into a very unlady-like squat with her knees resting against the insides of her elbows and her fingertips grasping her toes.

"This one's called the 'Monkey Stretch,'" Nick announced, watching as she lost her balance and toppled onto her side.

Once she righted herself, Mattie asked, "What else ya got?"

Sitting with his long legs extended into a "V" in front of him, he invited Mattie to sit facing him.

After pulling the hem of her sweatshirt down as far as it would go, she lowered herself into position.

"Put the bottom of your shoes against mine," he instructed before holding his hands out to her.

Looking as if she had just sniffed sour milk, she observed, "This is couples stretching. I've seen it on TV."

Nick shook his head. "It's instructional stretching, just until you're comfortable doing it on your own."

When still she hesitated, he urged, "Come on, Mattie. Ya gotta trust me."

She pressed her size five shoes against his. As she leaned forward, holding out her hands, she felt his shoes press back.

When Nick grabbed a hold of her fingers and enveloped them in his grasp, tingles traveled up the length of her arms, and she let out an involuntary gasp.

Eddie had rarely laid a finger on Mattie, and when he did, tingles were not the result. Maybe because any intentional physical contact on his part always seemed so forced, so obligatory. Even after they were engaged, the only time Eddie had agreed to sleep with her was after he had downed nearly half a bottle of one hundred-year-old cognac. While she had spent much of her young life looking forward to the magical moment when she would finally lose her virginity to the man of her dreams, the experience was, at best, awkward and, for lack of a better word, platonic.

Such a schmuck.

"Breathe," Nick coaxed as he studied her face. "You're not breathing."

Mattie winced. "Easy for you to say."

"Just a couple of more seconds. You can do it. Just relax."

"This isn't helping, Nick. It's making it worse."

Frowning, he eased her back a bit.

"All right. This ought to do the trick. Lay on your back."

"Excuse me?"

Nick put his hand on her shoulder and nudged her backwards. "You heard me. Lay down."

When she was flat on her back, he knelt next to her and grabbed the heel of her right foot.

"What are you doing?"

"Making it all better. Straighten your leg."

He slowly lifted her foot. By the time her leg was perpendicular to the ground, she was arching her back and digging her nails into the track's rubber surface.

"Uncle!"

"You're not breathing. Breathe. In through your nose, out through your mouth."

Mattie gritted her teeth while Nick knelt idly by, holding her foot mid-air. "Come on Mattie. I don't have all day."

No raise is worth this.

Taking a deep breath in through her nose and exhaling through her mouth, she felt something happen. The tightness in her muscles actually started to dissipate. She did it again. Even better. Her eyes popped opened, and she flashed a smile at the vaulted ceiling of the field house.

Nick eased her leg back to the ground and started raising the other one. After a quiet moment, he said, "This would all go much easier if you'd stop fighting me."

Mattie considered her options. She could continue to be aloof, whiny, and uncooperative for weeks, just to be difficult, but what would that prove except perhaps that Nick was right to advise his brother against marrying her?

She looked at him. "Do you promise never to make me this sore again?"

Nick thought for a minute then shook his head. "No."

He dropped her foot to the floor.

Coach one, Mattie zip.

Flinging an arm across her face, she mumbled, "Fine."

"Excuse me?"

She pulled herself into a sitting position and looked at Nick.

"You heard me. I surrender."

He reached down and extended his hand to her. "Good. Now let's get to work. We'll take it nice and easy today. Come on."

While Mattie shuffled along, sweating and panting, Nick walked next to her, talking the entire time.

"I want you to think about setting some goals for yourself..."

I'd like to not jiggle when I jump up and down.

"...For motivation..."

I'd like to be light enough for the man of my dreams to sweep me off my feet.

"...Like 5ks, 10ks, and a half marathon."

Oh.

"I checked around. There's a 5k in February. You should be ready for that by then."

"A 5k?" Mattie huffed. "How far is that?"

"Three point two miles. Piece of cake."

To put her mind in a happier place, she pictured a large piece of three-layered red velvet cake with loads of frothy cream cheese frosting.

"In April, there's a 10k along the lakefront. That's just over six miles."

Mattie began to feel as if an elephant had parked on her chest. "Do you know CPR?"

"Yep, I'm certified. Let's see. There's a half on the Fourth of July."

"Half?" Mattie asked, hoping for the best.

"A half marathon. Thirteen miles."

"You're a sadist," she managed between gasps for air.

Wiping her forehead with her sleeve, she announced, 'There's no way I'll be able to do all that."

Nick started jogging backwards so he could face her. "You know, it's exactly that kind of thinking that will cause you to fail. This isn't about anything other than what you think you're capable of."

No selling yourself short.

She was doing it again. Defeating herself before she even started. And he saw right through her. To make matters worse, with him jogging backwards in front of her, it created the illusion in her caffeine-starved brain that she was chasing him. The thought made her stomach lurch.

She gave her head a quick shake, but it didn't help. Nick was still talking. And she was still chasing him.

"You've got to get over whatever it is that's holding you back. It'll trip you up every time."

Mattie tried waving him off like he was a pesky mosquito. "You know so much, you tell me," she panted. "What's holding me back?"

Nick resumed his position beside her, doing little more than jogging in place to keep up with her.

"I've known you for a long time, Mattie, but I gotta tell ya, I could never understand why you always settled for less than you deserved."

"What?" If she sounded annoyed by the accusation, she didn't care. His observation was spot on, and it unnerved her. She started running through the list of lies she had designed to keep herself from getting hurt again.

I'm happily married. I love my job. I love my life. I couldn't be happier.

But Nick wouldn't let up.

"So tell me. What are you afraid of? What's holding you back from demanding the very best for yourself?"

This is so much worse than a tape measure.

"I'm not afraid of anything."

"Sure you are. And the sooner we get it out of the way, the better."

He not only touched a nerve, but he was dancing right on top of it. As she chugged along, images of her father storming out the door for the last time, her classmates faces as they teased her, and Claudia confirming that Eddie had indeed stood her up on their wedding day flashed before her. She pressed her sweat-soaked sleeve across her face hoping to catch the drops from her eyes and drips from her nose in one swipe.

"I'm not…" She tried, but couldn't verbalize the rest: *…ever gonna be loved.*

"You can't let fear cheat you out of being the best person you can be, Mattie. Don't you think you deserve better than that?"

Nick was facing her again. He jogged backwards a few steps before stopping.

"Look at you. Is this you not being afraid?"

"Shut up," she panted.

She never hated anyone as much as she hated Nick DeRosa at that very moment. Too worn out to slug him, she tried slogging right passed him, but he caught her by the shoulders and said matter-of-factly, "Congratulations. You just ran half a mile."

CHAPTER FIVE

———

"I come from a family where gravy is considered a beverage."
– Erma Bombeck

Nick was sitting in Miss O'Dell's third grade class, minding his own business, when the girl sitting behind him yanked his shirt collar back and stuffed a folded up piece of paper in his hand.

"Don't read it," Mathilde Ross, the new girl, hissed. "Give it to Eddie for me, OK?" Nick didn't know much about her. He had only heard a rumor about her not having a dad, but he didn't know why. The one thing he did know was that she only had eyes for his brother. It was as if he didn't even exist.

When Nick gave Eddie the note, he read it, scribbled a reply, and handed it back. "Give it to her," Eddie ordered.

Nick wouldn't take it. He held up his hands and said, "I ain't givin' it to her. You give it to her. She likes you, not me."

But Eddie persisted. "Give it to her, or I'll tell Mom you were the one who spilled grape juice on the rug."

"Go ahead. She knows I'd fess up if I did it."

"Fine." Eddie sneered at his twin. "But don't blame me when you get arrested."

"What?"

Nick spun around and saw four uniformed police officers with guns drawn. "You have the right to remain silent," one began.

Panicking, Nick, now an adult, laughed nervously. "Hey, wait. Don't I get a phone call?"

"What for?" another officer asked. "She won't answer. She doesn't even know you exist."

Nick awoke to a knock on his door and a harsh, "Everything ok in there?"

It sounded like his neighbor Frank, a trombone player who frequented many of Chicago's legendary blues clubs.

Rubbing his hands over his face, Nick threw his blankets back and trudged barefoot across the cold hardwood floor of his oversized studio apartment. Wearing only pajama bottoms, he opened his door just a crack and squinted at the bright light streaming in from the hallway.

He was right. It was Frank.

"Sorry, man, but it sounded like you were in some kind of trouble in there."

"Nah, just a bad dream." The memory of it was already evaporating like vapor.

Opening the door a little wider, he noticed Frank was wearing his rumpled black suit and white shirt, no tie, and holding his horn case. That he reeked of cigarette smoke, tipped Nick off to the fact that the non-smoker had just spent a couple of hours in either a bar or a lounge. Since he didn't detect the smell of alcohol, he asked, "Did you have a gig tonight?"

"Yeah, down at Kincaid's. Packed house." After a prolonged cough, he added, "Just two dozen seats, but they were full."

Nick smiled. "Nice. All right, Frank. I'll see ya 'round."

He started to close the door when Frank asked, "Hey, you got any plans for Thanksgiving? I'm going to my brother's down in Cicero. I'm sure he wouldn't mind if I brought a friend."

"Oh, thanks, but I'm going to my folks then volunteering down at the shelter. Maybe next year, huh?" With that, he tried closing the door again, when Frank used his foot as a stopper.

"Hey, man. One more thing. "

Nick rested the side of his face against the doorframe and lifted his eyebrows expectantly. "Shoot."

"Who's Mattie?"

* * *

"Happy Thanksgiving," Mattie called out after letting herself in the front door of her home away from home. Like so many other houses in the Lincoln Square neighborhood, Claudia and Tom's had a narrow, but deep floor plan, and its décor was warm and inviting. The air was filled with the intoxicating aroma of sage dressing, roast turkey, and pumpkin pie. She closed her eyes, inhaled through her nose and groaned.

As she made her way down the foyer hall toward the kitchen, Tom blocked her path and greeted her with a warm hug.

"Hey Matt. How are ya? Let me take your coat. Claud's in the kitchen."

"Thanks, bro. I'll go see if she needs help."

"And I'll go watch the game," he replied as he snuck in the opposite direction toward the family room.

The bag of salad Mattie had brought dangled haplessly at her side as she entered the kitchen. It was her only contribution to the otherwise starch-laden feast.

She found Claudia standing in front of the kitchen counter that jutted between them. With one hand, she had a white-knuckle grip on the rim of an over-sized stainless steel bowl that, by the smell of it, was filled with the ingredients for their mother's traditional sage stuffing recipe. In her other hand, she held a large stainless steel spoon. Mattie watched in awe as her sister stirred with the intensity of a high-speed blender.

Given the size of the bowl and the angle at which Claudia was gripping the spoon, she suspected her diminutive sister was standing on a step stool. It was likely the same one she used to reach items on the top shelves of her kitchen cabinets.

Strands of Claudia's otherwise smooth blonde hair had fallen across her pink, sweat-beaded face. When her eyes darted from the contents of the bowl to her sister, she cried, "What's that?"

Mattie jumped. She dropped the bag of salad on the counter and backed away slowly, out of Claudia's spoon-swinging radius.

"What does it look like?"

After dumping the ingredients from the bowl into a greased roasting pan, Claudia shoved it in the oven, slammed the door shut and responded, "I know what it is, but why did you bring it? We never have salad on Thanksgiving. The whole day is about indulging, not dieting. I made three different kinds of pie, for Pete's sake."

She ripped a paper towel off a nearby roll and dabbed her forehead, waiting for a response.

Mattie looked forward to this day of unbridled gluttony more than any other. Even Christmas. Gritting her teeth, she replied, "I know, I know, but I'm in training. Remember?"

"All right," Claudia conceded. "But you got to have at least one piece of pumpkin pie. Pumpkin's a vegetable, right? Or is it a fruit?"

After a week of following Nick's rules to the letter, Mattie had already managed to lose three pounds. Still, it took every ounce of will power she had to keep from lunging for the whipped cream canister she knew was in the refrigerator and spraying the entire contents of it into her open mouth.

Something distract me, quick.

"Where are the kids?"

"Tommy's napping, but I think the twins are with Tom, watching the game."

Watching a football game without the usual beer, chips and dip at her fingertips held little appeal. She decided to try a different tactic.

"How about I set the table?"

Claudia wiped her hands on her apron. "I did that first thing this morning."

Mattie peeked into the dining room. The table, draped in a gold, lightly patterned tablecloth with matching napkins and candle tapers, looked exquisite.

"Wow. All that's missing are little pinecone turkey napkin holders," Mattie teased, as she did in her column that ran the week before, off-handedly dissing stay-at-home moms who have too much time on their hands.

"Look behind you," Claudia said dryly.

There, on the kitchen table sat seven perfect little pinecone turkey napkin holders.

Mattie picked one up and examined it. "How cute. Did the kids make these?"

Claudia folded her arms and tried to look upset, but burst out laughing instead. "I don't want to talk about it. How about some wine before Aunt Viv gets here?"

Before Mattie could reply, she poured them both a glass and asked, "So how's it going with you? Tell me about the training."

"I have to admit it's going really well. I hardly get sore at all anymore and can almost run a mile without feeling like I'm going to die."

"Almost a mile? Already?"

"Without stopping," Mattie boasted.

"I'm impressed. And jealous. I haven't been able to work out since I had Tommy."

Setting her glass on the counter, Claudia snapped her fingers.

"Oh, I almost forgot. I was going through clothes for Goodwill when I came across the workout stuff I wore when I was expecting the twins. Would you be interested in any of it?"

"Ouch," Mattie exclaimed. "Do I look pregnant with twins to you?"

"Of course not. I had to stop exercising when I was in my fourth month, so they're technically not even maternity clothes. Besides, I'm not using them. I put everything in a bag for you by the front closet. Just remember to grab it when you leave later."

Mattie's spirit brightened. She was getting tired of having to wash the same sweats night after night.

"So, what's your coach like?" Claudia asked. "Would you recommend him?"

Mattie looked away and stammered, "He's uh, well, you know, he's OK. He's the first trainer I've ever had, so I don't really have anybody to compare him to."

Her sister leaned forward and whispered, "Is he hot?"

Taking another sip of wine, Mattie sank into a kitchen chair and examined one of the turkey napkin holders. "I don't want to talk about it."

"What's the matter? Is he a jerk?"

Mattie knew it was now or never. If she didn't tell Claudia the truth, she'd learn about it with the rest of her readers when the feature kicked off in January. And that would be bad. Very bad.

She sat up. "No, Claud. It's just that, well—" She took a deep breath before blurting, "It's Nick."

Her sister stared at her. "Nick who?"

Taking another deep breath, Mattie clarified. "DeRosa. My coach is Nick DeRosa."

Claudia covered her mouth with her hand. Her eyes were as wide as saucers.

"Oh. My. God," she shrieked. Lowering her voice, she asked, "When were you going to tell me?"

Tom came bursting into the kitchen in full paramedic mode. "What happened? Everything OK?"

Claudia started fanning herself with an oven mitt, smiling at Mattie who was five shades of red and covering her face with both hands.

"I knew I shouldn't have told you," her muffled voice moaned.

Shooing her husband away, Claudia exclaimed, "I'm so excited for you."

Truly concerned that her sister could be so clueless, Mattie scrunched her face in disbelief and asked, "Why?"

Having successfully paired an old college buddy with her best friend's brother, a union that blossomed into marriage, Claudia fancied herself a matchmaker. Mattie did not. Still, it didn't keep Claudia from giving it her best shot.

She beamed at her little sister. "Just wait. You'll see."

Laughing, Mattie held up her hand and said, "Please, don't embarrass yourself on my account. The man despises me."

"He does not."

"He does. Claudia, he does. On so many different levels. I'm sure he's as eager to get this assignment over with as I am."

Her sister smiled at her and sipped at her cabernet.

Mattie continued, "Okay. Whatever. Listen, this leads me to my next question."

"What's up?"

Mattie took a long slog of wine this time. When she felt a wave of intoxication warm her face and melt her reserve, she asked, "Is the offer to move in with you guys still open?"

Her sister seemed relieved. "Of course, hon, anytime. You know that. For how long?"

"Ten months?" she ventured.

"Oh. Wow. Sure. Absolutely."

"And Tom would be okay with it?"

"Are you kidding? You know he loves your cooking. Besides, having another adult around to watch the kids, take them to and from school, and help with the chores? He'd be ecstatic."

Wait a minute...

Claudia nodded. "So what's your game plan? Are you subletting your apartment?"

"My apartment?"

Claudia frowned. "Yeah. You just renewed your lease didn't you?"

Mattie hadn't thought that far in advance. She hadn't thought much beyond what Dianne had said. Moving in with her sister and her family so she would remember that she's supposed to be a married working parent suddenly didn't seem like a very good idea, especially if it would mean losing her beloved Lincoln Park apartment.

Responding with the only truth she knew, Mattie sighed, "I haven't gotten that far yet."

She was spared from further questioning by the sound of the doorbell.

The sisters' eyes met.

"Aunt Viv," Claudia announced with a smile.

Contrary to her gruff exterior, their aunt was the only one who had welcomed the girls into her home with open arms and raised them as her own after Mattie and Claudia's mother had died unexpectedly. As such, they were exceedingly fond of her despite her lack of social graces.

After dinner, the family matriarch sat at the head of the table opposite Tom. Her dark blond hair, infused with white strands, was pulled into a bun at the nape of her neck making the lines in her face more pronounced and her features more severe. Square-shaped, gold clip-on earrings covered her earlobes. With her elbows on the table, she surveyed the empty platters and bowls that just a few minutes before had been brimming with whipped garlic potatoes, candied sweet potatoes, green bean casserole, homemade drop biscuits, and roast turkey you could cut with a fork.

"Well, Claudia, you may not be the cook your sister is, but you have definitely mastered your mother's Thanksgiving menu."

Claudia rose from her seat, kissed her on the check, and replied, "Thanks, Aunt Viv."

Mattie took a more direct route to deliver the compliment. "Everything was fantastic, Claud."

After their Dad walked out on them, Thanksgiving marked the one day their mother considered cooking for her girls a joy, not a burden. Every bite was a soothing balm, taking away the sting of rejection and replacing it with just a couple of unwanted pounds. In Mattie's mind, this always seemed like a fair trade, and this year was no exception. Deprived of the starches, sugar, and alcohol for the past week, each bite was a culinary dream.

"Listen, girls," Aunt Viv said after setting down her napkin. "I was going through some old things. Books, letters. You know."

Mattie glanced at Claudia who had already started clearing dishes.

"Uh-huh," she prodded.

"And I found some pictures of you, dear," she said pointing to Mattie. "I was thinking maybe you could stop by if you wanted and pick them up." Vivienne then launched into an unsolicited update on her own daughter. "Did I tell you Linda is staying at her in-laws until Helen recovers from her hip surgery? I told you Helen had hip surgery, right? The doctor thought she should have both hips replaced, but he'll only do one at a time. And of course, Medicare will only pay for—"

"Aunt Viv?" Mattie interrupted, while Tom got up to help Claudia clear. "You found some pictures?"

"Oh, right. Well, I thought if you weren't doing anything tomorrow…"

Thinking of the train-bus-another-train-cab route she'd have to take to get to her aunt's after her morning workout, she replied, "Oh, Aunt Viv. I'm sorry, but I have plans tomorrow. Maybe some other time?"

"Sure. Another time then."

Craning her neck to see that Claudia and Tom were out of earshot, Vivienne whispered, "And tell your sister to stop spoiling her children. They'll be walking all over her before she knows it."

"Yes, Aunt Viv. Are you finished with that?"

Mattie reached over and took her aunt's plate that looked as if it had been licked clean and retreated into the calamity of the kitchen.

After the last dish was cleaned and put away, Tom offered to drive Aunt Viv home so she wouldn't have to take the bus. Claudia asked Mattie if she wanted to help put the kids to bed. Considering they were still bouncing off the walls at the news that Aunt Mattie might be coming to live with them, she begged off and headed for her train.

* * *

"Hey, Mr. D. What you got for me today?" The homeless man with a few teeth missing from his smile stood before Nick holding a tray with an empty plate on it.

"Hey, Happy Thanksgiving, Cyril. How about some turkey?" He lifted a generous portion onto his plate.

"God bless you."

Nick watched as the man shuffled over to the large vat of steaming mashed potatoes. After grabbing a dinner roll, he sat at a round table already crowded with five others, all regulars, except one. The youngest-looking one in the bunch dove into his food with ravenous abandon.

Leaning over to his friend Scott Murphy, Nick asked, "Who's the new guy?"

Scott, the manager of intake services at the shelter and a former teammate of Nick's, glanced at the young man with short blond hair hunched over his plate. "I'm not sure. I haven't seen him here before, but I like his shoes."

While Scott hoisted an empty serving bin out from the rack in front of him and replaced it with one brimming with hot mashed spuds, Nick looked back at the table.

Running shoes.

When it was time for his break, Nick approached the table. "How's everybody doing? Got room for one more?"

He pulled up a chair next to the new guy and held out his hand. "Hi. I'm Nick."

On closer inspection, Nick could see that he was more boy than man. Seventeen years old, maybe eighteen. When he looked up, his expression was a mixture of defiance and shame. He smeared his right hand against the thigh of his dirty jeans before shaking Nick's.

"John."

"Nice to meet you, John."

The boy nodded and shoveled more food into his mouth.

The two sat in silence while the rest of the guests discussed everything from politics to religion to the latest episodes of reality television shows.

From what Nick could tell, John seemed to be a young healthy kid. He wondered what brought him to the shelter, but knew better than to pry. Instead, he asked, "You a runner?"

Putting his fork down, he responded. "Listen. I don't want any hassles."

Nick smiled and shook his head. He hadn't meant to imply that John was a runaway. Pumping his arms back and forth, he asked, "Do you like to *run*?"

Shifting in his chair, the boy replied, "Yeah, I used to. In school. Not good enough for college, though."

"So what happened?"

John let out a short laugh and stared at his plate. "Nothing. That's what happened."

"Listen. You got a place to stay?"

"Sort of."

Not wanting to drive him away with any more questions, Nick pointed to Scott. "See that guy over there? He works here and can set you up if you need a place to crash."

John nodded. "OK. Thanks."

Standing up with his tray, Nick added, "And if you ever want to go for a run, I can meet you here most mornings around eleven."

"Good to know. Thanks."

* * *

As Mattie's train pulled into her stop an hour later, she heard her phone buzz, indicating that someone had just texted her. It was Nick.

"Happy Thanksgiving."

She stared at the words. They agreed to skip their workout for the day, didn't they? Why was he texting her? Feeling an awkward obligation to reply, she typed,

"Same to you."

When the doors on her train opened, she stuffed her phone in her pocket, grabbed the bag of Claudia's old workout clothes, and got off. She was halfway down the stairs when she felt another buzz. Given the sparse number of people in the area and the time of night, she kept her phone in her pocket and decided to wait until she got home to read his message.

It didn't stop her from wondering what he wanted, though.

A reminder to not eat any pie?

Too late.

An addendum to his list of rules to eliminate wine, water, and breathing?

Wouldn't be surprised.

Or maybe it was another one of his tough-love, bumper-sticker philosophies.

Spare me.

When she got home, she flopped on her couch, and pulled out her phone to look at Nick's text.

"Forgot school closed tomorrow. Meet me at Y on Marshfield @ 9 for pool work."

"Not on your life, pal," she muttered to herself.

Her thumbs flew over her keypad.

"Sorry. No bathing suit."

Mattie 1, Coach zip.

Feeling rather smug, she had no sooner set her phone on her coffee table and was reaching for the remote when Nick responded.

"Get one. And bring a towel."

The only thing Mattie hated more than buying new clothes was buying a new bathing suit.

Where am I supposed to find a bathing suit first thing in the morning on the day after Thanksgiving? In Chicago?

She grabbed a nearby throw pillow and screamed into it until she emptied her lungs of all that was in them. Sinking even deeper into her couch cushions, she remembered the one thing she hated even more than bathing suit shopping.

Wearing said bathing suit in the presence of Nick DeRosa.

She tugged the bag of clothes her sister gave her closer and started pulling out each item one by one, hoping to find something that could pass as swimwear. A pair of black spandex capris, two sport bras small enough for Mattie to use as ponytail holders, a pair of shorts with little panties sewn into them, and several long and short-sleeved Dri-FIT shirts in an assortment of colors. No bathing suit.

Next, she reached for her laptop and checked store hours. Many opened at five in the morning. Since she was already getting used to functioning at that early hour, she set her alarm and headed for bed.

Eight hours later, she was on a bus bound for a shopping mall not far from her apartment, her legs still stinging from being shaved for the first time in she didn't know how long.

The mall was packed with people. As she elbowed her way into a department store, she followed the signs to the women's department. A harried clerk pointed her to the sorry display of bathing suits they had in stock.

She found a rack on which hung the only one-piece bathing suits in her size that she could find. All were either in a gaudy floral print or solid black. Whimpering, she checked her watch. It was already 7:30. While she made sure to wake up on time, she sorely underestimated how long it would take to shave her legs.

Panicking, she jogged to a sporting goods store at the opposite end of the mall. As providence would have it, not only did they have a generous amount of tasteful, affordable one-piece suits, they were giving extra discounts to purchases made before 8 a.m.

Mattie grabbed four that she liked and ducked into a fitting room to try them on.

The one in which she looked the least awful was plum-colored and had a special tummy-trimming feature with a little bit of a skirt on the bottom that hid the razor burn along her bikini line.

Sold!

Rushing home, she put it on under her workout clothes, grabbed the largest beach towel she could find in her linen closet and zoomed to the pool, hell bent on getting into the water before Nick even arrived.

The first thing that hit Mattie when she entered the YMCA building was the intense odor of chlorine. While it didn't prompt any particular memory, it gave her an inexplicable urge to slather herself with suntan lotion. The second sensation to hit her was the humidity. The windows were thick with condensation, causing the curls in her hair to become more coiled with each step she took toward the pool entrance.

"Excuse me, you can't go in there," the girl behind the desk gurgled after swigging her iced coffee. She was wearing a gray tank top and jean shorts over her royal blue racing suit. The employee identification card and shiny silver whistle dangling from her neck made her look like a professional beach bum.

Mattie, who had been trying to sneak into the woman's locker room behind a pack of lithe, chlorine-bleached swim team members, stuck out like a sore thumb.

"Why not?" she said in her best take-no-prisoners tone. Peering at the girl's ID, she added, "Samantha."

"Because there's a meet," the attendant snapped back. "Swim team members only."

Laughing with the joyous exaltation of a schoolgirl who had just been informed that it was a snow day, Mattie asked, "Really?"

The girl behind the desk did not share her in excitement. "Really," she droned while examining her nails.

Mattie 1, Coach double-zip.

"Is the weight room open?" a low voice behind her asked.

Mattie spun around. It was Nick. His hair was tousled and the scruff on his face indicated that he hadn't shaved for the past few days. Still, wearing snow-white sweat pants and a matching hoodie that had the Olympic emblem in the upper left-hand corner, he looked, much to Mattie's chagrin, quite magnificent.

Oh, who are you trying to impress?

He spoke over her turned head to the girl behind the desk who had abandoned her iced coffee and gushed, "Hi, Nick."

"Weight room?" he repeated.

The girl nodded like a bobblehead doll. "Yep, it's open."

"Thanks, Sam," Nick replied with a full-wattage smile-and-wink combo.

Addressing Mattie, he simply said, "Come on," before stepping away.

When the girl's eyes finally fell on Mattie, still standing at the counter, dressed in her usual gray sweats and her hair twisted into two braids tucked behind each ear, a vague curiosity creased her face into a frown.

Mattie knew that expression all too well. It meant, "*You're* with him? How is that even possible?"

And just like that, she was back in high school, standing in front of Marina Buckley, a cheerleader whose favorite afterschool activity was berating Mattie and accusing her of stalking her boyfriend, Eddie.

"He'd never go out with someone like you," she would announce in front of all of her other beauty-queen wannabes. Then she'd explode in a haughty, oh-this-is-too-good-to-be-true laugh while her minions joined in.

Drowning in the memory of one of her many high school horrors, Mattie was frozen to the spot. Just as she was about to sink into a familiar puddle of nothingness, Nick re-appeared.

In what seemed like slow motion, he draped his arm across her back, gripped her shoulder with his hand, pulled her close, and said just loud enough for the attendant to hear, "This way, babe."

When Mattie felt his lips press firmly onto the top of her head, she surrendered to the tumble of emotions at war within her and melded into Nick as he led her away.

For the first few steps, she relished the warm sensation of his body moving against hers and the eyes that watched in wonder as they passed.

Take that, Marina Buckley.

When they turned a corner, though, the jilted working girl in her returned. Slipping out from under him, she demanded, "Just what do you think you're doing?"

"You shouldn't let people treat you like that," Nick scolded.

Mattie's cheeks flared, "Oh, and your solution is to just waltz right in and whisk me away, is it? I suppose you expect me to bow down and thank you for rescuing me."

Nick stood before her, nostrils flared, jaw clenched.

When he said nothing, Mattie added, "And you kissed me!"

She swatted her hand over the top of her head as if a bug had just landed on it.

"You know, I can manage just fine on my own," she continued. "I don't need you or anybody else to police my level of self-esteem. Got it?"

Nick just smirked at her and shook his head. "I just realized something."

"What?" By now, Mattie was certain her cheeks were crimson, but she so didn't care.

"You've never had any problem standing up to me," he said quite calmly.

Out of words, Mattie put on her best exasperated expression. "Whatever. I think we should talk about boundaries."

"Knock yourself out."

"First and foremost, kissing. Highly inappropriate."

He jutted out his chiseled chin. "And why's that?"

Mattie held up the ring finger on her left hand as if to issue an expletive.

Nick looked at her coolly for a moment.

"If it wasn't for that," he said, nodding at her ring, "I would've gone straight for your mouth."

He held the door of the weight room open for her. "After you, slugger."

But she couldn't move. The air had left her lungs and her bones had turned to cement.

That kiss.

The night of her wedding rehearsal, she should've known it wasn't Eddie when he didn't resist her. Maybe a part of her did know, and she kept kissing him, regardless. Either way, she never forgot the feel of Nick's bristly but soft face in her hands, his lips parted against hers, his breath in her mouth. Taking in the very essence of him all in one fleeting instant.

Apparently Nick hadn't either.

He stood patiently waiting until she was ready for her first ever lesson in the benefits of resistance training.

* * *

When an unseasonable warm spell blew into the Windy City right before the holidays, Nick informed Mattie that they would be running outside and arranged to meet at an intersection in Lincoln Park. From there, the pair jogged slowly down Fullerton Avenue passing elegant row houses, coffee shops bustling with early morning commuters, and students from a nearby university.

Mattie felt like she was in a fish bowl. Certain that all eyes were on the short, out-of-shape girl huffing and shuffling next to the clearly in-shape Olympian barely jogging next to her, every jiggle seemed magnified ten-fold. Each gasp for air seemed like an unspoken plea for an oxygen mask.

She glanced up at Nick. He wasn't even breaking a sweat.

"I don't like it out here."

"Why not? It's gorgeous. And, last time I checked, the marathon is not being run on a track, so you'd better get used to running outside."

On their way toward the lakefront, Nick pretended to check his watch while glancing at her as often as he could without being obvious. Since their run-in at the YMCA, their verbal exchanges had become sparse.

"How ya feeling?" he asked every half mile or so.

"Fine," she replied.

Traffic noise and pedestrian chatter punctuated the rhythm of their feet hitting the pavement in unison. To fill in the gaps, he'd toss out some pointers, doing his best to sound encouraging.

"Don't hit the ground with your heels. You'll get shin splints."

"Slow down your breathing."

"Relax your shoulders."

"Stop clenching your fists."

When they hit the asphalt path that skirted Lake Michigan, he pointed to their right, and they both swerved south.

* * *

With each passing day, Nick pushed her to go a little farther, reminding her that distance, not speed, was the goal. With each passing day, he saw her determination and resolve. But, with the wall she had erected between them, he felt little in the way of accomplishment.

As he tried explaining to his mother one evening over her homemade ravioli, "She's working hard, making good progress, but she's definitely not enjoying herself. Her whole approach is to get each workout over with as quickly as possible."

"Well, why don't you talk to her about it?" Lucy prodded.

Nick dismissed the idea. "It wouldn't do any good."

"Remember that coach you had in college? The one who was there when you first started? What was his name?"

Nick remembered the renowned running expert who gave little in the way of anything other than criticism and most of it not constructive.

"Coyne. Coach Coyne."

Lucy snapped her fingers. "That's right. Remember you didn't like him because he never told you how you were doing. No matter how hard you worked, it never seemed good enough?"

Nick knew where his mother was leading their conversation. "I know, Ma, but this is different. She doesn't like me."

Perplexed, his mother asked, "How could she not like you?"

Under his breath, he answered, "She never has."

Lucy paused. "She never has? Am I missing something here? How about you tell me who this girl is, huh?"

Nick looked long and hard at his mother. Resting his fork on his plate, he said, "All right. You're gonna find out sooner or later. It's Mattie. Mattie Ross."

He narrowed his eyes and braced himself for her response.

Lucy slapped her hand on the table, startling Nick. "I knew it."

"You did not. How could you have?"

His mother pointed to him and said, "You talk in your sleep."

Nick fell silent.

"I've been praying for that poor girl for so long."

Hearing this, he found his voice. "Poor girl? Have you forgotten that she sent me to the emergency room where I had to get ten stitches? Have you also forgotten that she didn't return any of my calls when I couldn't get a hold of you and pop to vouch for me? Where's your loyalty?"

Lucy held his chin in her hand and squeezed. "Your cut healed. Your criminal record is no more. But Mattie? She still has a hole in her heart that will never go away. First her father leaves her, then your brother. And, in between, her poor mother passes."

She picked up her plate and brought it to the sink. Turning around, she smiled and said, "But now, maybe things will start looking up for her. God put you in her life for a reason, Nicky. And you have a chance to make everything right."

He grimaced. The image of Mattie flipping him off with her ring finger was still very fresh in his mind.

"I don't think so, Ma."

"Oh, yeah, Mister Smart Guy? How come?"

"Well, for starters, she's married." The words hung in the air. He still couldn't believe it.

Lucy's plate slipped out of her hands and into the sink with a clank. "To who?"

"I don't know."

"How is that even possible?" she exclaimed. "It's only been, what, two years?"

"Just about," Nick sighed.

"Well then, how do you know she's married?"

"I saw his picture on her desk. And she's got a ring on her finger."

"Huh," Lucy replied, frowning as she wiped her hands on a nearby dish towel. "Well, it's her loss then."

Nick hung his head. "Thanks, Ma. It doesn't matter anyway. Even if she weren't married, it wouldn't work. I'd always be wondering if she was thinking of Eddie when she was with me."

He stood up and rinsed off his plate. "Right now, my only focus is to get her across the finish line in October so I can get my bonus and move on with my life."

Strictly business.

* * *

Ever since Mattie had surrendered herself to Nick's coaching prowess, her life seemed more unsettled. Everything was different. Some changes were for the better, some not so much. For one, despite having to dip into her alcohol and take-out-food funds to buy healthier fare, her clothes were beginning to feel baggy. While this should have been cause for celebration, she had few funds with which to replace them. Second, while her column's fan base was growing, her familiar snarl had abandoned her.

And there was something else. Something far more disturbing. Like her clothes, her identity no longer seemed to fit. Because of her two-carat crutch and the faux family gallery on her desk, she could hardly play the *wronged woman* card with

Nick. Staying angry with him while pretending to be a happily married career woman was already proving to be more than Mattie could manage.

Perplexed by this unsettling shift in her universe, she confided in her sister. That she chose to have this conversation while they waited in line to see Santa with Claudia's kids at a crowded State Street department store was her first mistake.

That she was expecting assurance and comfort was her second.

"Maybe," Claudia began over the shrill of screaming children and blaring holiday music, "you're finally realizing that the fabulous life you thought you missed out on with Eddie isn't anywhere near as great as your life is about to get."

CHAPTER SIX

———

"Seize the moment. Remember all those women on the 'Titanic'
who waved off the dessert cart."
– Erma Bombeck

"You're launching the new feature on the first Sunday after Christmas, and you still don't have a title for it?" Lester's face was pinched in disbelief as he gripped the back of his office chair.

He didn't mind being called a lot of things—opportunist, cheapskate, Republican, but the one thing he did not want to be called was "liar." If this promotion didn't fly, it would be the first time he didn't come through on a promise to help someone bolster their career. He did it for a number of writers on the staff who went on to become esteemed editors and even a couple of Pulitzer Prize winners. And he so badly wanted to help Nick, a man who had made such a tremendous difference in his troubled son's life.

Dianne sat on the opposite side of Lester's desk, staring him down with the steely determination of a bargain hunter on Black Friday.

"Mattie wants 'Running Down a Dream,'" she announced. "And I like it."

Lester grimaced. "Overused and clichéd. You need a gimmick. Something catchy. Something our readers can relate to. Something that will *sell*."

His face grew red as he gripped the back of his chair and looked toward the ceiling. "Let's see. We got the Comeback Kid coming in to train the Plate Spinner to run a marathon."

"That's not a story. People train for marathons all the time," Dianne interjected.

Lester pointed a finger at her. "Exactly. What makes them so special?"

When Dianne didn't respond, he folded his arms and kept talking.

"Let's see. Nick is trying to launch a new career. Fresh start. Mattie wants—" He looked at Dianne. "What does she want?"

"Well, to begin with, a raise. Beyond that, she wants to move over to something more challenging, like investigative work."

Lester thought for a minute. "No, nothing there."

Dianne rolled her eyes, and Lester checked his watch. "Listen, I've gotta run to a meeting. You need to nail this down by today. Meet me back here at two. No one goes home until it's final."

* * *

Dear Plate Spinner—

My fourteen-year-old daughter has a weight problem. I don't know what to do to get her to stop eating, but I know she has to. She gets teased a lot. She just started high school and has given up on finding any friends. I try not to have junk food around the house, but I'm a single mom. I work two jobs, and I don't have a lot of time to cook or shop, so we eat a lot of take out and pizza. But when I tell her not to eat so much, she gets upset. I'm at the end of my rope. I love my daughter and just want her to be happy. Can you help?

Signed,
Desperate

Mattie read the letter again, covering her mouth with her hand and swallowing hard on the lump in her throat. Before she knew it, her hands started racing over the keyboard.

Dear Desperate—

First, know that you're not alone, and neither is your daughter. High school is hard enough with a healthy self-esteem, but when a child's is low, it can feel like hell. I speak from experience. When I was her age, the kids used to tease me about my weight, too. Well, bully really. They'd shout a cruel name at me when I walked by, then laugh and laugh. I usually ducked into a bathroom stall until the bell was about to ring, then rush to my class before anyone else could hurl more insults my way. I'll be honest. To this day, I'm still self-conscious about my weight, but I'm learning to respect myself, both physically and mentally, remember that I'm awesome, and do my best to stay positive. If you can help your daughter do these things, she'll learn to never ever settle for anything less than she deserves.

"Who are you, and what have you done with my favorite columnist? Are you starting some kind of support group?" Dianne asked as she read over Mattie's shoulder.

Putting Desperate's letter back into view, Mattie pointed to it and whispered, "Dianne, that's me. This could've been from my mother."

After a quiet moment spent remembering the look of helplessness in her mother's eyes every time she'd offer to try the latest fad diet with her daughter, Mattie knew she had to do something to help not just this girl, but all kids who were shackled with low self-esteem.

She looked at her editor. "I hate to say it, but Nick got this one right."

"What one? What are you talking about?" Dianne asked as she peered at the email.

Standing up, Mattie asked, "Has Les finalized the campaign?"

"No, but he gave me until two to come up with something, bless his greedy little heart."

Mattie was texting faster than her thumbs could keep up. When her ring tone signaled a reply, she hissed, "Yes."

She squeezed Dianne's arm and said, "I'll have it for you after lunch."

And with that she was gone.

* * *

Nick had just finished changing the oil in his mother's sedan in the alley behind his apartment building when his phone signaled that he had received a text. Wiping his hands on a rag, he picked it up. It was from Mattie.

"Nick! Can you meet me for lunch? It's urgent. My treat."

Without hesitating, he responded.

"When and where?"

He didn't have to wait long for the reply.

"Whatever's easiest for you."

After he checked to make sure the text messages were indeed coming from Mattie, his curiosity got the better of him. For the past two weeks, she had barely said a word, and now she wanted to take him out to lunch?

Maybe somebody stole her phone.

He texted back that he could meet her at a sandwich shop not far from her office in half an hour. After seeing himself in the mirror, he added fifteen minutes to his estimate.

Forty-five minutes later, he stepped inside the bustling sandwich shop. It was one of those noisy chain places with exposed-brick walls and blond wooden tables and booths. The afternoon sun streamed through a large picture window facing the street.

Given that he had to park four blocks away, he stood under the vent just inside the entrance, relishing the blast of warm air blowing on him with the force of a hand dryer in a public washroom. From this vantage point, he scanned the crowd, looking for Mattie. When he didn't see her, he checked his watch to confirm that he was on time.

"Nick."

Hearing his name, he looked up, searching again for a familiar face. Not finding one, he turned around. Mattie had just walked in.

He barely recognized her. In high heels, her face was in much closer proximity to his than it was on their morning runs. She slipped off her overcoat and flung it over her arm, revealing a cranberry-colored sweater set and black dress pants. Her hair, usually pulled back during their workouts, bounced over her shoulders in soft curls.

Wow.

"Thanks for coming."

"Sure." He paused before asking, "Everything okay?"

"Never better."

Nick caught a sparkle in her eyes he hadn't seen before. Not when she was talking to him anyway. He struggled to pull his gaze away.

Get a grip.

Nodding at the menu hung on the wall, she asked over the din of voices, "Do you know what you want?"

Just then, a crush of customers pushed into her. When she lost her footing, Nick's hands flew to her elbows to steady her.

With his eyes still on her, he replied, "Yeah, I do."

Mattie caught her breath, and he took note of the pink hue fanning over her cheeks when she looked up at him.

"To eat," she clarified.

You can let her go now.

As the blush spread over the bridge of her nose and up her forehead, she clarified, "For lunch. Here, at the restaurant."

Release. Your. Grip.

He let his hands drop to his sides. Regaining his composure, he replied, "You'd better ditch the high heels. We can't afford for you to twist your ankle."

Addressing the girl behind the counter, he announced, "I'll have the turkey club. No chips."

"And I'll have the chicken Caesar, dressing on the side."

After she paid for their food, the girl gave Mattie a number card to place on their table.

Nick found a booth for two near a window overlooking the holiday shoppers traversing the sidewalk and asked, "So. What's the occasion?"

As Mattie slid into her seat, she whispered, "I need your permission."

Although her expression didn't reveal any hint of excitement, her eyes were still ten different kinds of sparkly.

"For what?"

"To use your rules."

Nick made a reeling motion with his hand, signaling her to keep talking. "For…?"

Mattie gave her head a quick shake. "Let me back up. Dianne, my editor, has been stumped on what to call this new feature about—"

Unable to find the perfect words to describe their unlikely collaboration, she finally blurted out, "Us. The whole marketing campaign has stalled because of it. We're really behind the eight ball. Then, this morning, I got a letter from a reader."

"Here you go." A lanky man wearing jeans and a polo shirt with the restaurant's logo on the front set their orders in front of them.

"Can I get you anything else?"

"No," they replied in unison.

When he was gone, Mattie asked, "Where was I?"

Nick, still wondering if Mattie herself had an evil twin or perhaps a family history of multiple personality disorder, prodded, "You got a letter from somebody."

"Oh. Right. So, it's from a mom who needs advice on how to help her fourteen-year-old daughter who is overweight and miserable."

Nick leaned forward and rested his elbows on the table. "Wait. Back up. You're an *advice* columnist?"

Taking a deep breath, Mattie exhaled, "I am."

"Do you always get this excited about getting a letter?" He took a large bite of his sandwich, waiting for her to reply.

"No, I don't. But you're missing the point. I started writing a reply to this mother about how to help her daughter, and that's when it hit me."

Nick, still chewing, raised both eyebrows and mumbled, "What?"

Given the wall she had erected between them after their run-in at the YMCA, he expected her to issue a scathing condemnation or blistering insult. He set his sandwich down, leaned back in his seat, and held out his hand, inviting her to continue.

Almost dunking her sweater into the little cup of Caesar dressing that came with her salad, Mattie leaned forward and said, "Your rules."

Nick snarled, "Yeah? What about 'em?"

"I cribbed my whole reply from them."

The way she bit down on her lip, raised both eyebrows, and clenched her fists after she said it, he could tell she was pulling out all the stops to avoid getting gushy in front of him.

Still not sure why she wanted to meet with him, he kept his mouth shut and waited.

She pushed her salad and overflowing dressing cup aside, leaned even further forward, and clasped her hands on the table in front of her.

"As much as I hate to admit it, they're pretty powerful."

Nick, uncomfortable with the direction the conversation was going, muttered, "Geez. I never got this kind of reaction from my guys. I'm not even sure they read them."

Mattie rolled her eyes and flashed him a smile that made his heart skip a beat. "How many times do I have to remind you I'm not a sixteen-year-old boy?"

Never.

Suddenly wishing they had taken a table out on the frigid sidewalk, Nick cleared his throat and asked, "So what does this have to do with me?"

"Tell me the truth. Are you sure you came up with these rules all on your own? I don't think it would be in either of our best interests to be slapped with a plagiarism lawsuit."

"Yes, I came up with them all on my own." He ran a hand through his hair and sat back in his seat, adding, "Well, mostly. They're my favorite quotes from my favorite coaches. Every time I heard something I liked, I'd write it down in my notebook. Over the years, I had quite a few to pull from. They saw me through some pretty rough times."

Mattie shot back, "Do I have your permission to use them?"

Nick shrugged. "Sure."

Satisfied, Mattie leaned back in her seat. After picking at her salad for a minute, she looked him in the eye. "Can I ask you something?"

He tried to assess from her expression if he was about to be sucker punched. Hoping for the best, he repeated, "Sure."

"I know you don't think I have a chance in hell of ever completing this marathon, but—"

"I never said that." His eyes grew wide as he continued, "The thought never even crossed my mind."

She lowered her chin and looked across the table at him. "Look, running may be your thing, but self-deprecation is mine. I'm really good at it. I've been doing it since I was ten."

Before she barely got her last word out, Nick replied, "Yeah, well, I've been a runner since I was ten, and I'll make damn sure you cross that finish line, even if I have to drag you by your hair every step of the way. So what's your question?"

Mattie appeared a tad horrified at the image he invoked. "I'm not so sure I want to ask it now."

They stared at each other for an uncomfortable minute.

She started slowly, carefully choosing her words. "Do you think I can——"

"Yes."

Mattie gasped. "You didn't even let me finish."

"I didn't have to. You want to know if I think you can finish the marathon. I don't think you can; I *know* you can."

More uncomfortable silence ensued.

When she glanced out the window, Nick leaned forward and clasped his hands together. He caught the surprise in her eyes when they met his. "I wouldn't be here if I didn't think so."

The corner of her mouth curved into a slow smile. Pointing her fork at him, she said, "You want to know what I think? If we play this right, we can change the world."

Nick let out a hearty laugh as he eased back in his seat. "What are you talking about? All I'm on the hook for is getting you across the finish line in October."

"And all I'm on the hook for is to write about it. But with your rules and my column, we have the power to make a huge difference in people's lives."

She waved her hands over the table, adding, "Bolster confidence, raise self-esteem, eradicate bullies. All the things you keep yelling at me about."

"I don't yell at you."

"You do, Nick. All the time. And it's all right. That's what coaches do, right? They yell. And you're my coach, so..."

You're my coach.

He liked how that sounded when she said it. It made him feel a little warmer on the inside. Even if her passion was directed more at his rules than at him, he liked being on the receiving end of it for a change.

Picking up his sandwich, he asked, "So what does this have to do with what they're doing at the paper?"

"They've been looking for an angle, a gimmick."

She scrunched her face up and asked, "How does 'Team Plate Spinner' grab you?"

He frowned at her and set the last bite of his sandwich back down. "Wait a minute. *You're* the Plate Spinner?"

"Yep, going on two years now."

He studied her, recalling the caustic tone of the few columns his mother had shared with him, mostly for their entertainment value. He made a mental note to look up the rest online.

"I thought you always wanted to be a big time journalist," he started.

Then, looking as if he had just taken a swig from a pickle jar, he asked, "Why are you writing an advice column?"

Given Mattie's reaction, he may as well have asked, "Is that really your natural hair color?"

The rare and wondrous light that had been sparking in her eyes clicked off. Just like that. He could barely hear her when she looked down at her nails and said, "I thought we were keeping the past in the past."

Nice going. Why don't you ask her how much she weighs while you're at it?

Back-pedaling as fast as he could, Nick offered, "Well, my Mom is a huge fan. She loves your column. She reads it all the time. She even keeps a binder of her favorites."

Schmoozing was not his forte.

"That's because she doesn't know I'm the one writing it."

Nick shook his head. "Not true. She likes you. A lot." He cringed at the slip.

Just stop talking.

"What? How do you know?"

"Listen, forget about that. Tell me more about your idea for the promotion."

He waited, hoping for the spark to return.

Instead, she checked her watch. "You know what? Never mind. I'd better get back to work. Thanks again for meeting me on such short notice. I'll see you in the morning."

"Oh. Yeah. Sure."

Nick watched her leave, wanting nothing more than to find a way to re-ignite the light in her eyes. What he found instead was what she had left behind.

* * *

Rushing straight to Dianne's office, Mattie found her editor sitting at her desk with her head down and bouncing her knee while twirling a pen between the fingers of her right hand.

"Hey there. Ready for my idea?"

Dianne started. "Hold that thought. Les is waiting for us."

"No, please. I need to run it by you first." Mattie dumped her coat in a nearby chair and made her pitch. She left nothing out—Nick's rules and the profound affect they were having on her all the way through to her promotion ideas, including use of the banned video clip of her first workout and hosting beginner running clinics.

After waiting an interminably long time for a response, Mattie watched as Dianne squinted at the ceiling.

"Team Plate Spinner? I like the sound of that."

Mattie scooted up to the edge of her chair. "I know, right? We can sell T-shirts, sweatshirts, caps, beach towels. All sorts of stuff."

Dianne smiled and asked, "And you have his permission to use his rules?"

"Yep."

"Seriously. Are you sure about this, kiddo? A couple of weeks ago, you were begging me not to use your picture. Putting your name and face out there, it's a big risk. That kind of exposure always comes with a price."

Gripping the arms of her chair, Mattie announced, "I'm not worried. Besides, what's the worst that can happen?"

Dianne considered this for a moment, resting a hand on her throat before responding, "You mean besides losing our jobs?"

Mattie dashed around the desk and gave her a quick hug. "You worry too much. If this takes off the way I think it will, we'll be able to start our own media company."

Patting her arm, Dianne chuckled, "All right. First things first. Let's see if it'll fly with Les. If it does, rest assured, I'll have your back. But if it doesn't, we're back to square one."

The two women made their way up to Lester's office and burst through the door without knocking.

Dianne announced, "I've got it."

Lester was sitting with his feet up on his desk and his hands folded in his lap. He couldn't have looked more serene if he had just gotten a deep tissue massage. Smiling at her, he replied, "Too late."

Dianne dropped into the same chair she had occupied earlier that day and gasped, "It's not even two o'clock. You said to meet you back here at two."

That was when Mattie noticed they weren't the only ones in the room. In the corner behind them, leaning on Lester's credenza, was Nick.

Feeling goose bumps spread under the sleeves of her sweater, she asked, "What are you doing here?"

He held up a bag from the restaurant. "Your salad. I thought you might want it later."

"Oh. Thanks."

When Mattie reached out to take it from him, she noticed a sleek dark brown leather clutch resting against his hip. "What are you doing with my purse?"

He picked it up. "This? You left it on your seat. I went to your cube first, but you weren't there."

She tried yanking it from his grasp, but he held firm.

Not letting go, she whispered an obligatory, "Thank you."

His reply was hushed. "You're welcome. I didn't open it, I swear."

As he released it, her mind flashed back to the note he delivered to her on the playground when they were kids.

I didn't read it, I swear.

He leaned forward and whispered in her ear, "I'm lying. I had to open it just a little to make sure it was yours, *Mathilde Jean Ross.*"

Mattie gasped. Her heart plummeted into her stomach.

"You looked at my driver's license?" she hissed.

Nick DeRosa was now in possession of two vital pieces of information she would have killed to keep private—her weight and her address.

Breathe, in through your nose, out through your mouth.

As she tried to recall if there was any other item in her purse that would provide fodder for recrimination, like a crumpled french fry wrapper or a receipt from her favorite pizza place, she heard Dianne ask again, "What do you mean I'm too late?"

Lester nodded toward Nick and said, "According to Coach, Mattie's already nailed it."

Mattie peered hard enough at Nick to drill holes into the wall behind him.

I did?

Nick nodded his head in Lester's direction. "You're on."

Mattie faced Lester. "Yes, I did."

After pitching the story to him, much the same way she did to Dianne, Lester looked at Nick and said, "You're right. I think that title is a perfect fit."

"Title?" Mattie glanced at Nick, frowning.

"The title," Lester shot back. "It's catchy, personal, familiar, and provocative. It's exactly what I was looking for. You know, I really admire you for putting yourself out there like that."

Confused, Mattie spun back toward Nick who was still leaning against the credenza with his arms folded. He raised his eyebrows as if to ask, "What?"

Holding a hand to the side of her face to prevent Lester from seeing her, she mouthed, "Team Plate Spinner?"

Nick shook his head back and forth before looking down at his shoes.

Running out of patience, she let out a sigh, turned back to Lester and said, "I'm sorry, Les, but I came up with a couple of different titles. Which one are you referring to?"

"You know, I wish I had known earlier that you were bullied as a kid."

She was perplexed. "Uh, well, it's not exactly the kind of thing that comes up in everyday conversation."

"I gotta tell you," he continued, "Nick is the perfect medicine for what ails you. I should know. I speak from experience. What he did for my son."

Lester paused to look at photo of Bobby, beaming in his cross-country uniform, on his desk.

"With what you've gone through and Nick's enormous talent, you two are made for each other. I couldn't have asked for a better pairing for this piece. Our numbers are going to go through the roof on this one."

Edging closer to him with her eyes narrowed and hands balled into fists, Mattie asked, "What's the title, Les?"

He continued as if he didn't hear her. "Damn shame you're already married. You two are a match made in heaven."

Standing directly in front of his desk, Mattie leaned down and placed her hands on top of it. "Tell me the title."

Lester grinned like a man who had just won a lifetime supply of hundred-year-old scotch. Shifting in his seat, he put both feet on the floor before announcing, "We're going with 'Fatty Mattie Meets the Comeback Kid.'"

To Dianne, he said, "Run it."

"What?" Mattie gasped.

After making an uncharacteristic fist pump, Dianne was already on her way to the production department, and Lester was busy dialing his phone.

Next thing she knew, Nick was at her side. Taking her by the elbow, he escorted her out of the office.

In the hallway just beyond, she stopped and faced him. Flabbergasted, she asked, "Do you mind telling me what just happened in there?"

He checked his watch. Then, focusing on his jacket zipper that hadn't worked right since she snagged her dress on it, he replied, "Sure. You just got what you wanted. All you have to do now is run with it."

Mattie let out a short laugh and clapped her hands together. *That was way too easy.*

Adrenaline pulsed through her veins. So much to do. She had to tweak her first piece, setup a special blog and social media page, and plan out her monthly submission schedule from January through October.

As her mind raced, she heard Nick say, "Yeah, well, you can thank me later."

He turned toward the elevator bank.

About to burst with excitement, Mattie tugged the arm of his jacket. "Nick. Wait."

What would a married woman do?

With perhaps a bit too much exuberance, she took both of his hands in hers, squeezed them and said, "Thanks so much."

Then, in a move that surprised even her, she reached up to kiss him on his cheek. His clean-shaven, deodorant-soap-scented cheek.

Hesitating for just a second, Nick leaned down to receive it when Mattie remembered the boundary she herself erected between them.

No kissing.

Her forehead bumped against his jawbone. Releasing his hands, she smiled at him again and turned away flustered, but certain of one thing.

I am so selling this ring.

CHAPTER SEVEN

―――

"I always cook with wine. Sometimes I even add it to the food."
– W.C. Fields

As expected, the Gazette launched the new feature on the Sunday prior to the New Year. It got a prominent mention on the front-page banner and made the front page of the weekend section. Mattie had to admit that the high school photo from her freshman year that she volunteered certainly was impactful. Under a mound of hair pulled back by two woefully inadequate barrettes stationed on either side of her head, was the weak half smile of a chubby, self-conscious teenage girl.

During the week that followed, a few walkers and runners braving the cold blowing off the frozen waters of Lake Michigan spotted Mattie and Nick as they jogged along their usual route. Some pointed. A few even waved. Considering the many layers that covered them from head to toe, Mattie found this surprising. By the second week, a dozen or so actually followed them. By the end of the third week, people stationed themselves along the path just to, cheer her on.

Mattie loved it. Nick, not so much.

With her first 5k a little over a week and a half away, he was hoping to push Mattie to go three miles without stopping. Instead, they were interrupted three times by fans either wanting to take a picture with her or have her autograph something.

"We're gonna have to change our route," Nick told her during their cool down.

"You're just jealous that nobody asked you for an autograph," Mattie observed.

Her attempt to impress him with her spot-on deductive reasoning fell flat.

"Unlike you, I'm not in it for the recognition." His voice was gruff as he leaned against an overpass pylon to stretch the backs of his legs.

Mattie put her gloved hand on a streetlight pole and pulled her right ankle up behind her with her right hand.

With her defenses already on high alert, she let out a laugh, "Since when? From what I recall, you could never get enough."

The dark cloudy skies above cast a menacing shadow across his face. "That was a long time ago."

Releasing her right ankle and pulling on her left, Mattie replied, "I see. So, now, you're just in it for the money. Is that right?"

"Damn straight."

"That must be one hell of a bonus they've promised you."

"Now who's jealous?" Nick huffed as he bent down and grabbed the tips of his shoes.

The horn of a car tearing through the intersection nearby blared as a taxi cut into the flow of traffic. Exhaust fumes filled the air, and Mattie started feeling tiny pelts of sleet sting her already-raw cheeks.

Tired of his crabby mood and the repartee that was not going in her favor, she tried changing the subject. "Any exciting plans for the weekend?"

Nick stood up straight. "No. You?"

Since Tom had to work the graveyard shift, Mattie planned to spend the night with Claudia, watching a chick flick marathon until he got home. Big fun.

"No," she sighed.

Wiping his forehead with his sleeve, Nick asked, "Really? Nothing?"

Then, citing topics of *Plate Spinner* columns past, he continued, "No family game night or cookie-baking for kids or making chores fun with Mr. Plate Spinner and all your little saucers?"

If Mattie's eyes could throw knives, he would've been a dead man.

Instead, Nick stood before her with his hands on his hips, sweaty and bothered—about what, she wasn't exactly sure, but she was about to find out.

"I've been reading your old columns."

A cold chill ran through her. "And?"

"I noticed the damnedest thing."

She was afraid to ask, but did anyway. "What?"

"You were already married when you were about to marry my brother."

* * *

"So what did you tell him?" Claudia gasped as she lifted a sleeping baby off of Mattie's chest. An empty bottle tumbled to the floor, depositing drips of formula on the hardwood.

"Nothing. I was speechless. I just walked away."

"Very smooth."

Claudia patted her youngest son's back until she heard a burp, then turned to deposit him upstairs in his crib. "I'll be right back."

Feeling a chill where a warm little body had just been snuggled against her, Mattie leaned over and wiped the formula off the floor, then got up and added another log to the fire. After depositing the baby bottle in the sink, she sat back down on the couch and spread the afghan their mom had crocheted in happier times over her legs.

Not exactly the ideal way to spend a Friday night, but she understood Claudia's concern about Tom working so late in one of the roughest neighborhoods for first responders.

"How about a glass of wine?" Claudia asked when she returned.

Mattie tried to remember the last time she had any. Thanksgiving was her best guess. Even though it was on Nick's "to-don't" list, she was feeling more than a little rebellious.

"Sure, why not? I get to sleep in until seven tomorrow morning.

Returning with a bottle tucked under her arm and two glasses, her sister handed one to Mattie, sat next to her on the couch, and uncorked the wine.

"I told you no good would come from wearing that ring."
Mattie nodded. "Yes, you did."

She looked at her once-coveted relic. The gleam was gone. She couldn't recall the last time she cleaned it.

"How many weeks have you been running now?" Claudia asked.

Mattie looked toward the ceiling and thought for a moment. "Eight."

Crinkling up her nose, her sister tilted her head. "Really? It seems longer than that."

"It does, doesn't it? Well, there's no looking back now. I'm just glad they decided to start off small with the campaign then build to a big crescendo in October. I'm not sure I'm ready to see my face plastered on the side of a bus."

"I still can't believe you agreed to let them use your old nickname."

Tugging the afghan a little higher on her lap, Mattie took a big swig of her wine. "'Old' being the operative word. That's not who I am anymore. Besides, if it can help somebody else, even if it's just one person, it'll be worth it."

Claudia, about to take a sip, lowered her glass. "Who are you, and what have you done with my sister?"

Recalling Dianne's reaction to her first column on the topic, Mattie frowned and replied, "You know, I'm getting a lot of that lately."

"Admit it. Nick's been a good influence on you. If this is how you're feeling after just eight weeks, I can only imagine how you'll feel in ten months."

"Nine," Mattie yawned as she stared into the fireplace.

"All right. Nine."

"You know, I've been trying to imagine what it will be like, crossing the finish line at the marathon. I actually have nightmares about it. People laughing at me."

"But you have Nick," Claudia cried. "He won't let that happen. You said it yourself in your article. He's going to be with you every step of the way."

Mattie grimaced. "In my nightmares, he's the one laughing."

The next morning, Mattie woke up, bleary-eyed. Lifting her head from the couch cushion, she tried to remember where she was. The answer came to her slowly, poking its way through the cotton webbing that seemed to have enveloped her brain.

Claud and Tom's, but what day is it?

"Saturday," a little voice in her head whispered.

Groaning, she pulled herself up into a sitting position. Her head throbbed, and her stomach threatened to do terrible things. Checking her phone, she saw that it was 7:45.She had slept right through her alarm.

Oh no.

She considered texting Nick to tell him she was sick, but after their exchange the day before, the last thing she wanted to do was validate any suspicions he had about her. Before attempting to stand, she tried recalling what she could of the discussion she had with her sister just hours before. They never did get around to watching any movies. It wasn't until the two empty bottles came into focus in front of her that she remembered.

It had taken half of the first bottle for her to admit to Claudia that it was a bad idea to let Nick believe she was married. It took half of the second bottle for her to realize that Nick not being anything like his brother wasn't such a bad thing after all.

After changing into her running clothes and downing a couple of aspirins, she ducked out the back door. In one hand, she clutched her water bottle, in the other, her train pass.

Once on the train, she tried filtering out the sounds of other people talking and the rattle of her seat as they sped over the rails. Looking out the window only revived the nauseous sensation she felt when she woke up.

The more she remembered, the more she realized she shared way more than she should have with her sister. Worse, she didn't feel any better off for having done so. All she wanted to do was go home, crawl under her covers, wake up on Monday morning, and go to work.

That Claudia maintained the upper hand throughout their conversation didn't surprise her. After just one glass of wine, her role morphed from inquisitor to confessor.

So Mattie should have nipped Nick's misunderstanding of her marital status in the bud. But she didn't. She tried explaining to her older, authentically married sister that her faux marital status was her armor, and her ring was her shield. It was when Claudia tried opening her eyes to the fact that Nick might have feelings for her—other than animosity and disdain—that she began to lose her grip on both.

"And," the elder sibling concluded before calling it a night, "you're going to blow it because you're afraid of getting hurt again."

She rested her head against the back of her seat and waited for the aspirin to kick in.

By the time her train pulled into her station, she was filled with dread. The blissful buzz she enjoyed just hours before was a very distant memory.

Clutching the staircase railing as she descended to the street, she took one step at a time, doing her best to minimize any swaying. Her sunglasses did little to shield her aching eyes from the morning sun or the sight of Nick pacing back and forth on the sidewalk below, alternately checking every direction, then his phone.

To say he looked a little agitated would be like saying the Grand Canyon looked a little impressive.

Mattie froze. After doing a stellar job adhering to Nick's list of commands, she blew it all on one wanton evening of sibling bonding, complete with soul-baring confessions, and way too much cabernet. Still sporting smudged makeup from the day before, she hadn't even taken the time to brush her teeth. Her thoughts flip-flopped between, "He's gonna quit," and "I think I'm gonna be sick."

Spotting her, Nick stormed over to the stairwell and waited. He did not look pleased. When she was two steps from the bottom, he opened his mouth and seethed, "Do you have any idea how—"

But before he could say another word, she held up her hand. "I know. I'm late. I'm sorry."

Her apology did little to dampen his anger.

"Why didn't you return my texts or answer your phone?"

Mattie patted her hands over her empty pockets, covered her throbbing temples with her hands and groaned, "Oh no. I forgot it."

Standing eye-to-sunglass-covered-eye, Nick lowered his voice and stared hard, trying to look past his reflection in her lenses. "Did the thought even cross your mind that I might be worried about you?"

Mattie cringed. She couldn't tell who he was more upset with—her or himself.

"Can you please stop yelling at me? I already apologized."

Apparently beside himself, Nick shook his head and stared at his shoes for a moment. When he raised his eyes to hers, he asked under his breath, "It's not like you to be late and not let me know. What's the matter with you? Are you all right?"

He still looked like he was ready to haul off and punch something.

The last thing she wanted to do was admit to Nick, the bastion of all things healthy and disciplined, that she was hung over.

The last thing she wanted *him* to do was quit on her. The thought of tanking yet another relationship made her stomach take a nauseous tumble.

When her only response was to bite down on her lower lip, he reached over and lifted the sunglasses off of her face.

Unable to look him in the eye, she took a deep breath, in through her nose, out through her mouth.

Nicks lips curled into a disgusted sneer, "Have you been drinking?"

Lifting her chin, Mattie said nothing. Instead, she tugged her sunglasses from his hands and returned them to their rightful place, hoping to shield the blow she knew was due her.

A vision of restraint, Nick's tone was firm, his message pointed.

"Your first race is a week from today. I'm going to ask you one more time, are you all right?"

Mattie nodded. It took everything in her to stifle the self-pitying sob she had been holding back since she got off the train. "Sorry. I won't let you down again."

Finding a crumpled tissue in her pocket, she turned away from him to dab at her nose. When she turned to face him again, she took off her glasses and looked him in the eye. "I mean it."

Nick relaxed his shoulders, and the scorn left his face.

"You haven't let me down," he said quietly. "We all make mistakes." He gave her shoulder a quick squeeze. "Speaking of which, I owe you an apology for the way I acted yesterday. We agreed to keep this strictly business, and I crossed the line."

Who are you and what have you done with Nick DeRosa?

"No worries," she whispered.

Holding out his hand for her to complete her descent, he asked, "Think you can manage a walk?"

"Yeah, to a coffee shop."

"Don't push it."

Two blocks later, he was back in full coach mode. "Come on, Mattie. Longer strides, you've got to get your heart rate up, otherwise we're just wasting our time here."

Feeling all was once again right with her new normal world, she smiled. Despite having fallen off the marathon-training wagon, Nick had yanked her right back on.

She quickened her pace.

"Whatever you say, Coach."

* * *

Dawn broke on the morning of the 5k through a glorious red and orange infused sunrise. Mattie sprang out of bed before her alarm went off and put on her brand new running gear. The matching tights and jacket, dark grey with purple accents, were a gift from Claudia as a means of showing her support and apologizing for getting her baby sister drunk the weekend before. But first, she pulled on two gifts from Dianne—a long-sleeved T-shirt and matching black knit headband with "Team Plate Spinner" printed across the front and the *Gazette* logo on the back.

Catching a reflection of herself in the mirror affixed to the back of her bedroom door, she groaned, "I can't believe I'm doing this."

She laced up her shoes and headed to Old Town, a storied neighborhood south of where she lived, to meet Nick at the corner of North Avenue and Southport Street. From there, they'd walk the remaining blocks to the event together.

She arrived before him and stood watching runners make their way to the registration table on Wells Street, a north-south thoroughfare that was blocked off for the run. While she waited, the skies began to cloud over and the wind picked up. A few snowflakes danced through the air.

Runners were everywhere, some wearing more layers than others, but nearly all had their heads and hands covered. Mattie folded her arms across her chest and began bouncing up and down to stay warm. It occurred to her that she had no idea how Nick was getting there. Come to think of it, she had no idea where he even lived. He just told her where to be and always showed up before she arrived.

A knot began forming in her stomach. She reached for her cell phone to see if he had called or texted. Nothing.

Weird.

She texted him.

"Where are you?"

Staring at her phone, she waited for his reply. Scores of runners began passing by, laughing and chatting, making their way to the registration table. She checked her watch. Thirty minutes until the start time and they still had to pick up their packets and warm up.

Where is he?

The thought of shuffling for three point two miles alone in a crowd of strangers unnerved her. She'd just as soon go back home and crawl under her blankets than endure the embarrassment of huffing and puffing her way through the course solo.

"Hey, Mattie."

Turning in the direction of the voice, she was disappointed to see Charlie Clarke, a staff photographer from the *Gazette*.

"Hey, Charlie. What are you doing here?"

"Crenshaw sent me. Wants shots of you during the race, at the finish line, and with your family at the after party."

Mattie gulped. "My family?"

"Yeah, he's planning a big spread for your first race."

Feeling like she was in an elevator plunging a dozen flights a second, she stammered, "Well, uh, Charlie, my family isn't here."

Not cutting her a break, he asked, "Can you call 'em? Les insisted."

"No, I can't."

"Why not?"

Because they don't exist.

"Because," she tried formulating a viable excuse that Les would buy, "well, they, have a thing."

Charlie made a face, "Huh?"

"You heard her, pal. Her family has a thing."

It was Nick.

Mattie lit up. "Hey."

Nick gave her a nod. "Sorry I'm late. The train was packed."

"That's OK."

Trying not to let him see how happy she was that he showed up was more of a struggle than she expected. It wouldn't have surprised her in the least if witnesses later reported having seen her levitate just a few inches.

"Who are you?" Charlie asked, looking small and seedy as he stood next to Nick.

"Her coach. Nick DeRosa." He held out his hand, and Charlie shook it vigorously.

"Oh, hey, nice to meet you. I used to cover you in high school. You were outstanding, man. Just outstanding."

"He still is," Mattie interjected frowning. "Just you watch."

The two men looked at her, surprised at her ferocity.

With that, the trio made their way to the registration table. Rifling through her packet, Mattie pulled out a Dri-FIT shirt with the race logo on the front and the event sponsors listed on the back. She held it in front of her and posed for Charlie.

She pulled out her bib number next.

Dangling it in front of her, she asked, "What do I do with this?"

Nick took the envelope from her. "Oh, here. There should be safety pins in there. Let me see."

After digging them out, he started pinning it to her T-shirt, just below "Team Plate Spinner."

She marveled at the way the sun glinted off his hair, making it seem more dark strawberry blonde than brown. She never noticed that with Eddie's hair, maybe because he always had so much product in it.

She held out her arms as he anchored the first corner of the square. With his face precariously close to her left breast, Charlie's camera clicked all around them. Other runners paused as they walked by to see if a celebrity was in their midst.

Mattie wondered if this was anything like the corsage-pinning photo sessions she missed out on in high school.

"You poke me, you die."

He stopped what he was doing and looked up at her. "You know how many of these I've pinned on in my life? I could do this in my sleep. Now hold still."

It only took him a minute.

"There. Now you're official. Time to warm up."

Noticing Nick had neither a bib nor a packet, she said, "Hold on. Where's yours?"

He frowned. "I'm not running this. You are."

Mattie clutched his arm and pulled him close.

"What do you mean you're not running?" she whispered. "I'm not doing this by myself. I can't."

Looking puzzled, Nick asked, "Are you nervous? Don't be. You can do this. I'll see you at the finish line."

His ambivalence unnerved her. In full fly-or-fight mode, she gripped his arm like it was the only thing between her and a slow painful death. "I gave up drinking coffee for you. I swapped pizza for produce," she sputtered, "and this is what I get in return?"

Nick tried to explain, "Mattie, think about it. Coaches don't run with their team. They stay on the sidelines and, well, *coach*."

She knew he was right, but it never occurred to her that she'd have to go it alone.

Releasing his arm, she growled, "Fine."

Nick smiled and checked his watch. "I tell ya.what—I'll warm up with you and then, like I said, I'll watch for you at the finish line, ok?"

She shuddered against a cold gust of wind. The day that had started so full of promise suddenly seemed quite the opposite.

"Beggars can't be choosers," she muttered.

"That's right. Come on."

He led her to an open pocket on the sidewalk where they could stretch. When they finished, he walked with her to the starting line, reciting pointers all along the way.

"Now, remember, don't gulp your air. Just breathe like I taught you. Nice and easy. Find your rhythm and keep your pace slow, but steady. The goal is to finish without stopping, no matter how long it takes. And don't pay attention to anybody else around you. Just take it a mile at a time, OK?"

She nodded and gave him one last pleading look.

In the midst of the loud, enthusiastic crowd of runners milling under the balloon-festooned start line, many of whom were wearing "Team Plate Spinner" paraphernalia, he took her by the shoulders, leaned down and spoke into her ear. "Listen. Your hard work got you here, not me. No matter how you do, I want you to know I'm really proud of you. Even if you come in last."

She squinted and shouted, "What?"

As the crowd pressed against them, Nick took her face in his hands and, emphasizing each word, said, "You can do this."

"Nice one," Charlie exclaimed, holding his camera in front of his face.

Annoyed at the intrusion, Nick stood straight up, gave her one last nod, and disappeared into the crowd.

When the start gun went off, Mattie was no longer afraid of being embarrassed; she was afraid of being trampled. Runners of all shapes, sizes, and ages seemed to be flying past her on either side. Doing her best not to panic, she fell into her familiar shuffling stride and followed the crowd running ahead of her. A fog of their warm breath hitting the cold February air floated behind them.

Recalling the course map Nick had shown her, she knew she'd have to run south for a few blocks, then head east toward Lake Michigan, then back north, and finally west to Wells. Before long, the bulk of the runners were out of sight. When she turned the first corner and only spotted a few in her line of vision, she wondered if she had made a wrong turn. By the time she rounded the second corner, she was convinced that someone had mis-measured the course.

This is way longer than three point two miles.

But, still, she plodded on, careful not to rush. She concentrated on her breathing, praying for patience and endurance.

As she turned onto what she presumed was the last leg of the run, she wondered if she was the only runner left on the course. She wondered, too, if the finish-line balloon archway would be dismantled long before she got there. Would the spectators be gone, too, leaving nothing but heaps of empty plastic water bottles in their wake? Even Charlie might get tired of waiting, but she knew Nick wouldn't abandon her. She imagined finding him alone, staring with his stopwatch while he awaited her arrival.

Not seeing anyone on either side of her, she started obsessing whether anyone was actually behind her or if she was indeed destined to come in last.

Don't pay attention to anyone else around you.

Mattie glanced over her shoulder to see if anyone could possibly be running slower than she was. Much to her surprise, she saw several people in her wake. Some were pushing baby strollers. Some were even walking. Some, like her, were just shuffling along.

Seeing at least two with shirts that read, "Team Plate Spinner" on them, she smiled and waved.

"Keep it up," she called over her shoulder.

"You, too," they yelled back.

The well wishes echoed in her muffled ears.

I made the team.

The very thought propelled her along, albeit at a snail-like pace. In the distance, she could see the rainbow of balloons arched over the finish line and hear the strains of a rock band playing some rousing classic at the already well-attended post-race party. The crowds of onlookers thickened as she approached, cheering her and the other stragglers on. But Mattie was only focused on one thing—the sight of Nick waving her toward him from just beyond the finish line.

Almost there.

Her mouth was parched and her legs felt like Jell-O.

Just a little bit farther.

She sensed another shuffler coming up behind her and heard Nick yell, "Close the gap, Mattie."

Ignoring him, she continued to chug along until the other runner was alongside her.

That's when she heard him yell even louder, sounding more angry than encouraging.

"Come on, Mathilde Jean, where's your kick?"

Her eyes widened. What other bits of private information would he be sharing with the crowd today? Her weight? How about her address?

She couldn't believe he called her that in public. And shouting it like that so everyone in a one-mile radius could hear it. Her mother didn't even call her by her full name, not even when Mattie had her at her wit's end or she did something horrific like polish off a tub of store-bought buttercream icing on the eve of Claudia's eighteenth birthday party.

Chugging along, she tried to remember if she had done it to forget something awful that happened at school that day, or if she did it simply to upset her uber-popular sibling. Just as she was trying to recall which flavor of icing it was, her eyes drifted up from the pavement in front of her to the finish line about an eighth of a mile in front of her.

Nick was standing there, holding his hands out in front of him as if to ask, "Well?"

Focus.

Channeling the indignation she felt to her legs, she somehow tapped into a reserve of energy she didn't know she had. She pumped her arms, lengthened her stride and burst forward in what would pass as a sprint if the rest of the world were going in slow motion.

As she crossed over the finish line and put her first 5k behind her, Nick swept to her side.

"34:11. Not bad. How ya feeling?"

Mattie's head was spinning. Runners were everywhere, laughing, talking, hugging, milling around her, making her dizzy.

"Water. I need water."

He jogged over to a large bin overflowing with water bottles and cracked one open for her. "Here you go. Keep moving."

Mattie took several swigs as they walked through the chute. With all the menace she could muster, she warned, "You call me that again, and I'll take you out."

Laughing, he asked, "What? Mathilde Jean? That's your name, isn't it?"

God, it's hard to be mad at him when he smiles like that.

She scrunched her face and said, "It's a horrible name. Do not use it again. Especially in public. Got it?"

Nick shook his head. "Nope. I'm gonna do whatever it takes to get you to cross that finish line."

Mattie thought for a moment. "Oh, so you're doing me a favor, is that it?"

"That's right."

"And what would you do for me if I called you by your full name? Yelled it, out loud for all the world to hear?" she asked.

Nick stopped and turned to face her, every bit the big bad coach his cross-country runners both feared and revered. "Nothing because I am never telling you my full name."

Mattie, noticing a mischievous gleam in his eyes, glanced at his jacket pocket. "Oh yeah? How about I take a peek at *your* license?"

When she reached for it, her fingers missed their target.

What they found instead was gold.

After her fingers dug into his side, just above his right hip, she watched, astonished and somewhat alarmed, as he recoiled and broke out into a little-girl giggle. It was then that she knew she had found a chink in his hard-assed coach's armor.

She waited as he composed himself, but even then he was beaming at her. His eyes sparkled like Christmas trees.

Eddie never looked at me like that.

She felt a heated blush cover her entire body, not that anyone would notice because any exposed skin was still red from the run and the cold.

"Come on. You want to get something to eat? They've got all sorts of food over there." He pointed in the direction of the post-race party already in full swing down the block.

Hearing the band and seeing the reveling runners, the enormity of what she had just accomplished settled on her like a nice warm blanket. All of a sudden, she didn't care what anyone, including Nick, would think if she were to hug him.

So she did just that. And she wasn't in a rush to let go either.

"Thank you," she mumbled, the side of her face smushed against him. When she felt his arms wrap around her, she added, "I couldn't have done this without you."

After a long moment, she felt a chuckle erupt in his chest. She pulled away, her defenses at the ready.

"What?"

"I just hope you remember this in a couple of weeks when I have you doing hill work."

Mattie took another swig of her water. "Bring it."

CHAPTER EIGHT

———

*"He that but looketh on a plate of ham and eggs to lust after it
hath already committed breakfast in his heart."*
– C. S. Lewis

Lester walked the circumference of his desk examining
the proof sheets from Mattie's 5k that were laid out on top of it.

He pointed to one of her holding up the race shirt from
her packet. "That one."

He paused before another. It was a perfectly framed shot
of her jogging mid-way through the course. She was in the
foreground smiling, and four "Team Plate Spinner" members
were in focus not far behind, all waving at the camera. "This
one."

Lastly, he selected a side shot of her just as she stepped
over the finish line. "And this one."

"That's it?" Charlie Clark was incredulous. "I took
dozens of pictures and you're just picking three? I thought we
were doing a slide show?"

Lester scowled down at the rest, his gaze lingering the
longest on one in particular. It was a close-up of Nick with his
hands cupping Mattie's upturned face. He actually looked like he
was about to kiss her. And she looked like she wouldn't mind at
all if he did.

"That's right," Lester replied. Sounding rather
preoccupied, he continued, "I'll hang on to the rest of these. We
can use 'em for the big year-end retrospective."

Throwing his hands up in the air, Charlie sighed, "You're
the boss."

After he left, Lester picked up another photo and stared
at it. Mattie was hugging Nick. Her eyes were closed tight and

her arms were locked behind his back. He couldn't see Nick's face, but he was bent over her, returning the embrace.

"Natural," Lester supposed, "given what she's been through and all the excitement."

But there was something about their body language that didn't sit quite right with him. He slid both pictures back in his desk drawer and picked up the phone to call Dianne.

* * *

Since crossing the finish line two days before, Mattie had yet to step down off cloud nine. It wasn't a great time, but as Nick said, "Nothing to sneeze at."

She couldn't wait to see the pictures. Feeling like a bona fide runner, she wanted proof that she actually looked like one and not just a vertical red-faced lump wrapped in dark gray spandex.

Nick had given her the day after the race off. Then he begged off running with her that morning. No reason. He just told her to get a couple of miles in. It was the first workout with her that he had ever missed. While concerned, Mattie was more than a little relieved. In the post-race euphoria, she felt like she was one careless slip away from shedding her marital armor, exposing her to all manner of potential heartache.

That morning, she took to the streets alone, shuffling along a different route through her neighborhood, doing her best to blend in with students from a nearby university. Now that she had a 5k under her spandex waistline, she was able to shed her self-consciousness. That she was wearing big black Audrey Hepburn sunglasses also helped.

By the time she made it to work, she was looking forward to diving into emails and responding to posts on her designated social media pages. Twenty minutes later, Dianne burst into her cube and hugged her tight. "Congratulations, Sweetie. I'm so proud of you."

"Thanks," Mattie replied as she sank into her chair. "It was incredible. I can't wait for the next one."

Leaning against her desk, Dianne asked, "When is it?"

"Either late April or early May. I don't remember. I'm not even sure he's registered me for it yet."

Dianne lowered her voice. "Correct me if I'm wrong, but you seemed to have lost every single misgiving you had about him being your coach."

Mattie's eyes widened. "Oh, I don't know. I wouldn't go that far."

"Well, I just thought, given the amount of praise you've been giving him in your column… "

There was something in her tone that gave Mattie pause. "Too much?"

"No, no. I'm sure it's well deserved. However, as your editor and chief back-protector, I feel it's my duty to remind you of your marital status."

She pointed to her own ring finger like she was revealing a secret handshake to an exclusive club.

Frowning, Mattie asked, "Why? What's going on?" Goosebumps started to race up her arms. She noticed Dianne had something in her hand. Papers and something else. A photo?

"Let me see."

Dianne handed two printed emails to Mattie. Each was a letter of complaint from readers asking, in so many words, why they changed the format of the *Plate Spinner* columns from a working parent advice column to a fitness column.

"What? How can they say that? I've responded to questions from working parents recently."

When Dianne didn't respond, she looked up at her and implored, "Remember? The road warrior dad who didn't feel like his family appreciated him?"

Dianne looked at her over her reading glasses. "You mean the one who you advised to take advantage of hotel fitness centers while traveling so he could try and bolster his self-esteem?"

"Yes," Mattie responded, her voice laced with defiance.

Dianne scooted further back onto Mattie's desk, then checked behind her to see if she had knocked down any of the prized family photos. Not seeing any, she turned and demanded with no small amount of alarm, "Where are your pictures?"

"Don't worry. I'm getting some new ones. What's with you?"

"That guy? The road warrior? The old Mattie would have reamed him up one side and down the other for feeling sorry for himself. What's with *you*?"

"Did you read his letter? I actually did feel sorry for the guy."

Dianne's expression softened. "Yes, but sweetie, there's no profit to be had in pity."

Frowning, Mattie handed the letters back to her editor. Nodding at what she was still holding in her hand, she asked, "What's that?"

Dianne handed her an 8x10 glossy from the race.

It was a shot of the crowd, but only Mattie and Nick appeared to be in focus.

Nice job, Charlie.

She remembered the moment exactly. Still, her heart did a tumble in her chest when, at first glance, it looked like he was going to kiss her. She finally began to understand what was upsetting Dianne.

Feeling the color rise in her own cheeks, she asked, "What's the problem?"

"I'll tell you what the problem is. Lester wants me to stop by this afternoon and explain to him why it looks like you two are about to lock lips. What do you suggest I tell him?"

Mattie's mind flashed back to her rehearsal dinner, then to the comment Nick made outside of the YMCA's weight room.

She rather liked being perceived as a bad girl for a change. It made her feel pretty, sexy, and popular—a trifecta of feelings she never had before.

A smile started at one corner of Mattie's mouth and worked its way to the other as she pointed at the picture and asked, "Does this make me a slut? I've always wondered what that would feel like."

"That's not funny."

Mattie laughed. "Yes, it is."

When Dianne didn't join in, she sighed and explained, "All right. Here's what happened. It was really noisy at the start line, and I couldn't hear a word he said, so he grabbed my face and said, 'You. Can. Do. This.' Honest. That's all there was to it."

Dianne narrowed her eyes and pursed her lips. After a moment, she nodded. "OK. That works."

"Good, because, trust me, if he did kiss me, I wouldn't be sitting here smiling." She pretended to shudder.

"Oh yeah?" Dianne stood up, and yanked the photo from Mattie's grasp. "Pull this one, and it plays 'Jingle Bells.'"

* * *

That morning, Nick had two reasons for stopping by the Knollwood High School field house. The second was to pick up items from the "long-lost-and-found box"—a repository of unclaimed clothing that was left behind in the locker rooms during the previous semester.

The first was to run a fast five miles to try and clear his head. Alone.

While the "business only" rule he and Mattie had in place prevented them from discussing their personal lives, it did little to keep him from wondering about hers. He couldn't put his finger on it, but she just didn't seem married. Not happily anyway. While he could explain away the pictures on her desk, he couldn't do the same with her wedding ring. But then again, lately, she rarely wore it.

He tried pushing Mattie out of his mind by convincing himself that she didn't have any feelings for him, but his thoughts kept drifting back to the way she almost kissed him outside of Lester's office. And then there was that hug after the race on Saturday.

Despite the many times during their workouts that he had come close to asking her, straight out, something always held him back.

Maybe it's better to believe she's married than find out she's still not interested in me.

An hour later, he arrived at the Lincoln Park Community Center to meet up with the members of an informal, albeit steadily growing, group of homeless runners, a large contingent of them had already gathered. While the group had started out as just a handful of wannabe runners, their number had swelled to almost two dozen.

"Hey, guys."

As he approached, he asked, "Anybody need shoes? Or sweats? Or socks?"

Digging through the box, he added, "Or shirts?"

As the men milled around him, he handed out all of the items until the box was empty. John, the young man whom he had met on Thanksgiving, approached him wearing a long-sleeved shirt from a cross-country meet that took place three years before.

He ran his hands over the sleeves like he was wearing a mink coat and said, "All the meets I ran in school, I never got a shirt. My parents could never afford it. "

Looking up at Nick, he said, "You have no idea what this means to me. Thanks."

Nick couldn't help but marvel at the affect one small act of kindness had on someone. While his own parents were by no means well off, they always made sure they had enough to get him a race shirt from every single meet he ever ran in.

He patted John's shoulder and smiled. "It's nothing. How's the job hunt going?"

John slipped a sweatshirt over his head, nodded, and said, "Good. It's going good. I've only been hitting running shoe stores, though. They don't seem to care what I look like. They just care that I know about running."

That was music to Nick's ears. He hated seeing kids down and out with no direction, no plan, and no future.

Nick fist-bumped him. He seemed like a new man, holding his head high. "Awesome. I'd be happy to put in a good word for you. Just let me know."

"Thanks, man, but I gotta do this on my own. No offense."

With a wink, Nick responded, "None taken."

"So how far are we going today?"

"You're the captain. What do you think?"

John addressed his team with a clear, confident voice Nick hadn't heard him use before. "I think six miles. Who's with me?"

A few of the men held up their hands. A few more shook their heads and groaned.

Laughing, Nick told him, "Looks like you've got yourself an 'A' team and a 'B' team. Take 'em out, Cap'n."

John smiled and gave Nick a mock salute, "Ay-ay."

Turning toward the men, he instructed, "Team A, follow me. Team B, follow Fitz. We'll meet back here for a cool down."

Nick watched as they took off down the street. With a surprising tug in his gut, he realized he missed Mattie and was sorry he wouldn't be seeing her until the next day.

Ducking inside, he dropped by to see Scott about obtaining a grant that would enable him to develop a formal running program at the shelter.

"I've got most of the paperwork already filled out. I just need your signature in a couple of spots," Scott told him as they sat in his cracker box-sized office. "If we can get it submitted by the deadline, I think you've got a pretty good shot at getting it approved."

Nick tried stretching his legs out before him but gave up when they kept hitting the edge of Scott's desk. "I really appreciate your help with this."

Looking up from his paperwork, Scott laughed. "Are you kidding? If it wasn't for cross-country, there's no doubt in my mind, I would've ended up in juvie. Running saved my life. I can only imagine what it might do for these guys."

Scott's recollection of what running did for him was not that far off the mark. Always in trouble with the high school administration, Nick remembered when the coach had misgivings about accepting him on the team. A known troublemaker, Scott smoked, swore, had gotten caught shoplifting and joy riding, and was as selfish as the day is long. But, man oh man, when he got on that course, there was no stopping him. It was as if Scott was chasing away his demons. Or running from them. Nick could never tell. All he did know was that Scott grew to become a strong, fast varsity runner and top student. During their senior year, the two sat side-by-side on signing day—Nick for Oregon and Scott for Illinois. And they never lost touch. More importantly, besides his parents, Scott was the only friend who ever came to visit him in jail.

Checking his watch, Nick asked, "So, until it gets approved, any ideas on how we can scratch up some cash for registration fees and maybe some new shoes?"

Scott looked up from the paperwork. "You think these guys will be ready to run the Chicago Marathon?"

Nick leaned forward and drummed his fingers on Scott's cluttered desk.

"Yeah, why not? Mattie said we had the power to change the world. I have to admit, I'm starting to believe her."

Scott turned the grant application around so it was facing Nick and handed him a pen. "You two are like the opposite of Bonnie and Clyde, you know that?"

Ignoring him, Nick asked, "So where do I sign?"

* * *

A few weeks later, Dianne held an impromptu staff meeting in her office.

"Skinny comfort food? Talk about an oxymoron." She looked over to the food critic seated across from her and asked, "Am I right?"

David Morse, the man who had the power to make or break any dining establishment in the entire Chicago metropolitan area, chuckled.

"You're right. It's a hot trend, though. People want to devour grandma's homemade macaroni and cheese but not suffer the consequences."

Dianne stood up and leaned against her desk, twirling a pencil between her fingers like it was a mini baton. "I'm thinking videos of Mattie remaking old favorites in the test kitchen. Posting them next to her column and linking it to the food section."

Mattie offered, "I've already gotten a couple from my readers." She looked around at the others as she listed them off. "Turkey meatloaf, sweet potato and quinoa chili, cauliflower mac and cheese."

"Yeah, but how do they taste? Do your kids eat them?" asked a skeptical Nancy Braley, assistant food editor.

Unable to recall if she had shared any with her sister to conduct a taste test with actual children, she evaded the question by asking another. "What's not to like?"

Nancy, a perky single middle-aged woman directed her attention to Dianne. "Well, if you're going the video route, you really ought to have Nick in them. I'm sorry, but that man is *hot*."

A loud, awkward laugh burst out of Mattie. "No, he's not."

All eyes turned toward her. "He's not," she muttered to herself.

"Well, of course a happily married woman wouldn't think so," Dianne replied. Addressing Nancy, she said, "That's not a bad idea. We'll float the idea past him. If that flies, we can move on to healthy brown bag options for kids, quick and easy dinner options, tips for feeding your child athletes. The list goes on."

Mattie, worried the ten extra pounds added by the camera would belie all of her hard work, nodded at Dianne. "I'll ask him."

"Good. All right. That's all for now. Thanks everybody. Mattie, I need you to hang back a second."

When they had the office to themselves, Dianne pulled an envelope out from under her desk calendar.

"What's this?"

"Just a little something to tide you over."

Mattie ripped open the envelope to reveal a check that was big enough to cover a month's rent. She looked at Dianne with her mouth hanging open.

"Lester put in for it after I convinced him that absolutely nothing untoward was brewing between you and your coach. The way he explained it, he'll cut you a check—an advance on your bonus, if you will—each time you finish one of your races. The longer the race, the bigger the check."

"Hang on. Are you saying that if Lester thinks something is going on between me and Nick, he'd withhold my bonus? A morality clause? In this day and age? Is that ethical?"

"Sweetie, you, of all people, are in no position to be asking if something is ethical."

Mattie knew Dianne was right, but she had one last question for her.

"Does the same hold true for Nick?"

Dianne smirked. "I'd assume so. I hear it was his idea."

* * *

By April, Mattie's everyday lexicon included phrases like, "hill work," "mile repeats," and, her personal favorite, "fartleks."

Motivated by money, she figured finishing the upcoming 10k race would net her double what she got for completing the 5k. That she felt herself transforming into a healthier, slimmer, more confident person with each workout completed helped. But, her biggest motivator of all was Team Plate Spinner. At last count, it had over two thousand enthusiastic members, not including the satellite teams that were sprouting up in Chicago's collar counties.

Since the new feature kicked off, Mattie highlighted a "Plate Spinner of the Month." By sharing their personal struggles and how they overcame them, entrants contributed to the valuable forum in which working parents shared ideas on getting fit. After tallying readers' votes, Mattie sent the winners a goody bag filled with certificates to spas, organic grocers, and athletic apparel stores. She had never expected to feel so fulfilled professionally and personally by this assignment.

With those very readers in mind, she was determined to finish another punishing hill workout on the steps of the Knollwood High School football field bleachers. After reaching the top one last time, she started her final descent and noticed Nick talking on his cell phone while he paced back and forth on the sidelines.

Another client? He must have a dozen by now.

Curious, she hopped down the steps, watching as he ended his call and jotted something on his clipboard. When he looked up at her mid-scribble, she asked, "Ordering a pizza? I'd like black olives and red onions on mine."

In reply, he nodded toward a grassy spot in the middle of the field and said, "Core work. Come on, you know the drill."

Making no attempt to hide her disappointment, she muttered under her breath, "Yes, I do. I was just trying to make conversation."

Since the 5k, their verbal exchanges had gone from friendly banter to curt one-sided directives with Nick issuing orders and Mattie obeying.

In short, he was being everything Eddie always told her he was—domineering and egotistical. After nearly two months of being at the receiving end, she had half a mind to storm Lester's office and tell him what he could do with his morality clause.

She wiped her face with a towel from her duffle bag and pulled out a bottle of water. After a couple of swigs, she spread her towel on the dewy grass and lay on top of it. Enjoying the damp coolness of the grass, she clasped her hands behind her head, raised her feet in the air, crossed her ankles, and began a set of crunches. After completing forty-five, she started lowering her legs.

"Feet up. Elbows out. Ten more," Nick said as he circled her like a hawk, inspecting her form.

When she was done, she started bicycle rotations, touching her right elbow to her left knee and alternating until he told her to stop.

At the end of the workout, she zipped her jacked and asked, "Where to tomorrow, coach?"

"Nowhere. Nothing now until the race on Saturday."

"Have you made up your mind about doing that cooking demonstration with me?"

He shook his head back and forth, but said nothing.

She examined his expression. "I'll take that as a no."

He dropped his clipboard to his side and locked his eyes onto hers for the first time in a very long time.

"Why? I didn't say I wouldn't do it. I just haven't made up my mind.'"

Huzzah! A conversation.

"You never struck me as the indecisive type."

He narrowed his eyes and lifted his chin. "Oh yeah? Well you never struck me as a⸺"

Mattie held her breath.

Nick checked himself. "Never mind."

"What? As a what?"

He turned his attention toward his gym bag and said, "I'll see you Saturday."

Mattie pressed her lips together and would've said something, but thought better of it. He wasn't interested in her, and that was that. Was she surprised? No. Was she disappointed? Hell, yes.

But, as Claudia was so fond of reminding her, "What more could an allegedly married woman expect?"

Maybe she imagined that something more was developing between them. Maybe the way he was making her feel about herself was spilling over into some residual gratitude that she mistook for something more. Maybe she'd quit her job and come clean.

Yeah and maybe the Cubs will win the World Series.

On the morning of the 10k, Nick rattled off the exact same advice that he had given to Mattie for the 5k, minus the smiles, minus the face holding, minus all warmth whatsoever. After depositing her at her start corral, he vanished into the crowd of runners. She wondered why he even bothered coming at all.

While alone in the crowd, Mattie was heartened by the fact that everywhere she looked she saw Team Plate Spinner shirts, hats, and shorts.

Before the starting air horn went off, she hopped up on a curb and turned to rally her team.

"Hey Team Plate Spinner! Who's a winner?" she shouted as loud as she could.

After the crowd shouted a mixture of "me" and "I am" in reply, she yelled, "Ya know why?"

Hundreds of men and woman shouted all around her, "Why?"

"'Cause you're a *spinner*!"

Again, the crowd thundered with cheers. On the opposite side of the road, she could see Charlie Clark clicking away with an enormous zoom lens affixed to the front of his camera. Nick was nowhere to be found.

Feeling like the coolest person on the planet, Mattie slipped on her sunglasses and got into position with her Team Plate Spinner peeps. When the blast of the air horn pierced through all other sounds, the runners poured across the start line, heading north on Columbus Drive. The air, still on the brisk side, was perfect for a race along Lake Michigan.

During the third mile, Mattie swept by a water station and grabbed a cup, splashing some in her mouth before crushing it with one hand and tossing it to the curb like a pro. By mile five, she opted for a sport drink station, downing as much as she could while jogging; the rest dribbled down the side of her face and chin. When she finished the sixth mile, the muscles in her legs began running out of gas, and she was starting to feel disoriented.

Following along with the pack of runners surrounding her, they headed south on Michigan Avenue for a few blocks before turning left to ascend the slope on Roosevelt Road that marked the southern border of the expansive Grant Park. About half way up, she was desperate to lay her eyes on the finish line.

Where is it? How much farther?

Slowing her pace, she panted to no one in particular, "I can't do this."

"Oh yes you can," said a woman twice her age jogging beside her wearing a hot pink Team Plate Spinner tank top. "Come on. Don't give up now. We're almost done."

Mattie looked up and there it was—the big beautiful finish line. The two women turned left onto Columbus Drive and started down the straightaway.

Sure enough, there was Nick, just on the other side of it, staring at his stopwatch.

When he looked up and spotted her, he let it dangle from his neck. Cupping his hands around his mouth, he bellowed, "Come on, Mathilde Jean, show me what you got."

She was dumbfounded.

The first thing he says to me in over two months that could pass for conversation, and he picks something he knows will piss me off?

The next thing she knew she was charging over the finish line and blowing right passed him. Charlie Clark couldn't click his camera fast enough.

Making her way straight to the table covered with water bottles, she uncapped one and kept walking through the chute, not looking back. She went directly to the gear check tent to pick up her things, leaving Nick in her wake.

All around her, runners were celebrating with their friends and families, enjoying the cool breeze coming off of the lake, hugging, taking pictures, laughing, drinking, and eating. After posing for several selfies with some of her jubilant teammates, she waved to others who greeted her as they passed by.

Music coming from speakers mounted on old-fashioned coach lights in the park started playing a popular love song that prompted several couples to start dancing all around Buckingham Fountain. Mattie stood watching the spectacle, feeling accomplished, but empty and alone. She tried to remember which lame excuse she had given Lester for her family's absence this time around. Was it an out-of-state soccer tournament or an in-law's birthday party?

I've told so many lies, what's one more?

She took one last swig of her water and started walking toward her train station.

A few weeks later, Dianne informed her that Nick had finally agreed to co-host a cooking segment. And she handed Mattie a check to cover roughly two months' worth of rent.

Looks like I won't have to sell my ring, after all, was her first thought.

Her second was, *So why am I so bummed?*

CHAPTER NINE

———

"I'm at the age where food has taken the place of sex in my life.
In fact, I've just
had a mirror put over my kitchen table."
– Rodney Dangerfield

On Memorial Day, Chicago's lakeshore was abuzz with concerts, newly opened beaches, and family picnics. People came out in droves to welcome summer in the city.

But all Mattie wanted to do was fall asleep on her couch.

It was ten in the morning. She had gotten up four hours earlier to meet Nick at Lincoln Park Zoo where he said little, but handed her a blue rental bike and a helmet. From there, she followed him up to Sheridan road, then all the way down to Burnham Harbor and back. Doing her best to look at anything besides his backside for the duration, she thought of how cold he had become toward her over the last four months and wondered how different things might be between them if she had simply told him the truth.

Still, given that they would be co-hosting their first-ever cooking demonstration that might actually air on their local news affiliate later in the week, she would've thought he'd at least try to make conversation.

From what she could gather from Nancy Braley, they'd be supplementing her series on skinny comfort food by making a healthy meatloaf. It was Dianne's idea, but when Mattie found out Nancy booked the studio with the one-person kitchen in it, she grew suspicious. All it had was a five-foot long food prep counter with a chopping block, a range and an adjoining sink behind which was a working wall oven and a fake kitchen window. When Mattie called her on it, Nancy, mocking all things coy asked, "Oh, are you cooking, too?"

After her shower, Mattie recalled their exchange as she opened all of the windows in her apartment. Mocking Nancy, Mattie made a face and repeated, "Oh, are you cooking, too?"

She flopped on her couch, enjoying the breeze. Just as her eyes were starting to close, her phone rang. She picked it up and looked at the number. With a groan, she draped an arm over her eyes and answered.

"Hey, Claud. What's up?"

She was accosted by her sister's, slightly congested, maternal scolding. "Mat, where have you been? I've been trying to call you for two hours."

Mattie sat up. Clearly aggravated, Claudia sounded like she had been crying.

She gripped her phone tighter. "What's wrong?"

"It's Aunt Viv. She died during the night."

Stunned, Mattie had trouble getting the news to register in her brain. "What?"

Claudia spoke quickly, speaking in staccato sentences.

"Linda just called. Said they had dinner last night. Aunt Viv seemed fine. Went to bed earlier than normal. Said she felt like she was coming down with something. Linda found her this morning. Thinks she either had a stroke or heart failure. She'll let us know about arrangements."

Mattie felt like the floor had opened up and swallowed her whole. Having already lost a parent, the thought of losing the next best thing, even if it was in the form of an overly critical, sometimes callous aunt, was still heart wrenching.

"I don't know what to say," she thought out loud. "I know, right? She was the only one there for us after Mom passed." The words caught in Claudia's throat. "Do you want to come over?"

Mattie swallowed hard. "Sure, yeah. I'm on my way."

She called Dianne who gave her the rest of the week off and pledged to postpone the cooking demo. Mattie started to text Nick, but decided to call his phone instead, certain that the sound of his voice would bring her some small degree of comfort.

After four rings, it went to his voicemail. While she couldn't keep her voice from breaking up as she left her message, she assured him that she'd meet up with him the day after the funeral.

On the train ride to Claudia's, she replayed all of the wonderful ways Vivienne had stepped up and taken over as mother to her two grieving nieces, opening her home to them, and making sure they felt safe and secure.

Two days later, she sat alone on a settee at the funeral home before the visitation had started. Her cousin, Linda, fifteen years older, sat down beside her and hugged her tight. "You were always mom's favorite, you know."

Mattie blinked back the tears. "I never told her."

"What, honey?"

"That I loved her."

Linda didn't let go. "Don't worry. She knew. You were the only one who could get her to laugh. Remember? When we were all in the kitchen making chocolate chip cookies and we completely forgot to add the flour to the batter? Or when we were baking, I don't remember what, and the broiler caught on fire?"

At this Mattie started laughing. "And she said not to use the baking soda to put it out because she was hoping insurance would pay for a new oven?"

"Good times," Linda chuckled.

Mattie nodded in agreement.

"Those are the memories that will get us through this."

Four hours later, when Nick arrived with his parents to pay their respects to their former long-time neighbor, he scanned the crowded room for Mattie. He had no idea what he'd do if he saw her. All he knew was that his parents insisted he join them. His mother called as soon as she got the news. In fact, he was on the phone with her when he saw Mattie's number pop up on his phone.

When he listened to her message, it took everything in him to not rush to her side.

But that wouldn't be appropriate considering she's a married woman and all, would it?

His suspicions of her marital status grew with each passing day.

She listed a woman named Claudia as her emergency contact.

She never mentions her husband or kids. Ever.

She rarely wears her wedding ring anymore.

Straightening his tie, he watched as his mother got in line to pray beside Vivienne's casket, while his father stood nearby, chatting with several other men from their neighborhood.

After picking up a prayer card, Nick made his way to Linda. He hadn't seen her in years.

Taking her hand in his, he said, "I'm so sorry for your loss. Your mom was a wonderful woman."

Linda tilted her head at him. "I'm sorry, and you are…?

"Nick. DeRosa. You used to babysit my brother and me. My folks are, well, *were* neighbors."

"Oh, of course I remember you," she exclaimed as she threw her arms around him. "You're a lot taller than I remember, though. How are your parents?"

"They're here, actually." He pointed them out in the crowd.

Linda nodded. "So you must know my cousin, Mattie, right? She came to live with us when her Mom passed, remember?"

Here we go.

Nick took a sharp breath. "Yes. I remember Mattie. Is she here?"

"No. The poor kid was beat. I sent her home about twenty minutes ago. I can tell her you stopped by, though."

"Oh, don't worry about it," Nick assured her. "You've got enough on your mind."

Linda gave him an appreciative smile.

It's now or never, dummy.

"So, tell me. What's she been up to?"

* * *

As promised, the day after the funeral, Mattie arrived at her and Nick's usual spot at their usual time. She had barely eaten for four days, wasn't especially wowed by the sunrise erupting in spectacular fashion over the lake, and hadn't given much thought to the cold shoulder Nick had been giving her since February. Feeling truly and completely like an orphan, it was everything she could do not to lose it.

Staring straight ahead, she didn't notice the other runners jogging by her, the cyclists whizzing past, or the dog walkers, and rollerbladers. And she didn't see Nick coming toward her. She only felt his arms when he wrapped them securely around her, holding her up and holding her together in a way she struggled to do on her own.

"I'm so sorry for your loss." He nuzzled into her hair.

It took everything in her not to collapse into a sobbing, guilt-ridden mess.

At that moment, there was nothing she wanted to do more, but she knew she couldn't bear having to raise her guard again as soon as his sympathetic mood lifted.

Several deep breaths later, she asked with the stoicism of a war-weary general, "How far today, Coach?"

He brushed an errant strand of hair off of her face, looked her in the eye, and asked, "You sure you're up for it?"

Her heart tumbled in her chest.

Nodding, she sighed, "I missed it."

I missed you.

For a split second, she felt like he was peering into her soul, searching for more, but she wasn't ready to deliver. Not yet.

* * *

Early the next week, Mattie popped into Dianne's office. "He should be here any minute."

Dianne, her eyes fixed on her computer screen, replied, "Good. And what are you making?"

"Lentil bean and turkey meatloaf with maple syrup glaze."

"Sounds yummy," she sang out while her hands flew over her keyboard. "Is the kitchen ready?"

"I guess." Truth was Mattie didn't have to do much more than bring Nick down to the kitchen and follow Pete the producer's directions. Why she was standing in the doorway to Dianne's office wringing her hands, she had no idea.

Punching the Enter key, Dianne sent the email she had been drafting and looked up at Mattie. "Sweetie, is something wrong? You look distressed."

Mattie left the open doorway and took a step closer to Dianne's desk. "Here's the thing," she started. "That morality clause, remember?"

Dianne nodded at her.

"Was that really Nick's idea or was it Lester's because I keep playing what you said over and over in my head, and I don't think you made that very clear."

Peering over her reading glasses, Dianne shrugged, "What does it matter? Either way, you play, you don't get paid."

It was times like this when Mattie was certain Dianne had been a member of the mafia in a previous life. She could just picture her wearing a fitted pinstripe suit with black and white spectator pumps while ordering hits on women who shopped at discount clothing stores or colored their own hair.

"That's extortion."

"No, sweetie. That's keeping our jobs."

Mattie sighed and hung her head. Strapped for cash, the *Gazette* had her over a barrel, and she knew it. But she didn't have to like it.

"It's only for what—four more months?" Dianne continued. "Besides, I thought you agreed that this was a simple business transaction?"

Four more months? Nick had barely said "boo" to her since the 5k. She thought she was resigned to the fact that he had no feelings for her whatsoever. Then he came at her with that bear hug the day after the funeral.

There was no business in that transaction.

Mattie stood firm and declared, "Dianne, I don't think I can do this any more."

In reply, her editor smiled at her through clenched teeth and pointed at the door.

Seeing this only stoked Mattie's frustration. "You want me to leave? Fine. I'll leave, but not until I say this: Nick DeRosa's one of the best people I know. He's changed my life in ways that I can't even begin to articulate, and I'm not going to spend the next four months pretending otherwise."

She glared down at Dianne who, by now, had covered her face with both hands.

Mattie lifted her chin and closed her eyes. "He's right behind me, isn't he?"

Damn. It.

She turned around and found herself face to button-down-shirt-stretched-over-chiseled-chest with Nick.

Fighting back the urge to unbutton him with her teeth, she willed her eyes upward until they met his. Aside from the crinkles in the corners that hinted at a slight sense of amusement, his face showed no expression whatsoever.

Her heart thumped wildly in her chest, her face fifty shades of embarrassed.

"How long have you been standing there?"

He raised his eyebrows and asked, "Kitchen?"

He was giving her an out, and she grabbed it with both hands.

Good man. Did I tell you he's one of the best I know?

"Right. Follow me."

Together, they made their way to the test kitchen. After Pete Fleming, the short, spindly segment producer, greeted them, Nancy Braley appeared out of nowhere, wearing a low-cut mini dress.

Mattie suspected that, over the years, Nancy's criteria for the perfect man had morphed from tall, dark, and handsome to breathing and walking upright. As soon as she laid eyes on Nick, she wedged herself up against him like a rabid fan out to get a selfie with her favorite rock star.

"Hi, Nick," she gushed. "My name's Nancy. I'm the *Gazette's* food editor."

"Assistant," Mattie corrected. "Assistant food editor."

Ignoring the distraction, Nancy guided Nick behind the food prep counter and pointed out everything she had already prepared. "Here's the recipe. I already made one that will be finished by the time you're done making this one, but you'll be making two because we always feed the crew after a show. The lentil beans are in this bowl. Here's the garlic you'll chop, and this is a grater for the onion. I used the food processor to dice the baby carrots, but the viewers might like to see you chopping them by hand. Any chance you can take your shirt off?"

"Nancy!" Pete and Mattie exclaimed in unison.

Ever the hunky professional, Nick smiled and said, "How about I just roll up my sleeves?"

Fanning herself with her hand, Nancy sputtered, "Oh sure, yeah, that'd be fine."

Clearly enjoying the unbridled adulation, Nick surveyed the ingredients, scratched the scruff on his face, and said, "OK, I think I've got it."

Mattie stood nearby watching as shades of the Nick she used to know and loathe started to manifest in the otherwise potentially adorable man. When he caught Mattie's eye and nodded her over, she joined him behind the counter.

"You're helping me out, right?" he asked under his breath as he edged them both out of Nancy's earshot.

Mattie frowned. "I'm not cooking this. You are."

Nick tightened his grip on her arm. Looking over at Nancy who was checking the oven temperature, he whispered with the urgency of a big game hunter who just realized he had no bullets, "What do you mean you're not cooking? I'm not doing this by myself."

Looking puzzled, Mattie asked, "Nick, are you nervous? Don't be. I'll be watching from right over there." She pointed to a chair behind the massive video camera aimed at him like a cruise missile.

Next, she recited his own words of wisdom. "If you don't think you can do this, you won't."

A crease formed between his dark arched eyebrows as he glanced at the chair. When he turned his big hazels on her, his anxiety was palpable.

You're lovin' me now, aren't ya?

Well aware that this would have been an opportune time to announce his full name at the top of her lungs just to get him to cooperate, Mattie did the next best thing.

She smiled and mouthed, "Gotcha."

Mattie 1, Coach zip.

Before she could gauge his reaction, Nancy held out his-and-her Team Plate Spinner aprons. "Okay, you two. Put these on. Now, this set was designed for only one cook behind the counter here, but Pete's going to pull back to squeeze you both in.

Nick shook his head in mock disapproval while he tied his apron behind his back. "Is that any way to treat one of the best people you know?"

Coach 1, Mattie zip.

"Now, above all, remember," Nancy whispered to them both, "this is all about easy-to-make meals, so you've got to get it prepped, in the oven, and taste-tested in under ten minutes. And don't forget to make it look easy and have *fun*."

"Ten minutes? You have got to be kidding me," Mattie said to Nancy's back as she left them alone on the set.

What followed were the longest ten minutes of Mattie's life. She struggled to maintain a sense of decorum—no small feat considering the heat of the oven pulsing behind her and the hot studio lights baking her from above. Her close proximity to Nick certainly didn't help matters. Try as she might, there was no way to avoid bumping into him.

When she felt his hands on her waist as he tried maneuvering around her in the miniscule space, she was certain she would spontaneously combust. The first time made her feel uncomfortable, like he was assessing her BMI. The second time, though, the gentle squeeze of his strong hands and the feel of him brushing up against her sent a low volt of electric current coursing throughout her.

I'm happily married. I'm happily married. I'm happily married.

By the time they were both squishing their bare hands in the large bowl of raw meatloaf ingredients, she finally began to understand the meaning of "food porn"—a phrase Nancy used regularly to describe her favorite cable food shows.

When a strand of hair fell across Mattie's face and she had no way to brush it back, she resorted to rubbing her forehead against Nick's upper arm.

"Sorry," she sighed when he looked down at her, his expression full of curiosity.

Turning to the camera, she continued, "You want to really get your hands in there good to make sure everything is mixed together thoroughly, otherwise the flavor won't be consistent throughout."

After a minute of squishing the goo, Nick looked at her and murmured, "Is this good for you?"

She couldn't bring herself to make eye contact for fear she would either jump him on the spot or burst out laughing.

"Yeah, that feels really good." She pulled her hands out of the mixture, certain that her cheeks were sporting blotchy crimson patches.

When Mattie turned to wash her hands in the tiny sink, Nick stood next to her with his hands in the air.

Thanks for the well-equipped kitchen, Nancy. Not.

"Just give me a sec—"

Out of the corner of her eye, she saw Phil mouth, "Two minutes."

The next thing she knew, Nick was standing behind her. With an arm on either side of her, he took her hands in his and started lathering them together.

"Sorry," he breathed into her ear.

Mattie stared into the sink, feeling the heat of his body press against her back, and watched as his hands enveloped hers under the cool water. After he scrubbed her palms, he worked his fingers between hers and slid his hands back and forth over them until they were clean. It was a utilitarian effort, but she had never experienced anything so erotic.

Phil turned to Nancy who was standing nearby, gnawing on the tip of a pen like a dog does a chew toy while she watched them get busy in the kitchen. "She's married, right?"

Nancy chuckled. "Yeah. I actually feel sorry for the guy, whoever he is. He doesn't stand a chance."

Blowing out a big breath, Mattie quickly dried her hands on her apron, tucked her hair behind her ears, and turned to slide the meatloaf into the oven while Nick retrieved the already-cooked one from the upper rack.

Per Nancy's instructions, he used a metal spatula to shimmy out a piece and slid it onto a plate that was waiting nearby. After he heaped a bit of it on a fork, he held it out for Mattie to taste. When she raised her face toward it with her mouth open, he said, "It's hot. You'd better blow on it first."

From behind the camera, Nancy groaned.

And so ended their first cooking demonstration.

After seeing it for herself and downloading a copy, Mattie could certainly see why Lester had instructed Dianne to shelve it. Nancy Braley, however, informed Mattie that she had received no such directive and went ahead and linked it to her "Quick and Easy Meals" page.

Even without advertising, it only took four hours for it to become the top-rated story by unique clicks for the day. By the next morning, it was the top-rated clip for the week. By the end of the second day, it was on its way to becoming an Internet sensation, and Mattie had the privilege of witnessing a historic moment when Lester himself did something he had never done before—admit to Dianne that he was wrong.

* * *

Three days before the half marathon, Mattie was about to wake up from a delicious dream. In it, she was being kissed, and it wasn't the sort of closed mouth peck Eddie used to impart; it was a long, slow, lovely, probing sort of kiss—the kind that leaves even the hardest of hearts breathless and the likes of which she had only ever experienced once before.

When she opened her eyes, she saw Nick's face above hers, but it was wrought with worry. "Come on, Mattie," he yelled, though his voice sounded far away. "Wake up. Don't leave me. "

She sat up with a start and looked around her empty bedroom. Grabbing her phone, she saw that it was six-twenty in the morning and someone had just texted her. It was Nick.

"Where r u?"

Dammit.

She leapt out of bed. Even with her windows cracked during the night, the air inside of her apartment felt muggy. Outside, it would be worse.

She pulled on a pair of fire engine red running shorts and a matching sport bra over which she yanked a gray Dry-FIT tank top. Grabbing her sunglasses and keys, she shut her door behind her, texting the entire time.

"Sorry. Overslept. Be there in 5."

If Mattie felt frisky after her dream, seeing Nick standing on their usual corner, shirtless and wearing the shortest of running shorts didn't help. Not many men could pull off that look, especially so early in the summer, but Nick, more muscular than the stereotypical string bean distance runner, was already tan and turning heads.

As she approached, he took off his sunglasses to reveal the same unsmiling expression she assumed he'd use to intimidate his high school runners.

It didn't work on her. Not bothering to suppress a grin, she cried, "How are ya?"

He frowned at her. His reply was self-evident. "I'm hot."

Mattie couldn't keep her eyes from sweeping his big guns, sculpted chest and chiseled abs. Forcing herself to look in his eyes, she pointed out over the lake behind him.

"Check out that gorgeous sunrise."

When Nick turned, she bolted in the opposite direction. When she was several yards away, she pulled off her tank top and yelled over her shoulder, "Come on, slow poke. What are you waiting for?"

Nick stood for a minute, wondering what had come over her. He'd never seen her like this. He laughed out loud when he saw her rip off her shirt like a seasoned pro in the midst of a long, hot run. Given the heat and humidity, most everyone out running that morning had already done the same. That she did it at all spoke volumes about how much more confident she had become.

The old Mattie never would've done that. Not in a million years.

It was the first time he saw her in anything besides baggy workout gear or loose-fitting business clothes. She looked good. She looked fit. With a full view of just how good of shape she was now in, he took his time catching up to her.

Ever since her cousin had informed him that Mattie wasn't married, his emotions had swung between elation and hurt and everything in between. Why hadn't she been honest with him? Was it about her job or was it about him? Why didn't she trust him with the truth? Was she still in love with Eddie? All questions he could've asked if he had waited for her to tell him herself. As it was, he cheated by taking advantage of a kind acquaintance at her own mother's wake.

How low can you go?

When he was right behind her, he stretched out his hand and gave her ponytail a light tug.

She glanced back at him, smiling. "Slacker. What took you so long?"

"Shut up and run," he chuckled. "We're only going as far as Montrose today."

As they bounded north up the path that cut through Lincoln Park, Mattie exclaimed, "I can't believe I'll be running a half marathon in three days."

The wind kicked up, doing little to alleviate the stifling humidity. To their right, swells of waves in Lake Michigan crashed against the breakwaters. To their left, the patches of sky between the Gold Coast high-rises looked as if someone had painted them dark gray.

Nick stared straight ahead. His eyes were on the path, but his mind was on what he would rather be doing with Mattie.

"Hello..." she sang out.

He glanced at her. "What?"

"The half. I can't believe it's in three days."

"Oh, yeah."

When he said nothing more, she prodded, "That's it? If you're trying to motivate me, I have to tell ya, I'm not feeling it."

Nick stopped abruptly and shot his arm out in front of her as a car turned onto the street they were about to cross over.

"Sorry. I've got a lot on my mind."

"Care to share?" she ventured as she jogged in place, waiting for the traffic to clear.

As desperate as he was to share his feelings with her, exposing himself to the kind of rejection he was expecting in return would be more than he was willing to deal with—especially with three solid months of training to go before the marathon.

Instead, he replied by wagging his index finger in her direction. "Uh-uh. Strictly business, remember?"

She either missed or completely ignored the mocking tone in his voice. "Right. Sorry."

She jogged along a bit more then asked, "Hey, any chance I can talk you into running the half with me?"

He was surprised by her question, but ready with answer.

"No. I only registered you."

This seemed to agitate her. Her mood darkened along with the clouds above. "Can't you just run with me anyway?"

"What's the problem, Ross?"

"Finishing the 10k was a lot harder than I expected. I'm not sure I'm ready for double the distance. Especially if it's this hot."

Nick dismissed her concern with an icy observation. "From what I saw, you did just fine at the 10k. You ran a 54:05. Do you have any idea how good that is for somebody who just started running a couple of months ago? Besides, if it's this hot, the organizers will be more than ready. Tons of water stations and emergency personnel."

Glancing in her direction, he added, "And me running with you won't make the distance seem any shorter or the air feel any cooler."

After several more yards, she tried using his own rules to persuade him. "What about 'you're not in this alone'?"

"Mattie," he started, his voice sounding sterner and more irritated than he intended, "How many times do I have to tell you, you're never gonna succeed if you keep telling yourself you can't?"

With that, they ran along in stony silence. By the time they passed Belmont Harbor, he noticed the path ahead and behind them was virtually deserted. Despite the wind whipping off of the lake, the air began to feel thick and charged with electricity. The sky to their left looked like a chalkboard that had just been wiped clean with an eraser. Thunder rumbled in the distance.

Nick slowed. "Come on. Time to head back. We shouldn't get caught in this."

Just as they turned around, the sky opened up. He grabbed Mattie's hand, and they ran over a quarter of a mile before taking shelter under a hidden prairie-style wood and stone structure on the northern shore of a secluded pond just to the west of the park.

Tucked away from the bustle of the city, the shelter was nestled in a dense, untamed wooded patch that curved around it like a green, leafy hug, open only to the serene pond that was carpeted with lily pads in full bloom. It was an unofficial habitat for many of the exotic birds at the zoo and a favorite place for weddings and couples looking for, um, privacy.

In the relentless downpour, it resembled a miniature rain forest, still and hushed.

Soaked through, Mattie backed herself into a dry corner trying to catch her breath. She undid her ponytail and fluffed her hair over her shoulders.

Nick stood dripping a few feet away watching the downpour, agitated and wishing he hadn't snapped at her. He cast a sideways glance in her direction as she stood against the wall made up of thin limestone slabs stacked like crackers. Even though she had pulled her shirt back on, her clothes clung to her like plastic wrap.

When a chilled gust of wind blew through, she gasped and crossed her arms across her chest, looking self-conscious and vulnerable—much like he remembered seeing her between classes in high school, hating who ever it was that had caused her to feel that way. Only this time, he knew there was no one to blame but himself.

"How can you be cold?" he asked, unable to keep the hard edge from his voice. "We just sprinted all the way down here."

Would you just shut up?

Mattie narrowed her eyes, emerged from her dry, secure corner and demanded, "If you have something to say to me, why don't you just say it?"

She was so close. Dangerously close. He could smell the rain in her hair and was very eager to find out if her lips tasted as sweet as he remembered.

I could take you right here, right now.

Nickel-sized hail started falling like snow, pelting the flowers lining the path circling the pond.

Barely able to restrain himself, he asked, "Aren't you the one who has something to say?"

Mattie blinked. Caught off guard, she lifted her chin. "I don't know what you're talking about."

He shook his head and let out of short laugh. "Like hell you don't."

As she stood there, staring at him, her narrowed eyes started to well up.

Nick held her gaze and leaned into her. "Come on, Mattie. Be honest."

Blinking back tears, she gasped, "I have to go."

She had just stepped out from under the shelter, when a bright white flash and an explosive, ear-popping crack of thunder forced her backwards with a cry.

Nick caught her and yanked her towards him. "I've got you."

As her body trembled against his, he held her tight. She felt warm and, tucked into him like that, fit like a missing puzzle piece. He rested his cheek against the top of her head and closed his eyes, pretending, if only for a few precious seconds, that she belonged to him and not some fabricated spouse.

After a short while, the rain stopped as suddenly as it started, and he eased his grip, but she stayed put and looked up at him, her face flushed.

"I'd better—"

Before she could get the words out, something in Nick took over, something out of his control. Shedding his fear of rejection, he slipped a big hand on each side of her face and spoke in a raspy whisper. "Mattie, I can't get you out of my head. I've tried, but I can't."

She looked like she was in the front seat of a roller coaster that was about to derail. "Nick. Don't. Nothing personal, remember?"

"That was your rule, not mine."

He kissed her tenderly at first, but when he felt her arms tighten around his waist, he hungrily covered her mouth with his. Clutching the back of her shirt, he lifted her off of the ground as he tried to consume every bit of her that she was willing to offer.

When he was finished, he brushed her mouth with a soft kiss, whispered, "See you Saturday," and was gone.

* * *

"Oh my God, he knows. How does he know?" Dianne asked before putting her face in her hands.

Mattie sat languidly in a chair facing her editor's desk, still basking in the glow of Nick's very intentional display of affection. "I don't know," she sighed. Then, staring out the window, she added, "And I don't care."

Dianne put both hands on her desk, "Did you kiss him back?"

Mattie just looked at her, cheeks aflame.

"Oh, you did, didn't you? I knew this would happen when you stopped wearing your ring. And you never replaced those pictures on your desk like you said you would. Didn't I tell you to move in with your sister?"

"Everything will be fine," Mattie replied. "Lester doesn't know, and I doubt Nick's going to tell him. He needs his bonus."

"Oh, and you don't?" Dianne shot back.

"I suppose."

Dianne, her face etched with skepticism, asked, "You're in love with him, aren't you?"

Gripping the arms of her chair, she lied, "As far as I'm concerned, our relationship is still strictly business."

Dianne nodded and said, "That's what I want to hear."

Mattie left, but after seeing Diane's expression, she'd have been a fool to think her editor believed her.

* * *

Later in the day, a rousing debate was taking place between the assistant fashion editor and three guys from the IT department who had clustered in the corridor near Dianne's office. The topic was what Mattie should wear for the half marathon. The choices were a sparkly red, white, and blue tutu or a "skort" with Team Plate Spinner embroidered across her derriere.

Looking to fill her water bottle at a nearby cooler, Mattie passed by and declared that the topic was not up for discussion. When she returned to her cubicle, she found a lithe, sweaty delivery biker waiting for her.

A jittery type with his hair slicked back into a greasy ponytail and his helmet dangling from his wrist, he sputtered with a thick accent of indiscernible origin, "Special delivery. You sign."

What now?

She held out her hand and took the large envelope from him. The return address was of a law firm in the Loop. Goosebumps crept up her forearms.

"Where do I sign?"

He held out a portable electronic signature pad.

Scribbling like a doctor writing a prescription, she waved him away and stared at the envelope, thinking of nothing but Claudia's warnings about fraud and misrepresentation.

She was certain Dianne would have given her a heads up if legal action of that magnitude were imminent.

Wouldn't she?

She held it up to the light, but was unable to see through the envelope. Curiosity getting the better of her, she took out her letter opener and sliced it open. She pulled out several photos and a letter with a notary seal on it. A smaller piece of paper wafted into her lap.

As she read the letter, the words "executor" and "Vivienne" jumped off the page in between a lot of "herebys" and "heretofores." With trembling fingers, she lifted the small piece of paper that was still in her lap.

Holding it at eye level, she saw that it was a check for $100,000.

Ducking into an empty conference room, she called her sister.

"Yep. I got mine this morning. Same amount," Claudia announced.

"I'm stunned. I feel like I just won the lottery. Where did she get all this money from? I didn't know school teachers made that much."

"Well, think about it. When she and Uncle Al got married, they stayed in the same house she grew up in. They didn't have a mortgage to worry about. They only had one child, no major disasters, rarely went on vacation…"

"But still." Mattie plopped into a chair and whispered, "I didn't see this coming."

Her eyes brimmed just thinking about her aunt's generosity.

"Me neither. I guess the kids will have a college fund, after all," Claudia laughed. "And you can finally pay off all your bills and still keep your ring, if you want. It's a win-win."

Paying down her financial obligations and being debt-free suddenly seemed like an attainable fantasy. As for her ring, she had stopped wearing it a several months back when it became too loose to stay on her finger. She didn't even miss it. She wasn't even sure where it was.

For the rest of the day, she thought about the implications of her inheritance.

I could quit my job, but I'd be letting my readers down.
I could tell Nick the truth, but he'd probably leave me.
I could just keep playing the game until marathon is behind me, then quit.

None of her options held much appeal.

Depositing the check in her bank account on her way home that night, she paid every single remaining balance she owed to the wedding-related creditors and still had plenty left over.

Feeling that an enormous weight had been lifted, she turned on her stereo, cranked up the volume, and began dancing around her tiny living room, debt-free and jiggle-free.

Just living the dream.

* * *

The night before the race, Nick had dinner with his parents. His father, a proud first-generation Italian, looked at him from across the kitchen table. "You sure you're all right, Nicoli? You don't look so good."

Glancing up, but not making eye contact, Nick replied, "I'm fine, pop."

Lucy eyed her son. "So, two races down, two to go, right?"

"That's right." Nick dug his hand into a wicker basket to retrieve a piece of steaming garlic toast and set it on his plate.

"You don't seem very excited about it. Everything going OK? How's Mattie holding up?"

"Oh, she's doing great. She's working really hard. Her times just keep getting better. You wouldn't even recognize her. She looks so—"

His parents waited for him to finish his sentence.

"Confident."

Exchanging glances with Lucy, his father said, "Why don't you bring her by sometime? Maybe for your mother's pasta before your next race. When is it? October? I'll bet she's never tasted food as good as your mother's before."

He gave his wife a quick smile while Nick stared off into space, considering the idea. "I don't know. Maybe. We barely even talk to each other. I coach, she writes. I think that's the way she wants to keep it."

Again, his parents exchanged eye contact. Lucy wrapped spaghetti around her fork, twirling it in her right hand while holding a tablespoon against it with her left. She looked down at her plate and asked, "You don't still believe that she's married, do you?"

Nick let out a long sigh. "No, Linda told me she's not."

He put his fork down, rested his chin on his hand, and stared at the table.

Lucy reached over and rubbed his back. "Well that's good news, right?"

"It would've been better coming from her."

"Ya, well, Good things come to those who wait, huh?"

Nick offered her a half smile.

"How about you stay here tonight?"

"No, thanks." Glancing at the kitchen wall clock, he added, "And I'd better get going. I have to get to bed early. It's gonna be a hot one tomorrow."

CHAPTER TEN

────

*"We can't all be heroes because someone has to sit on the curb
and clap as they go by."*
– Will Rogers

On the morning of the Firecracker Half Marathon, there wasn't a cloud in the sky, and the forecast called for temperatures to top out in the nineties. With the humidity providing enough moisture to steam a sauna, Mattie chose her clothes carefully— royal blue skort and matching sport bra with her white Team Plate Spinner T-shirt. While the local news blared in her living room, she braided her hair into a thick rope that started high above her neck and dangled to the middle of her back.

On Nick's urging, she had consumed copious amounts of water the day before. So much so, that she was up every hour on the hour all night long just to go to the bathroom.

So much for a good night's sleep.

She slipped a cap on her head, yanked her braid through the opening in the back, slipped on her sunglasses and said, "Let's get this over with," to her reflection in her bedroom mirror.

Twenty-five minutes later, she found herself in the midst of a mob of other runners in Millennium Park, just behind the Art Institute. It was seven-thirty in the morning. The trees offered no shade, and there was no breeze coming off the lake.

Volunteers, sporting T-shirts imprinted with American flags and carrying red, white, and blue squirt bottles with little battery-operated fans attached near the nozzles, were everywhere. Water stations lined much of the route, and EMT tents were so plentiful, the area near the finish line looked like a war zone.

The plan was to meet Nick at the gear check tent although Mattie had half a mind to ditch him. While she no longer cared about her bonus, the last thing she wanted was to be responsible for him not getting his. And, after what had happened between them just a few days before, she wasn't sure she'd be able to restrain herself. To make matters worse, since the *Gazette* was co-sponsoring the event, cameras would be everywhere.

Just two more races and I can just be me. No husband. No family. No stinkin' morality clause.

She figured all she had to do was give Nick a couple of nods while he delivered his usual coach's spiel. After that, she wouldn't have to see him again until the finish line. And after that, just a few more months of training, the marathon, and then they'd be done.

Piece of cake.

She zipped her phone into the little pocket on the back of her waistband and stood jangling her keys, watching for him. Before long, she saw him sauntering toward her.

Like most of the men milling around, he was shirtless.

Have mercy.

Then she noticed the bib pinned to the front right leg of his shorts.

What the——?

"Mattie. Listen. About the other day. We gotta talk," he started.

"Are you running this?" she interrupted. "Why are you running this? You said you weren't running this."

He handed his keys and wallet over to the gear check volunteer who put them in a clear plastic bag and put them in a box that corresponded with Nick's bib number.

Pointing to her keys, he asked, "Is that all you have?"

Before she could answer, he took them from her hand and asked the volunteer to put them in his bag.

"You don't have to run this," she reiterated. "I'll be fine."

"Not in this heat, you won't. Now take your shirt off."

"What? I don't think that's a good idea."

He held up a tube of sunscreen. "Take your shirt off."

She pulled her shirt over her head, careful not to dislodge her hat. Nick took it from her hand and handed it to the now exasperated volunteer.

"Sorry, could you add this to my bag, too, please?"

It came as no surprise to either of them that, just as he started smoothing the lotion across her shoulders, Charlie Clark and his most annoying camera appeared.

"Hey, Mattie. Nick. It's gonna be a hot one today, huh?"

Nick positioned himself behind Mattie, smearing the lotion across her back and around her waist while she plastered on a big smile for Charlie.

"How 'bout a nice one of the two of you? Nick. Stand next to her, huh? It'll just take a minute."

Standing up straight, he slipped on his sunglasses and folded his hands in front of him. The classic high school coach's pose.

"You look like you're her body guard. Put your arm around her or somethin', would ya? Loosen up."

Nick took off his shades and did as Charlie instructed.

Click, click, click.

After what seemed like an eternity, he announced, "I'm gonna go check out the start line. I'll catch up with you guys later."

When he was gone, Mattie snatched the tube from him and started rubbing lotion on her arms, neck, and face. The feel of Nick's hands caressing her body was not getting her into race mode. Not one bit.

"Hey, get my back for me, would ya?"

Are you frickin' kidding me?

"Turn around," she demanded.

She squirted some of the white goo into the palm of her hand and reached up to run it along the width of his shoulders.

Oh my.

"As I was saying, about the other day…"

"Forget about it."

He turned around and watched her for a moment before responding, "Not gonna happen."

When she looked away, flustered, he reached down and grabbed the sunscreen out of her hand.

"Hey, I'm not finished."

"That's all right. I covered myself before I walked out the door this morning," he said with a wink.

Mattie rolled her eyes. "You realize Lester probably has cameras lining the entire route."

Nick tilted his head. "If you're so worried about it, why didn't you wear your wedding ring?"

She clenched her bare left hand and stomped to her start corral.

I've got a very bad feeling about this.

Nick hovered over her, keeping her close. Given the heat, his presence was already starting to annoy her. What she practically begged him to do just three days earlier, she was now regretting with every fiber of her being.

When the officials opened the gate between the runners in their group and the start line, everyone moved forward like cattle.

She looked up at him. "So you're not worried about your bonus?"

"What?" he shouted

The blast of the air horn signaled the start of the race, and all of the runners in their wave started making their way north through Chicago's city streets.

Mattie charged out with a sprint, darting through the crowd.

Nick chased after her. When he caught her, he panted, "What the hell are you doing?"

"Getting this over with," she snarled.

"Haven't I taught you anything? You're gonna die out here if you don't pace yourself. Now, slow it down."

She resumed her usual pace which made the course feel that much longer and the air that much thicker.

After just a mile, Nick reached out for water from a volunteer holding out cups for runners as they passed by.

Holding it in front of Mattie, he barked, "Take it."

She took a swig then handed it back to him. He held up his hand in protest. "Finish it."

She splashed more in her mouth, crumpled the cup, and tossed it to the curb.

At each of the next three-mile markers, the same scene played out. In between, Nick kept a close eye on her, shouting things like, "slow down your breathing," and "relax your shoulders." By the fifth mile, she'd had enough.

"Would you just stop?" she sputtered.

"What?"

"God. It's just like when we were kids. Always getting in my way."

Nick was quiet for a while. At the next water station, he took a cup and downed it himself.

"You asked me to run with you."

Mattie's reply was nothing short of combative. "No, I didn't."

Nick looked at her, confused, his concern growing with each stride. She was beginning to labor in the heat. Her gait, usually rhythmic, was plodding.

"You oughta stop. You're getting overheated."

Mattie just shook her head. "Just like at the wedding."

"What are you talking about?"

She was breathing in short gasps. Despite her cap, sweat dripped into her eyes. "You sabotaged me then, and you're doing it now."

"Unbelievable." He took a cup of a sport drink from a volunteer standing on the edge of the course and held it out to her. "Mattie, please drink this."

She smacked it out of his hand and ducked to her left, blending into a dense pack of joggers. When they turned onto a narrower side street, the stream of them thickened, and she got what she wanted. She had ditched Nick.

By mile nine, Mattie thought the pavement rolling out ahead of her looked like shimmering pools. She chased it down, wanting so badly to dive into the cool water. Greedily accepting cups that were held out to her, she ducked with the rest of the runners under a cool mist station. This revived her just enough to make it to through to mile twelve.

The sun was baking the course. Mattie's feet felt like they were on fire. If she weren't so focused on the road that stretched out endlessly before her, she would've noticed runners starting to leave the race to her right and her left. Some were being helped off by volunteers. Others simply called it quits.

All Mattie needed was to see the finish line. Once she laid her eyes on it, she knew she'd find her kick and breeze right on through to the end, but until then, every step was a monumental effort. Her body felt like a volcano that was about to erupt. If she could just find a cool, shady spot and lie down.

"Just a little further," someone to her left said. Not wanting to lose her focus, she didn't dare turn her head.

When she finally spotted the finish line, she was dismayed to see that it was still so far away. She wanted to stop. Stop running. Stop lying. Stop being someone she wasn't. She just wanted Nick. As that thought crystallized in her overheated brain, tears tried to form, but couldn't.

When she didn't see him stationed in his usual spot, waving her in, she called out his name with a pathetic whimper.

"Come on, Mattie. We're almost there."

With everything she had in her, she glanced to her left. There he was.

As they approached the finished line, she reached for him and cried, "I'm so sorry. Please forgive me."

Once they both stepped foot across the line, Mattie crumbled like a rag doll. Nick scooped her up, looked into her face as her head hung lifeless over his arm and yelled, "Where do I take her?"

Within seconds, volunteers swarmed to escort them to an air-conditioned emergency medical tent.

Nick laid her on an empty gurney, checked her pulse, and made sure she was breathing. He then removed her hat and took her right hand in both of his. "Come on, Mattie. Wake up."

Beating himself up ten different ways for not pulling her off the course when he knew she was struggling, all he could think to do was kiss her forehead and whisper, "Stay with me. Please."

Blinking back the tears he felt sting at his eyes, he looked around and shouted, "Can we get some help over here?"

A nearby paramedic rushed over holding an IV bag in one hand and three ice packs in the other. Handing him the ice packs, he instructed Nick to place one under her neck and one under each armpit while he readied her for a much-needed infusion of fluids.

Another man burst into the tent. He was not in uniform. He wasn't even wearing a volunteer T-shirt. Standing opposite Nick on the other side of the gurney, he looked down at Mattie and muttered, "Oh, Jesus."

Alarmed, Nick asked, "Can I help you?"

The man looked at him and asked, "You Nick?"

I know you.

While his mind busied itself with trying to reconcile the recognition with the source, he released her hand and replied in a hoarse croak, "Yeah."

The man reached his hand across to Nick. "I'm Tom. Nice to meet ya."

Addressing the EMT, he said, "She's a southpaw. Better start that in her right arm."

How the hell would you know?

And that's when it hit Nick. He *had* seen his face before—in a frame on Mattie's desk.

Backing away, he watched as the EMT tapped a vein, inserted the needle, taped it to her clammy arm and left to hail an ambulance.

When he was gone, Tom stroked her cheek and called out, "Mattie. Come on, honey, it's me, Tom. Stay with me all right? You gotta stay with me now, sweetheart."

Oh my God, she is married.

Nick turned to leave, his heart crumbling in his chest, when he heard Tom say, "Shit."

He turned and watched as he patted down his pockets, then look at him imploringly. "Do me a favor? I lost my wife in the crowd trying to get in here. Can you call her and tell her to meet us at Chicago Memorial. Her name's Claudia."

"Your *wife*?"

"Yeah." Pointing to Mattie, Tom clarified, "Her sister."

Nick blew out a breath and nodded. "Right."

His overloaded emotional circuits flipped into autopilot mode. He pulled his phone from the back pocket of his shorts, punched in the number, and mechanically delivered the message.

When he hung up, Tom handed him the fluid bag to hold up high while he pushed her to the waiting ambulance. At Tom's urging, he followed him in and rode with them to the hospital. By the time they arrived, not only was Nick up to speed on Mattie's marital status, or lack thereof, he was certain of just one thing—he didn't want to play this game anymore.

* * *

Waking up to her six-year-old nephew Charlie serenading her with his rendition of "Wheels on the Bus," Mattie opened her eyes and scanned her surroundings.

"Mommy, she's awake," the little cherub shouted at the top of his lungs.

Claudia rushed into the hospital room. "Oh, thank God. How are you feeling, hon?"

She had never felt so exhausted in all her life. Her head throbbed, and she felt dizzy. Through her cracked lips, she croaked, "Nick?"

Her sister sat down on the edge of the bed. "He just left. He wouldn't leave until the doctor convinced him that you'd be OK. He called me from the medical tent."

Mattie moaned, "Oh no," and Claudia started brushing the back of her fingers against Mattie's cheek like their mother used to do when they didn't feel good.

"He's in love with you, Mat. You should've seen him." But, she didn't say it like an excited teenager divulging a secret. She said it like she felt sorry for him. "He's a wreck."

The tone of Claudia's voice was filled with an unarticulated, "I told you so."

Mattie contorted her face to hold back a sob. "He's not coming back, is he?"

After shaking her head back and forth, her sister got up and closed the curtain around them as Mattie turned onto her side and cried out all of the fluids the good doctors and nurses of Chicago Memorial Hospital had just replenished.

Early the next morning, she saw that someone had posted a new link on the Team Plate Spinner Facebook page. Apparently, one of her readers was a volunteer at the race. Not only did that person record Mattie and Nick crossing the finish line, but they also managed to follow them into the medical tent and record everything up until Mattie being loaded into the ambulance.

Underneath it, someone had typed, "Dislike."

Over three hundred people clicked that they liked that comment.

Over five hundred had clicked "Like" directly under the link itself and over fifty people had already shared it.

She replayed the clip at least half a dozen times before her buzzer rang.

She got up as quickly as she could, pressed the button, and said with her voice full of hope, "Hello?"

"It's me, Sweetie. I come bearing caffeine and refined sugar."

Dianne.

Unable to mask her disappointment, she pressed the buzzer and sat on the couch, waiting for her editor to arrive.

Letting herself in, Dianne asked, "How're you feeling, doll? I brought you some breakfast."

She set a large disposable cup and a small bag from a bakery down the street on the coffee table and sat beside her.

"I'm so sorry," Mattie whispered. "I've ruined everything, haven't I?"

"I wouldn't say everything. For starters, you're trending Facebook and Twitter. Oh, and you made the sports section. Well, the last page of the sports section."

Dianne handed it to her. "See? There, on the bottom."

After scanning it, she was grateful that the report on her dismal performance was limited to one picture. It was of Nick holding her seemingly lifeless body in his arms at the finish line. The expression on this face spoke volumes. He looked like he had just lost everything. Again.

Reading her thoughts, Dianne sighed, "Clearly not your typical client/coach relationship."

Mattie shook her head. "My readers must hate me."

Putting her hand on Mattie's shoulder, Dianne squeezed it and said, "How 'bout you get yourself cleaned up and into something fabulous. Lester wants to see you in his office at ten. I'll pop for a cab."

After a quick shower, Mattie put on a pretty floral-print dress and, since the temperature had finally dropped to a more tolerable level, a matching short-sleeved cardigan. Twenty minutes later, she made her way to Lester's office doing her best to prepare for her inevitable termination.

And possible criminal charges.

During their cab ride into work, Mattie hadn't asked about the fate that awaited her, and Dianne didn't offer. She only asked this: "What's the worst that can happen?"

Mattie had stared out the window as the tree-lined streets of the Lincoln Park neighborhood segued into the high-end storefronts of the Magnificent Mile and said, "It already has."

Feeling all eyes on her as she approached the administrative assistant's desk closest to Lester's office door, she gripped the small notebook she had brought with her.

Natalie Foster sprung up from her chair first. "Hi, Mattie. He'll be right with you."

"OK, thanks."

The admin moved her box of tissues to the edge of her desk closest to where Mattie was standing and whispered, "Good luck."

Frowning, she said, "Thanks."

Not a moment later, the door to Lester's office swung open and there was Nick, standing directly in front of her wearing jeans with a shirt and tie. Mattie caught her breath. His eyes were dark. He looked wounded and brooding. When he saw her, he folded a little piece of paper he was carrying and stuffed it into his shirt pocket.

With his voice low and gruff, he asked, "You OK?"

Sensing a collective swoon from the administrative pool behind her, Mattie whispered, "Can we talk?"

He turned and started making his way to the elevators. When she hurried after him, Natalie and her officemates craned their necks, trying to follow the action.

"Nick, please. I'm so very sorry. I never meant to hurt you."

She cringed at the cliché.

Ignoring her, he ground out, "I don't know why I never saw it before."

"What?" Mattie asked, wishing she had plucked a couple of tissues from Natalie's box.

"You and my brother would've been perfect together. A couple of con artists."

Ouch.

Reaching the elevator, he plastered on a fake smile and added, "Who knows? Maybe someday he'll come back, and you two can live happily ever after. Just like you always wanted."

Anger started pulsing through her veins. "How can you say that?"

She grasped his hand. "I don't want your brother. I want you."

Nick let out a short laugh. Pulling his hand away from hers, he jabbed the down button. "Is that right? Well, you have a crappy way of showing it."

The elevators doors opened, and he walked in.

"Wait." Mattie followed. When the doors closed, she hit the emergency stop button. "Are you leaving me?"

This was it. Her greatest fear was playing out before her very eyes. Another man she had lost her heart to was about to abandon her. This time, though, she knew it was no one's fault but her own. With her heart threatening to pound right out of her chest, she swallowed hard, barely able to contain the tears as she waited for his reply.

When Nick turned toward her, his eyes smoldered with hurt. "Why do you sound so surprised? You never expected me to stick around. Why else would you have lied to me this whole time?"

"I didn't lie to you. I never said I was married."
He gave her a disparaging look and released the button. "You never said you weren't."

"Nick, please." She spoke quickly, her pulse racing as they descended. "What was I supposed to do? The whole time we were growing up, you never liked me. You always just looked right through me. Then all of a sudden, you show up and act so surprised that I could be married—"

Pulling the emergency stop button, he turned on her and asked, "What are you talking about?"

She held her hands out in front of her. "Oh please. The note you handed me on the playground?"

Where the hell did that come from?

She winced, painfully aware of how pathetic she sounded.

When Nick's expression made it clear he had no idea what she was talking about, she rolled her eyes and began reciting, "There once was a girl named Mattie who looked like a great big—"

A deep crease formed between his eyebrows. "I never gave you a note."

Mattie took in a sharp breath as the memory she believed to be her reality for so long shifted like the colors in a kaleidoscope.

"Of course it was you. Who else could it—"

Eddie?

"All this time I thought—"

Nick released the button. "Yeah, well you thought wrong. About a lot of things."

Verbalizing her stream of consciousness, she blurted, "But you always came off so judgmental, so critical of me."

The doors opened and they stepped out. In a flash, Nick turned toward her, pinning her against the wall. "Only because you couldn't see that the only twin who ever really loved you was standing right in front of you the whole time."

With that, he turned, strode across the near-vacant lobby, and pushed through the revolving doors. Just like that, he was gone.

Damn.

Three reporters from the sports department, smelling of pepperoni, cigarette smoke, and beer sauntered into the elevator.

"Hey, could ya hit six, please?"

Mattie turned to look at the overweight, short-sleeved-plaid-shirt-wearing dolts, and said, "Press it yourself."

She made her way to the stairwell and stomped her way up all eight flights to Lester's office. By the time she had reached her destination, her despair had turned to fury—at herself for not being upfront with Nick, at Nick for walking out on her, and at Lester for thinking of this stupid idea in the first place.

With notebook in hand, Mattie marched down the hallway leading to his door and pushed it open. "You wanted to see me?"

Lester looked up from his computer. "Yes. Close the door. Have a seat."

She sat in the chair in front of his ginormous desk and glared at him, holding little regard for what was about to happen next.

Pointing to the morning paper, he said, "That was quite a finish."

Mattie raised her eyebrows expectantly.

Lester leaned forward with his hands clasped on the desk in front of him. "You know, you really had me fooled. Hell, you had everybody fooled. Even Nick."

Here it comes...

"Care to set the record straight?"

"Why? So you can run an exclusive?"

He narrowed his eyes, shook his head, and leaned back in his chair. Using the kindest tone she had ever heard come out of his mouth, he said, "No, Mattie. So you can restore your integrity. Because, for the record, I think it's worth restoring."

She looked at him. For the first time, she didn't see the conniving, manipulative publisher whose sole concern was how many hits her columns got per week. She saw a decent human being who seemed to truly care about her.

Who knew?

"Just a minute." She got up and dashed out to Jessica's cube to retrieve the box of tissues.

Sitting back in her own chair, fully stocked with nose-drying accouterment, she asked, "Where would you like me to start?"

Lester's expression softened, and he smiled. "How about the third grade?"

She told him everything, all the way up to the blowout she had just had with Nick. When she was finished, he frowned and asked, "So all this time, you thought Nick was the bad guy?"

Mattie nodded glumly. "I know. The one man I blamed for ruining my life actually saved it."

If her eyes weren't brimming with tears she would've noticed Lester scribble down what she had just said on a notepad. When he was done, he looked up.

"I think I know a way we can fix this, but first you have to hear the rest of the story."

Mattie shifted in her seat. "I'm listening."

"I don't know if you're aware, but Eduardo DeRosa is number five on the FBI's most wanted list."

Lester proceeded to detail the federal criminal allegations against Eddie, including money laundering and extortion, and the long list of wealthy women he was involved with during their engagement, each of whom filed civil lawsuits against him for fraud and forgery. Facts the *Gazette* had printed in its coverage of Eddie's dramatic disappearance that Mattie chose to ignore when she cut herself off from reality and became the Plate Spinner.

Lester paused and asked, "Does it bother you to hear this?"

While surprised to hear he was in so deep with the feds, she felt somewhat vindicated to learn that he had indeed cheated on her.

She took a deep breath. "No. Go on."

"Now, as you know, Eddie had invited Nick to stay at his place on the night before the wedding and asked him to house sit while you two were supposed to be on your honeymoon. What Nick didn't know was, by the time Eddie handed him the keys to his Ferrari so he could drive to the church in style, Eddie had already swapped their driver's licenses, passports, credit cards, and birth certificates."

"Why didn't Eddie go to the church with Nick?"

"Nick said he offered to drive him, but Eddie begged off saying he had one more errand to run before the ceremony."

"Like flee the country?"

Lester pointed at her. "Bingo. As soon as Nick left for the church, Eddie took Nick's car and drove to Toronto. No one's heard from him since."

He paused. "Still with me?"

Mattie nodded, and he continued.

"Nick, in the meantime, well—he got screwed. First, you deck him at the church, and then the cops arrest him in the emergency room. They hauled him away, and, 'cause Eddie forged his prints when he started at the investment firm, there was no way for Nick to prove he wasn't Eddie without a credible character witness. When he couldn't get hold of his folks, he called you, but you didn't pick up. Didn't reply at all."

Lester gave her a rather unsavory look.

"Go on," Mattie instructed, frowning.

"It took the defense well over a month to get the judge to drop the charges against Nick, but by then, he had lost everything. His place on the team, his endorsements, his money, his friends. He had to start at the bottom of the barrel. And that's where I found him. Coaching cross-country at my kid's high school. Who would've thought? The great Nick DeRosa, the Comeback Kid, coaching high school cross country."

He leaned forward across his desk and asked her, "Do you have any idea how insane that is? That's like finding Derek Jeter coaching peewee T-ball in a suburban park district league."

Mattie squirmed. She knew Nick was good. She just didn't realize how good.

"Well, he loved that job. He told me so himself."

Lester leaned back in his chair. "I know he did. He was great at it, too."

Then he asked something that made the little hairs on the back of her neck stand on end. "So you never heard from Eddie after the wedding?"

She narrowed her eyes. "Why?"

"Because it would make a hell of a story. For the right reporter, that is."

"Ya don't say." She clasped her trembling hands in her lap.

"One of our guys got a lead on a story. Rumor has it Eddie's run out of cash and is getting pretty desperate. The Feds think he might attempt a re-entry to liquefy some assets."

"Holy crap. Do they think he'd actually come back here? To Chicago?'"

Lester pulled a face. "Could be. He had a lot of friends here. It wouldn't be the first time a criminal returned to their old stomping grounds."

It was the first time Mattie heard Eddie referred to as a "criminal." She rather liked it.

Opening his desk drawer, Lester pulled out a business card and handed it to her. "Detective Rohmer was the chief investigator on the case. If you've got any ideas or information, I'm sure he'd be happy to hear it."

Tucking the card in her wallet, Mattie asked, "So you're not going to fire me?"

He shook his head. "To be honest, I could tell something was sizzling between you and Nick from the very first day. I was actually a little relieved to hear you weren't married. That would've been much stickier to deal with. But your readers…"

Mattie sat on the edge of her seat. "What about them?"

Lester grimaced. "Let's just say, some aren't taking it so well."

"So, what now?"

Pulling one side of his mouth into a smile, he shrugged and said, "I'm a firm believer in second chances.

Mattie let out a sigh of relief. "Thank you."

Pointing his finger at her, he added, "Don't get me wrong. You'll still need to make a public apology, and you should expect some backlash. But, it's been my experience, if you're honest with people, you'll win them back. Besides, you still have a marathon to run, young lady."

Mattie started. "But Nick quit."

Lester nodded. "Yes, he did. Damnedest thing, though. He paid back the advances on his bonus."

"What?"

"All he asked was to be reimbursed for the running shoes he got you," he explained with a smile spreading from one end of his mouth to the other.

"I don't understand."

Lester put the picture from the sports section on his desk and turned it in her direction. "They say a picture is worth a thousand words, but I think this one says just three, don't you?"

CHAPTER ELEVEN

———

"Most people run a race to see who is fastest. I run a race to see who
has the most guts."
– Steve Prefontaine

Nick had just finished running five fast miles on the field house track at Knollwood High School to try and clear his head. It had been a month since he had walked out on Mattie, but she was still under his skin, deep and inextricably. Who he thought she was, and who she turned out to be, why she did what she did, and what he was supposed to do about it were just some of the thoughts that kept turning his heart and mind into knots.

He stopped running and walked to his gym bag, catching his breath. Pulling out a towel, he covered his sweaty face and let out a groan.

Gotta get a grip.

Just then, a voice boomed across the cavernous high school field house.

"Mister D."

He turned to see several members of his former cross-country team approaching.

"Hey guys." He blotted his face and neck with the towel. "What are you doing here?"

After shaking hands with some and exchanging several high fives with others, Drew Bates, the team captain, asked, "Practice started a couple of weeks ago. What are you doing here, man? We thought you left us for good."

"Oh, hey, I told you—that wasn't my decision."

At least a dozen skeptical faces stared back.

"You don't believe me?"

"Whatever. Thing is, you gotta come back. Ginsburg's coaching cross-country and he sucks."

This was followed by a chorus of groans.

Nick laughed. "Aw, come on. He's not so bad."

"He's ancient, Coach," Drew pleaded as the other boys fanned out behind him. "We need somebody young. Somebody we can respect. Somebody who cares about us. We want you back."

He handed Nick a stack of papers. "And so do over two thousand other people."

Nick's eyes widened. "What's this?"

"A petition. We're presenting it at the school board meeting tonight. You should be there. Unless you got something better to do."

Scanning the signatures, he recognized several faculty names as well as parents of his former team members.

Who knew?

Wondering what would cause the tide of acceptance to wade in his favor, he asked, "Whose idea was this?"

When no one responded, Nick looked up from the petitions. Scanning the group, he didn't see Bobby Crenshaw, Lester's son.

"Where's Bobby?"

"Orthodontist."

"Was this his idea?"

The boys cast quick glances at each other before responding with a wall of defiant silence.

Smiling, Nick nodded his head. "Once a team, always a team, huh? I get it."

At that, the boys relaxed their stance.

Doubtful that the same school board that ousted him would reinstate him, he told them, "Guys, I'm touched, really, but I'm kinda into something else right now."

He looked into their faces, some hopeful, some already showing their disappointment. At the sound of the Coach Ginsburg's whistle, all but Drew scattered. Taking back the petitions from Nick, he pointed his finger at him and said, "We're still gonna present these tonight. See you at seven. All right?"

"Yoohoo, Coach. Over here." A skinny middle-aged bottle blonde who had spent too much time in a tanning booth waved at Nick from across the park.

As he approached, he clenched his jaw and checked his watch to confirm that he had enough time to meet with the guys at the shelter later.

This was his third session with Paige Sumner, his latest in a string of over-privileged clients and hopefully his last. With her girlfriends continually, and somewhat suspiciously, interrupting their first two workouts, it became clear to him that Paige wasn't as interested in becoming a better runner as she was in being seen running with him.

When a broken nail emergency cut their session mercifully short, he informed her that his services were no longer available.

That night, he pulled into the school parking lot promptly at seven. Well over five hundred parents, faculty, students, and other tax-paying citizens were packed into one of the district's middle school auditoriums. By the time Nick arrived, it was standing room only.

Not wanting to draw attention to himself, he leaned against the back wall not sure what to expect. While most everyone in attendance had their backs to him, one head kept turning around, looking toward the doors.

Bobby Crenshaw.

When Nick caught his eye, he saw him smile and mouth, "Yes."

Paul Quincy, the school board president called the meeting to order. After taking roll and addressing open items from last month's meeting, he asked if there was any new business.

On cue, all of the boys from the cross-country team stood up. Drew raised his hand.

"Mr. Quincy," he started, his voice sounding nervous, but determined, "I have here over two thousand signatures on a petition mandating the reinstatement of Mr. Nicoli DeRosa as coach of the boys' cross-country and track teams at Knollwood High School.

Nick beamed with pride for Drew, a boy who had overcome a severe stutter just a few months into practicing with the team last summer. As the crowd burst into applause, he backed deeper into a shadowed alcove at the back of the room. He wasn't even sure if he should be there. He only came because the boys asked him to.

Paul Quincy, a man nearing sixty with little more covering his head than the beam of the spotlight above him stood and approached the edge of the stage. "May I see the petitions, son?"

As Drew approached the stage, the other boys joined him until they had formed a cluster at the base of the stairs leading up to where the board was seated.

After flipping through the pages, the president turned and handed the pages over to the others. He then leaned over with his none-too-attractive backside facing the audience while they all whispered like crazed conspirators plotting the hostile takeover of a well-stocked ice cream truck.

Unable to see their faces, Nick looked on, amused, yet anxious about the outcome. To steady his nerves, he tried anticipating potential outcomes.

If they reinstate me, I won't have to coach adults and can move on with my life.

If they don't reinstate me, I can always move back in with my folks and figure out what to do next.

But this little exercise didn't seem to work its usual calming magic.

The only thing he knew for sure was that coaching high school boys was a breeze, and he loved it, but it wasn't nearly as great as coaching Mattie had been. Witnessing her transform into someone who felt good in her own skin took what he did for the boys to a whole new level. Especially since it was his own brother who had inflicted her with so much hurt and disappointment.

I just want Mattie.

He took a deep breath to try and push back the ache he felt when he heard, "...the Comeback Kid."

He missed what Mr. Quincy had said before that.

"But according to our bylaws," he continued, "we still need to put it to a vote."

Standing behind the podium, he adjusted the microphone and spoke into it. "All those in favor of re-instating Nick DeRosa to the position of boys' cross-country and track coach at Knollwood High School say 'aye.'"

The walls of the auditorium rumbled as the crowd shouted, "Aye."

Hunched over the microphone, the president stated the obligatory, "All those against reinstating Nick DeRosa, say 'nay.'"

A moment of silence ensued.

"The motion is carried. Let the record show that Nicoli DeRosa has henceforth been reinstated to his former position by a unanimous vote."

Before he had a chance to let it sink in, he heard a voice yell, "There he is."

He had no idea who that voice belonged to.

As people began turning to shake his hand and offer their congratulations, he heard the thumping sound of fingertips tapping against a microphone.

"Hey, Nick, why don't you come on up here and say a few words?"

That voice he knew.

It belonged to Lester Crenshaw.

* * *

The *Gazette* ran Mattie's letter of apology to her readers as a full page ad the week after the race.

Dear Readers:

For almost three years, I have been posing as someone I'm not—a married mom. Please accept my humblest apology.

As the Plate Spinner, I gave advice and tried to build a community in which you could commiserate with other working parents. While I stand behind every single word I wrote, I know I led you to believe that I was someone I'm not.

Your trust is a sacred thing, and I trifled with it. For that, I am deeply sorry.

Aside from your forgiveness, I ask only two things. First, please know that I acted alone. It is my hope that you will still consider the *Gazette* the premier news publication that it truly is. Second, know that I remain fully committed to running the Chicago Marathon. My own effort in this and my pride in Team Plate Spinner were and are completely authentic.

If my actions have in any way prompted you to reconsider your participation in this endeavor, please don't stop on my account. While you would be fully justified in returning or tossing any Team Plate Spinner gear, please do not let what I've done cheat you out of achieving this auspicious goal.

I hope to see each and every one of you at the start line in October.

Sincerely,

Mattie Ross

The only thing more daunting than continuing her marathon training was having to face it alone. The first day after Nick left was the hardest. She arrived at their usual corner at the usual time, half expecting, half hoping, to see him waiting for her; but of course, he wasn't. She waited for fifteen minutes.

When he was a no-show, she took to the path, trying to find her rhythm. Week after week, she kept at it, using a plan she had pulled off the Internet and counting the days until the big event.

"It's like I'm running with one leg," she tried explaining to Claudia while attending her nephew's soccer game over Labor Day weekend.

"You haven't heard from him at all?" Claudia ventured.

"No," Mattie sighed, her eyes welling up behind her sunglasses. "I'd give anything to see him again, Claud. I keep hoping I'll run into him, but I don't. It's like he disappeared."

"Just give him some time, hon. He'll come around," she soothed before yelling at the referee, "Off-sides. That kid was offside. How could you not see that? What are you, blind?"

In late September, Mattie set out for an early morning run. The sunrise over Lake Michigan was hidden behind a thick layer of clouds, and the wind was blowing in from the east.

As she headed north along the lakefront, a cramp started developing on her right side, just under her rib cage, and she heard Nick's voice—his low, encouraging, kind voice in her head.

"You'll be fine. Just breathe through it. Don't focus on it."

A gust of wind, smelling of seaweed and fish, stung her eyes. She slowed to a jog.

"On your left," a deep, husky voice announced from behind her.

A quick jolt of panic shot through her, and she veered out of the way. As she chugged along, a diverse, tattooed, and somewhat menacing crowd of men started passing by. They moved in a synchronized rhythm like a well-practiced military unit, minus the uniforms. Feeling more than a little intimidated, she slowed to a shuffle.

Must get mace.

Just as the last man blew past, he turned and glanced back at her. He looked to be in his late teens or early twenties. His short blond hair and sweet face belied his otherwise intimidating presence.

"Hey. You're that Plate Spinner, right?"

Huh?

She nodded.

"I thought so." He slowed to her pace and said, "You look just like your picture. It's Mattie, right?" he asked as he jogged alongside her.

Again, she nodded, astounded that her readership now included young adult men. "You read my column?"

"Oh, yeah. And Nick's always talking about you."

"Nick?" Her heart raced. "Nick who?"

The young man shook his head. "Not sure what his last name is. We just call him Nick. Or Mr. D. Or Coach."

A smile crept over her mouth.

"Hey guys. It's Mattie the Plate Spinner."

A couple of them turned and waved.

"I can't wait to tell him we ran into you."

"How do you know him?" she panted.

Waving his hand toward the guys running ahead of him, he replied, "He started this group. We're all from the shelter on Fullerton Parkway. Nick volunteers there. A lot. "

Mattie thought for a moment. "Do me a favor, huh?"

"Sure."

"Tell him Mathilde Jean can't find her kick."

The young man frowned and repeated, "Mathilde Jean can't find her kick. Got it."

Not sure he'd follow through, she looked at him and said, "Promise? It's important."

Smiling, he replied, "I promise." After a few more strides, he added, "Hey, maybe we'll see you at the marathon. I'm John, by the way." He held out his hand to her.

"Nice to meet you," she huffed as she shook it.

"Well, I'd better go. I'm gonna lose my team. Catch you later."

She watched as he caught up to his group and waved. "Catch you later."

Certain that John would make good on his promise to deliver her message, Mattie was filled with anticipation. She happily busied herself with helping Nancy sort through the avalanche of recipes that had been pouring in since she had announced the first official "Team Plate Spinner Carb-Loading Recipe Contest." While her numbers had initially dipped at her outing at the half-marathon in July, the bulk of her readers, it seemed, were card-carrying members of Lester's church of second chances.

The top three winners of the contest would have their pictures and recipes printed in the *Gazette's* food section the week before the marathon. The first place winner, however, would also get to have dinner with Mattie at Salvatore's, the exclusive Italian bistro in the city's River North district, the Friday night before the Sunday marathon.

Banking on John delivering her message to Nick, she checked her phone frequently for messages and missed calls as she sifted through every pasta-based dish imaginable.

When her stomach growled, she asked Nancy, "How do you stay so thin? Just reading this is making me hungry."

"You sure you don't want to be a judge? Looks like it's going to be a close competition."

"I can't. It has to be impartial. However, when you're looking for judges for the Christmas cookie contest, you know where to find me," she said with a wink.

By the end of the day, Mattie's cell phone hadn't received a single call or text, and her anticipation fizzled into disappointment.

After work, she left her cool, air-conditioned building behind and stepped into unseasonably balmy air. When she finally made it to her apartment, she was sticky and tired. Her arms full of groceries, she balanced one bag on her knees while she fished in her purse for her keys.

Despite the sauna-like conditions outside, her living room felt tolerable. She had learned soon after she moved in that keeping her shades closed from June to October kept her place from baking.

Eager to take a nice long cool shower, she set the bags and her phone on her kitchen counter and started down the short hall to her bedroom.

If it weren't for the snoring, she would've missed the man sleeping on her living room couch altogether.

Her heart leapt to her throat. She stood frozen, debating which to grab first—her baseball bat or her phone, each in an opposite direction. Gripped with fear, she couldn't quite wrap her head around the fact that the intruder crashed on her couch posed no imminent threat.

After taking a few deep breaths, it occurred to her that the guy might have been out partying into the wee morning hours before mistakenly breaking into her unit while she was at work. She tiptoed over to the couch to get a better look.

Whoever it was had his back to her. Peeking over his shoulder, she saw that his head was partially buried in one of her favorite throw pillows that would now have to be either dry cleaned or disposed of. But she could still make out his profile.

Oh. My. God.

She hadn't laid eyes on him in three years. Still, his hair seemed wilder and more untamed since she had last seen him, and he looked to be sporting a full beard.

Icy cold fingers of panic locked themselves around her neck.

The man rolled over.

Oh God. Oh God.

Her mind raced. The trap had actually worked. Working in concert with Lester and Detective Rohmer of the F.B.I., Mattie had agreed to act as bait. Through some clandestine network that she didn't really want to know about, they put the word out that she had recently come into a large sum of money.

Per the detective's instructions, if Eddie did show up, the first thing she was supposed to do was to call him and then act natural until he showed up with reinforcements. That was well over a month ago. When he didn't reply, she figured Eddie had somehow been tipped off to their ulterior motives. She had nearly forgotten all about it.

Now, she just had to make sure she didn't end up getting caught in her own trap. With no time to lose, she dialed Detective Rohmer's number and set her phone on the kitchen counter next to her still-bagged groceries.

Just as she was about to dash down the hall and grab her Louisville Slugger from under her bed, the man on the couch called out to her.

"Hey, gorgeous."

Her heart pounding, Mattie turned and faced him, making sure she spoke loud enough to be heard on the other end of the line, but not so loud as to raise his suspicions. "Eddie DeRosa. I can't believe my eyes."

It wasn't hard for her to sound genuinely happy to see him. He had greeted her like that so many times before, pretending she was a sight for sore eyes when all he really wanted was a free meal, someone to do his homework while he went out on a date, or somewhere to hide when he was in trouble.

Old habits die hard.

He sat up. The megawatt smile he shot at her fell more than a few amps short, and its affect was far less dazzling than it used to be.

"God, you're a sight for sore eyes."

Bingo.

"It's so good to see you," he blathered. "I've missed you more than you can imagine."

If he had shown up a year earlier, this would've been, hands down, the best day of her life. As it was, all she wanted to do was flatten his head with her cast-iron skillet.

"Uh, how did you get into my apartment?" she asked as if she was just realizing the enormity of his infraction.

He dug into his pocket and held up a key.

She had completely forgotten that she had given it to him. Maybe because he had never used it.

Remembering the detective's instructions, she forced herself to calm down and do whatever she could to stall him. "Oh, right," she chuckled. "My bad. So, how've you been?"

He ran his hands across his face, took a deep breath, and smiled. "I've been better."

Wanting to stay close to the phone, she asked, "Can I get you anything?" She opened her fridge. "Water? Or, um, well, I really don't have anything besides that."

"How 'bout you come over here?" Eddie patted the couch cushion next to him.

Mattie looked at the spot and folded her arms. She had no intention of getting anywhere near him if she could help it. "How about something to eat? You must be hungry."

He stood up.

Maybe it was because her apartment was so small, but he seemed taller than she remembered. And, given his homeless-guy-wearing-Armani look, he was seriously creeping her out.

"Yeah, I wouldn't blame you for being upset," he said. "I hope you can forgive me."

Mattie lifted her chin and did her best to sound perky. "It's been three years, Eddie. Water under the bridge."

Her eyes darted to her phone. She was beginning to wonder if she hit the Talk button. As he edged toward her, she struggled to remember what had attracted her to him in the first place.

"So, what are you doing back in Chicago? Miss the deep dish?"

Eddie looked around her unit. She noticed his gaze hone in on her phone. "I'm meeting up with some old business partners and need a place to stay. You were always after me to spend the night." He held out his hands in front of him and said, "Here's your chance."

Scum. Bag.

She didn't even try to hide the grimace she felt spreading across her face.

In a pathetic attempt to sound coy, he added, "And I'm a little strapped for cash."

She backed up against her kitchen counter.

"You're welcome to stay her for a couple of days, but I'm still paying off the wedding, Eddie. I don't have any money."

Desperate to get her baseball bat, she forced a laugh and said, "I'll go get some sheets."

When she reached over to grab her phone, he caught her arm and pulled her against him.

Putting a hand on either side of her head, he worked his fingers into her hair and breathed, "That's a lie. I happen to know you came into some cash recently. Your Aunt Vivienne, right? I could never stand that old bag. Who knew she was loaded?"

His eyes bore into her as he shoved her back against the counter. He lowered his hands, running them down the length of her neck. "You look so different. Let's say we go into the bedroom and get reacquainted. It's been so long."

Feeling his hot breath on her skin, she shut her eyes. How long had she yearned for this kind of contact with Eddie? How long had she fantasized about him wanting her as much as she wanted him? Now that he was here, all she could think about was Nick.

"Not yet," she urged. "You just got here."

Ignoring her plea, he groped her breasts.

As Mattie tried pushing his hands away, she heard the faint swoosh of the side entrance door opening.

So did Eddie. He froze and asked, "What was that?"

Taking advantage of the distraction, she pushed him off her. He staggered back and leered like a horny frat boy at his first kegger party.

"What's the matter? You don't like my new look?"

Sneering, she replied, "I didn't know snakes could grow beards."

At that, he lunged for her. Lifting her up on her kitchen counter, he started kissing her neck while reaching under her dress.

She tried fending him off with her right hand while she stretched her left hand behind her, grabbing at anything she could use to inflict pain.

Just as he released her to undo his own pants, her fingertips found the perfect deterrent—her two-carat, pear-shaped wedding ring, lying forgotten between her rarely-used toaster and coffee pot.

Slipping it on her finger behind her back, she gave him another hard shove.

Guess all those pushups paid off.

Before he realized what was happening, she slid off of the counter and said, "This is for what you did to me," and kneed him as hard as she could in the groin.

Contorted in pain, he started to crumple in slow motion. When his face was in striking range, she said, "And this is for what you did to Nick."

She cocked her left arm back and slammed her fist against his jaw with everything she had in her.

Eddie toppled back, tripped over her armchair, and landed on her living room carpet.

Better not bleed on it, was her last thought before she felt herself sink to the floor, trembling, and cradling her left hand.

Two police officers had burst through the door, guns drawn, just as she knocked out her former fiancé. Detective Rohmer followed. After checking to see that Eddie was no longer a threat, he knelt before Mattie.

Grabbing a sweater she had draped over the back of her kitchen chair, he wrapped it around her shoulders. "That took a lot of guts, young lady. You OK? Let's take a look at that hand."

When Eddie let out a pathetic moan, Mattie heard the detective call over his shoulder, "Cuff him. And get an ambulance over here."

* * *

By late September, the faces of the residents in Chicago's Wrigleyville neighborhood were already bearing the all-too-familiar "maybe next year" wistfulness of seasons past.

Sitting at a sports bar near Clark and Addison, Nick's friend and former classmate Scott Murphy hypothesized, "Rooting for the underdog, it's who we are. It's what we do."

He held up his bottle. "To the underdogs."

"Underdogs." Nick held up his beer and clinked it against Scott's, his mind elsewhere.

He had paid a visit to the shelter earlier in the day. After accepting Scott's invitation to watch the last Cubs game of the season with him that night, he ran into John, the captain of the shelter's running team.

"Hey, Nick, you'll never guess who I saw today."

"Gimme a hint."

John thought for a minute. "Pretty."

Nick shook his head. "I'm drawin' a blank."

"Uh, runner?"

Narrowing his eyes, Nick repeated, "Runner. A pretty runner. Male or female?"

John made a face.

"Sorry. I'm just messin' with ya. Give me another hint."

Thinking for a minute, John pointed at him and said, "OK, I got it. And if you can't guess after I give you this one, I won't bother telling you what she told me to tell you."

This peaked Nick's interest. Fighting back the urge to grab John by his shirt and shake it out of him, he instead took a deep breath and said, "Gimme the hint."

"Writer."

"Mattie Ross?"

"Bingo, man."

"Where'd you see her?"

"Running on the lakefront. This morning. With the guys. I think we scared her."

In his don't-make-me-hurt you voice, Nick asked, "Why? What did you do?"

"Nothing. It's just—there were a lot of us and just one of her."

Nick had shadowed her most mornings, but not that one. "What's the message?"

"It was weird. Didn't make any sense."

"Tell me."

"Mathilde Jean can't find her kick."

His heart twisted into a knot when he heard it. She needed him, but as her coach or something more?

Hours later, he was still contemplating how to respond to her when Scott nudged him.

"Hey, look. You're on the news."

Nick looked at the flat screen TV over the bar and saw a picture of Eddie in a business suit, then a video clip of him being led away in handcuffs in front of a two-story house tucked next to a gray stone apartment building.

"Jesus," he muttered. "Hey, can you turn that up?" he asked the bartender.

"…most wanted list captured tonight at this near north side residence by none other than Mattie Ross, a member of our very own Griffin Media team. Miss Ross, taken to an area hospital where she is being treated for non-life threatening injuries she suffered in the attack, was unavailable for comment."

"Holy shit," Scott exclaimed.

Nick would've heard him, too, if he weren't already storming out the door.

It had been many months since he got a good look at Mattie's driver's license, but her address was still burned into his brain.

2535 N. Bailey Court, Apt. 2

By the time he arrived, just one squad car remained, and two officers stood next to it, talking. When one of the officers spotted Nick approaching, he immediately reached for his gun.

"Easy. I'm not who you think. I'm his brother. I can prove it."

When he reached for his wallet, the officer barked, "Keep your hands where I can see 'em."

His partner approached Nick and started to frisk him.

With both hands in the air, Nick said, "Check my license. Back pocket. Right side."

After checking his credentials, the first cop to pull a gun on him said, "You're a dead ringer, man."

"Not exactly," Nick replied. "I got this." He pointed proudly to the scar Mattie had given him.

The cop shook his head. "That's not gonna work for you anymore, pal. After tonight, your brother's gonna have the same thing."

Nick shoved his wallet back into his pocket. "Is Mattie all right? Can you tell me where I can find her?"

The second officer responded. "Sorry, we can't give out that information."

Nick looked away for a moment. "Listen, he didn't—? Did he—? Was she—?"

He couldn't bring himself to articulate his greatest fear.

The officer shook his head. "No worries, man. We got there just in time."

"Oh, thank God." Nick ran both hands through his hair.

"She should be fine once they get the cast on."

"Cast?"

"Yeah. She broke three fingers on her left hand when she slugged him. I saw it happen. Knocked him out cold."

Both officers frowned as Nick let out a laugh.

That's my girl.

CHAPTER TWELVE

———

"Life itself is the proper binge."
– Julia Child

After learning what he could about Mattie's condition from the police, Nick's first instinct was to call her sister. Claudia invited him to join her at the hospital. He agreed, but on one condition.

"Don't tell her I'm coming."

Claudia agreed and told him to text her when he arrived.

Hopping into the back of a nearby cab, Nick shot out, "Chicago General."

Having convinced himself for so long that should Eddie ever re-emerge, Mattie would run to him with open arms, he spent the entire ride to the hospital trying to take in what had just happened.

Twenty minutes later he stood in the emergency room full of energy, his mind clearer than it had been in months.

"Hey, Nick."

As Claudia approached, he saw that her eyes were damp and bloodshot, and she looked like she had a bad case of bed head. He could only imagine what kind of condition Mattie must be in.

Alarmed, he gave her a quick hug and asked, "Is she all right?"

Dabbing her nose with a tissue, Claudia declared, "She'll be all right, thank God." Her eyes welling up, she continued with a wobbly voice, "If the police hadn't gotten there when they did, I hate to think what would've happened."

Nick clenched his jaw. The thought of his brother laying a hand on Mattie made his blood boil. He took a deep breath and said with a tight voice, "Well, thank goodness they did, right?"

Claudia nodded. "They just gave her a painkiller, and she went out like a light. I can take her home as soon as she wakes up."

He led her to a couch and sat down next to her. "So what happened?"

Claudia shared as much as she knew. "I had no idea she was working with the FBI to capture him."

In a low voice, Nick reasoned, "I'm sure she didn't want to worry you."

Her eyes welling up, she laughed and said, "Well so much for *that* plan."

Nick looked longingly toward the room in which Mattie was sleeping. "Mind if I check on her?"

Claudia gave him a warm smile. "Not at all. She was calling for you before she fell asleep."

Standing in the doorway of the dimly lit room, he could see that she was partially turned on her side, facing the door. Her left hand was encased in a soft cast that protruded out from under the thin blanket.

He went in and sat on the edge of her bed and brushed away the long curls that had fallen across her face. His heart beat wildly in his chest like it knew it had just located its true owner. A lump formed in his throat. He took her unbandaged hand in his and kissed it.

Mattie's eyes fluttered open. When she whispered his name, a warm wave rushed over him. He cupped her cheek with his hand and said in a rough whisper, "Hey, slugger."

He felt his own eyes well up as he watched a sleepy smile creep over her mouth.

She closed her eyes and sighed, "Love you."

Nick drew in a sharp breath and clutched her hand against his chest.

After a long minute, he leaned down and kissed her cheek. "Get some rest, beautiful."

Stepping into the sterile, brightly lit waiting room, Nick resumed his seat on the couch next to Claudia but turned so he was facing her.

"Listen, Claudia. Since you're the closest thing Mattie has to a parent, there's something I have to ask."

It was close to midnight. Mattie's sister yawned and then sat up a little straighter. "Sure. What?"

He lifted his chin and looked her straight in the eye. "Do I have your permission to marry your sister? If she'll have me, that is."

Raised by old world, old school parents, Nick wanted to do this right.

Claudia blinked and let out a laugh. "Really? Oh my gosh, yes. Of course." When tears started down her cheeks again, she sniffed, "I'm sorry. It's been a long night."

Nick leapt up and grabbed a box of tissues from a table across the room. Once she had calmed down, he filled her in on his plans.

Much to his relief, she was all in.

* * *

Two days later Claudia sat hunched over Mattie's laptop, pecking at the keyboard with her two index fingers.

"Slow down. You're talking faster than I can type."

Mattie rested her head on the back of Claudia's couch. "Sorry. Just read me that last bit again."

"DeRosa, charged with multiple counts of embezzlement, money laundering, home invasion, and sexual assault was taken to the Dirksen Federal Building where he awaits sentencing."

"OK. That's good. Can you email it to Lester, please? His address is in my contact list."

"Sure thing."

"Thanks, Claud. You're the best."

Her sister laughed. "Tell that to your nephews. Hey listen, I'm gonna swing by your place to pick up some more clothes for you and make sure there's nothing rotting in your fridge. You sure you're gonna be OK?"

After nodding her head up and down, Mattie closed her eyes and let the painkillers do their thing. Claudia kissed her on the head, checked on Tom and the kids, and headed out the door.

* * *

The co-conspirators agreed to meet in front of Mattie's apartment. By the time Nick made it to her leafy, well-appointed block, he spotted Claudia sitting on the front porch steps under the shade of a half-green, half-gold sycamore tree.

"Hey, future brother-in-law," she called out, grinning and waving.

Nick grimaced. "Don't jinx it. How's she doing?"

Claudia shrugged. "Pretty sore, but she'll be fine. The doctor said she'll still be able to run the marathon."

"Thought so. Listen, I've got just about everything in place. You sure she doesn't suspect anything?"

"Not a clue. She told me she dreamed that you came to visit her in the hospital."

Nick let out a hearty laugh. "Are you serious? Even after I carried her from the car to your couch and practically tucked her in?"

Claudia scrunched her face and shook her head. "Pain killers. Gotta love 'em. She didn't wake up until eleven the next morning."

As they started up the stairs to Mattie's apartment, she couldn't help but turn and squeal, "I can't wait to see the expression on her face. Oh, and here's the ring. They had to cut it from her finger."

Nick examined it, before shoving it in the front pocket of his jeans. His Uncle Vito knew a guy down on Jeweler's Row who owed him a favor. He just hoped he'd be able to get it back in time.

Claudia unlocked the door and made a beeline for the kitchen. Peeking into the two bags of groceries Mattie had brought home two nights before for anything perishable, she pulled out a ripe bunch of bananas, a mushy bag of previously frozen broccoli, and a package of room temperature chicken breast.

"Ewww." Tossing the last two items into the garbage, she turned and opened the refrigerator. "Did you want to take the yogurt and milk? If not, I'm just gonna dump it."

Nick stood in Mattie's living room, looking around. "Yeah, I'll take it."

"OK, I'm going to grab some stuff from her bathroom."

Following her down the hall, he stepped into Mattie's bedroom. His eyes fell on her bed. Covered with a patchwork quilt, she had four pillows stacked in a heap against the brass spindle headboard.

It looked so Mattie. Comfy and cozy. Rather like how he had come to feel whenever she was around. A pang from deep within tugged at him. It didn't feel right being there without her.

While Claudia pulled pajamas, underwear, shorts, and tops from Mattie's drawers and put them in an overnight bag, Nick walked over to her nightstand and picked up a framed eight-by-ten photo. He remembered exactly when Charlie took it—at the 5k start line. He stared at it, remembering the feel of her face in his hands.

"Nick, I think I found it."

He set the photo down and looked up.

Claudia had pulled Mattie's red sweater dress with a nickel-size hole on the front of it out of the closet.

"Yep, that's the one." He found himself smiling at the memory of their fateful collision. "My mom said she can fix that."

Examining it, Claudia observed, "She might have to take it in for her, too."

Watching as she continued to rifle through the items hanging from the rod, his eyes landed on large rumpled shopping bag tucked in the corner up on the shelf.

Curiosity got the better of him, and he tugged it down.

Looking at the lacy, beaded jumble of white satin bunched inside of it, he sighed, "Thought so."

Claudia looked up at him. "Think your Mom can fix that, too? It's a gorgeous gown."

"Oh, I remember, but let's leave it here. *Really* don't want to jinx anything."

After he shoved it back into place, he said, "I'm good. Let me run the garbage out back, and we can go."

Like a couple of well-intentioned thieves, they locked up behind them and left with their loot.

* * *

A week later, Mattie was back in the office trying to type her last Plate Spinner column with the fingers on her right hand.

"You sure you wouldn't rather dictate that to someone, sweetie?" Dianne asked.

"No, not for this one. It's personal," Mattie winked. "Thanks, though."

"Suit yourself. I absolutely love the pictures you're running with it. Wherever did you get the one of you and Nick when you were kids?"

Mattie pulled up the picture on her screen. "My aunt had it. I don't remember her taking it at all."

Dianne laughed, "Well, no wonder. You don't look at all pleased to be standing next to him. You probably blocked it out of your memory."

Her mother had taken the picture on the night of their parish's fifth grade Christmas pageant. While Mattie, dressed in a white flannel angel costume, posed for the camera, Nick had snuck into the shot, put his arm around her, and plastered a big devilish grin on his face.

"Adorable," Dianne assessed. "Absolutely adorable."

* * *

Two days before the marathon, John was sitting on the steps of the Lincoln Park Community Center reading the *Gazette*, when Nick walked up and asked, "Hey, shouldn't you be at work?"

John stood and shook his hand. "Just got off. How you doin'? Ready for the big day?"

"Absolutely. You sure everything's in place?"

"Are you kidding me? We'll be like a well-oiled machine. Besides, how many runners will there be with casts on their left hands?"

Nick pursed his lips together. "You do realize there will be over thirty-five thousand runners on the course?"

"Between our guys and your Knollwood team, we'll have eyes everywhere. You've got nothing to worry about. Especially after this." He held up the paper.

Nick took it from him. "What?"

"Read it for yourself."

Dear Plate Spinners, With the Chicago Marathon fast approaching, I wanted to take this opportunity to congratulate all of you who have trained with me, cheered me on, and provided me with immeasurable inspiration. I'm truly touched. I'm so proud of each and every one of you who were courageous enough to follow along, smart enough to know that you have to love yourself before you can love anybody else, and loyal enough to stick with me even when I faltered. We've radically changed our lifestyles, pushed ourselves to the limit, and found out that we're made of stronger stuff than we realized. I know when I stand at the marathon starting gate, I'll be thinking about how far I've come, what I lost, and what I found. But most of all, I'll find strength in knowing that I didn't have to travel this road alone. To that end, I want to extend my heartfelt thanks to my coach, Nick DeRosa. Believe it or not, I used to blame him for ruining my life. Now, however, I know that he actually saved it, in more ways than one, and I will be forever grateful.

Right next to the column were two pictures of Nick with Mattie. The first was the one in which he photo-bombed her in the fifth grade. The second was of one Charlie had taken of the two of them before the half marathon.

As he stared at them, John said, "If that's not proof that you two belong together, I don't know what is."

Nick took a deep breath, handed the paper back to him and asked, "Mind if we run through the plan one more time?"

* * *

Late for dinner with the Plate Spinner's Carb-Loading Recipe Contest winner, Mattie played her broken fingers card to hail a cab during rush hour on a Friday night on Michigan Avenue. Within seconds, one zipped to the curb in front of her.

"Delaware and Rush, please."

Between prepping for the marathon and pondering her post-marathon career plans, she didn't check to see who had won the contest. She only knew that Dianne had made the reservation under "The Plate Spinner."

"Can you please step on it? I've got to get there by six."

"Doin' the best I can, lady," the cab driver droned.

Pulling a small notebook out of her purse, she called the assistant food editor.

"Nancy? What can you tell me about the contest winners?"

The cab driver looked at her in his rear view mirror when she raised her voice and said, "I know. I've been a little busy. Can you tell me who won and what their recipes were, please?"

Holding her phone in the crux of her neck, she started scribbling with her right hand while repeating everything Nancy told her.

"Third place. John L., a single dad from Sycamore for his bowtie pasta with prosciutto dish named, 'Hipster Ham.' Seriously? OK, who's next? Second place. Kelly F. from Evanston for 'Pesto Poultry.' Nice. And who am I having dinner with? From Chicago…"

The connection went dead.

"Nancy?"

Mattie growled at her phone and was in the middle of dialing her back when the cab driver announced. "We're here, lady."

Right on time.

After paying the cab driver, she walked through the door a valet held open for her. Dark and intimate with candles on the red-linen topped tables, the interior had a classy, Old World feel to it. Dean Martin crooned in the background.

"Can I help you?" A dark-haired hostess-slash-supermodel asked.

"I have a reservation," Mattie announced.

"The name?"

"The Plate Spinner."

"Oh," she smiled. "Your guest has already arrived. Right this way."

She guided Mattie toward the back of the bustling dining area. As they approached the table, she spotted a petite, fully accessorized woman at a table for two. She had her head bent down as she glanced at a menu, but Mattie could see that her hair was short and dark, peppered with lots of trendy highlights. She wore a tasteful black and gold print blouse and looked to be in her late fifties, early sixties.

Oh, dear God.

Mattie stopped when she reached the table.

Through a forced smile, she managed, "Mrs. DeRosa. How nice to see you again. Congratulations on winning the contest."

Not sure what else to do, she held out her right hand.

The woman accepted it and replied, "Have a seat."

Before Mattie had a chance to drop into a chair, a waiter appeared at her side.

"I am Aldo," he announced with a thick accent and a great deal of flourish. "Would you like a cocktail?"

She looked at Lucy. "What would you like?"

"Already ordered."

Acutely aware of the delicate nature of their imminent exchange, Mattie responded, "I'll have whatever she's having."

After holding her seat out for her and trapping her snuggly under the table, Aldo dashed off and left her alone with her guest.

This is going to be one long night.

Pressing her lips together, Mattie tried smiling and said, "Talk about a small world."

Lucy pulled her attention away from the menu in front of her and looked at her over her reading glasses.

"How's your hand?"

Mattie looked at her cast. "Oh, it's healing."

"No permanent damage?"

"No. I'll probably have some stiffness for a while, but—"

Lucy cut her off. "Glad to hear it."

Mattie narrowed her eyes and bit her bottom lip, trying to discern if the woman sitting across the table loathed her or loved her. She suspected the former.

"Here we are ladies."

Aldo swooped to the table with two ridiculously large wine glasses filled only a fraction of the way.

Mattie breathed a sigh of relief. Wine, she could handle. Hard liquor, not so much.

Lucy took one look at hers and said, "I'll take mine in a Manhattan glass."

He looked at Mattie.

"Ditto?"

Hesitating, Aldo did a quick bow and said, "Yes, of course."

Again, they were alone.

Mattie took a deep breath and made another attempt to break the ice.

"So, tell me about your recipe. Is it an old family favorite?"

Lucy closed her menu and leaned forward with her hands clenched on the table before her.

"So, tell me—are you in love with my son or not?"

Ice broken.

"Excuse me?"

Lucy cocked an eyebrow at her. "You heard me."

Mattie nodded. "Nick. I'm in love with Nick."

She felt her eyes water, but it felt good to say it out loud. It had a liberating affect, even though she had no idea what his mother's reaction would be.

She braced herself, but there was no need.

Aldo returned to their table and deposited two Manhattan glasses filled with chilled Pinot Grigio.

Lucy pulled on his arm before he could get away and, into his frightened face, demanded, "Bring us a bottle."

Addressing Mattie, she said, "So, you want to know about my recipe?"

Mattie nodded.

"Well, technically, it's not mine. It's my mother-in-law's. She gave it to me as a wedding present when Lorenzo and I got married, but the recipe itself is very old, passed down from generation to generation."

What followed was an encapsulated version of the DeRosa family history, dating all the way back to the seventeenth century, complete with territorial land grabs and at least two other instances of sibling rivalry involving love triangles and criminal convictions.

She listened, mesmerized, hoping Lucy didn't ask her about her own broken home and tiny family whose history, as far as Mattie knew, only went as far back as the 1950s when her mother was born.

Two hours later, over espressos and a shared hunk of decadent tiramisu, Mattie was finally able to get a word in edgewise.

"I've got two questions for you."

Lucy pointed to the edge of her mouth to let Mattie know she had a smudge of whipped cream on her lip.

"Go ahead. Ask away."

After a quick swipe of her napkin, Mattie asked, "Who's older—Eddie or Nick?"

"Eddie. By two minutes. And he never missed the chance to rub it in Nick's face."

She stared off into the distance for a brief moment, and added, "When Nick was born, the doctors were sure he wouldn't make it. He was much smaller. He didn't even cry when he came out. We had Father Iuzzi come and gave him Last Rights. We were terrified we would lose him. But, the good Lord had other plans for him."

She paused and made the Sign of the Cross.

"Still, it took Nicky a long time to catch up to his brother, size wise. The whole time, he adored Eddie. He'd follow him around everywhere."

She raised her eyebrow and continued, "But Eddie always resented him. Maybe because Nicky got all the attention when they were babies."

She held up her finger. "But, still, that is no excuse for what he did. Nothing will ever excuse that. But now, thanks to you, maybe he can learn from his mistakes, huh? Mend his ways."

"Yep, he'll have plenty of time to reflect over the error of his ways," Mattie said, thinking of the lengthy sentence the judge had just handed down.

Looking wistful again, Lucy smiled and said, "But, my Nicky. He's a survivor."

Picturing Nick in his running shorts, shirtless, Mattie couldn't help but agree.

"He sure is."

Just as Mattie was about to ask her next question, Lucy looked at her over the rim of her espresso cup and asked one instead.

"So tell me, what makes you think you deserve him?"

Hanging her head, she replied, "I'm not sure I do."

Lucy took a long look at Mattie. "And why's that?"

"He's everything I'm not. He deserves someone as patient and kind and selfless as he is."

His mother shook her head and said, "I think he deserves—well, I think we all deserve someone who's going to rattle our cage and drive us crazy every once in a while. Couples need to push each other to look at life differently so they can grow, not just together, but as individuals, too. Take Lorenzo and me. We go at two completely different speeds. He's always rushing this way and that. Me? I like to take my time. Yet, we complement each other beautifully. Sometimes, he drives me absolutely nuts, and I'm sure I drive him completely bonkers, but still, we love each other with all our hearts."

Mattie wasn't sure if it was the wine or the liqueur from the most excellent tiramisu, but Mattie felt emboldened enough to ask, "Mrs. DeRosa, are you saying what I think you're saying?"

Lucy smiled warmly and asked, "What was your second question, dear?"

* * *

Mattie spent much of the next day resting and hydrating, trying not to dwell on the fact that she would be running twenty-six point two miles the following morning. Still very much hoping to hear from Nick, she couldn't help checking her phone for messages every fifteen minutes despite having the ringer turned all the way up.

When the only phone call she got was from Tom who stopped by to re-wrap her fingers for her on his way home from work, she went to bed that night resigned to going it alone and, no matter the outcome, putting the race and all that led up to it behind her.

The next morning, she woke up well-rested and ready to go. The sky was a brilliant blue, and the high temperature was not expected to top sixty degrees. Perfect running weather.

She took her time putting on her gear—shorts and a tank top covered by a long-sleeved shirt, both emblazoned with Team Plate Spinner.

"Dress in layers," Nick's voice echoed though her mind. "That way, you can just peel 'em off as you warm up."

She clipped a belt with a small pouch on the back for carrying keys, gels, and bars around her waist. Lastly, she pinned her bib on and headed out the door.

Twenty minutes later, she found herself strangely at peace in the middle of the festive chaos welling up in her starting gate.

It was such a beautiful day, and she had no intention of rushing through the event. Unsure of what lay before her afterwards, she just wanted to finish, no matter how long it took. While she had declared her love for Nick to Lucy, she did not reciprocate on his behalf.

As it was, her heart was all sorts of empty.

An air horn blast sliced through the air, and the runners burst forward. Mattie found her stride early on and just kept with it through most of the relatively flat course. The twenty-mile training run she had completed a few weeks back wasn't anywhere near as difficult as she expected, so her hopes were high that she would be able to complete the marathon in a relatively decent time.

After passing the first few water stations, she grabbed a cup at four miles from a nice boy wearing a Knollwood Knights T-shirt, a detail that didn't register in her brain until she hit the next water station at mile eight.

Another Knollwood Knight, but this one was talking on his cell phone.

Huh. Must be some kind of service project.

By mile twelve, the soft cast on her hand started to itch. By mile fourteen, she was ready to rip it off. By mile seventeen, she did, revealing her three taped fingers. The relief was exquisite.

* * *

Nick paced back and forth near the finish line, trying to hear what Drew Bates, his team captain stationed at mile eighteen, was saying.

"Sorry, coach. I didn't see her."

"She should've passed by there at least twenty minutes ago," he shouted over the din of excited spectators. Then, after nodding, he added, "OK, check with Pete for me, would ya, and then call me back."

"Everything OK?" Claudia asked.

"Naw, the guys lost her after mile sixteen. Drew's gonna check with Pete at nineteen."

He ran his hands over his face. "This waiting is killing me."

Claudia gave his arm a squeeze. "Everything's gonna be fine. She'll turn up. The runners are really starting to thin out as they come up the straightaway."

"I just hope nothing bad happened. Maybe her hand got to be too much?" he shot her an anxious look.

Claudia laughed. "Relax. She's not gonna let a couple of broken fingers stop her now."

But Nick couldn't. Staring down the gaping expanse of the straightaway stretching out before them, he said, "I've got John, one of my guys from the shelter, waiting at twenty-one. I figure that's when she's gonna need a buddy to keep her going."

"Can he just jump on the course like that?"

"I registered him. He's got a number. He'll just look like he's getting back on the course from a water stop or bathroom break."

Nick checked his stopwatch for the hundredth time when his phone rang.

"Yeah?" he barked into the phone.

Sticking his finger in his other ear so he could hear, he listened for a minute then shouted, "All right. Great."

When he hung up, he shot both arms in the air. "She just started mile twenty."

He quickly dialed John's number. "Get ready, man. She's coming."

* * *

Jogging at a steady pace through Chicago's ethnic neighborhoods, Mattie tried to be in the moment, notice her surroundings, and enjoy the experience. She was in the zone, not thinking about her past, present or future. The fwap-fwap of hundreds of shoes hitting the pavement lulled her into a meditative state.

After grabbing more water at mile twenty from another Knollwood Knight, she had just turned east on 33rd street when she heard footsteps dash up next to her.

"Hey, Plate Spinner," the man panted.

Surprised, Mattie turned her head to see the guy from the shelter she had met on the path a couple of weeks back. "John. Hi."

After a few more paces, she exclaimed, "How'd you find me?"

He looked straight ahead and smiled. "Would've found you sooner if you kept your cast on."

"What?"

He didn't respond.

Still, she was happy to have a companion, even though she doubted her ability to carry on much of a conversation.

They curved south onto State Street where the crowds of spectators were beginning to thicken. She was still feeling good. But by the time they curved left and started north on Michigan Avenue, the familiar finish line panic started bubbling up inside of her.

"How much farther?" she asked John. "I gotta see the finish line."

"About two and a half miles, I think," he panted next to her. "You can do it."

"Ok, ok." She wiped her brow and focused on the road in front of her. After what seemed like an hour, they passed the twenty-four mile marker.

Just put one foot in front of the other. You can do this. You can do this.

When she saw the twenty-five mile marker, all her happy self-talk abandoned her.

"I can't do this," she gasped, her voice strained with anxiety.

"Sure you can," John laughed, "if you tell yourself you can't, you won't."

He was channeling Nick.

They turned east onto Roosevelt Road. This slope in the road had tried to claim her before. She worked hard to remember that she had already conquered it.

Chugging along, Mattie asked, "Hey. Did you give Nick my message?"

John didn't answer until they took a left on Columbus Drive. The finish line was several yards ahead of them.

"What do you think?"

Mattie could no longer feel her feet, but her heart leapt.

Through her sunglasses, she peered ahead, scanning the mass of people lining each side the course, all yelling and cheering. But she didn't see him.

"Where?" she gasped.

"There," John pointed to an area just beyond the finish line that was clear save for a few race officials.

And Nick.

He was standing there, in his coach clothes, complete with a stopwatch, shaking his head back and forth. If it weren't for the grin on his face, she would've thought he was still angry with her.

Cupping his hands around his mouth, he yelled, "You call that a kick? Have I taught you nothing, Mathilde Jean?"

She let out a laugh. She squeezed John's hand and, summoning the last ounce of energy she had in her, she rushed to the finish line. After she crossed it, she put her hands on her hips and walked towards him.

"Seriously?" she panted. "How many times do I have to tell you not to call me that?"

Handing her an open water bottle, he walked alongside her and asked, "OK, how 'bout M.J.?"

She took a long swig of her water. "M.J. Ross? Nah, I don't think so."

"How about M.J. DeRosa?" He stopped and faced her, taking her hands in his.

Mattie gasped. She was still sweating, but somehow trembling at the same time. When she noticed several familiar faces come out of the crowd, she covered her mouth with her hand. Claudia and Tom, Lucy and Lorenzo, Dianne, and John, along with several guys from the shelter and several members of Nick's Knollwood Knights cross-country team, all stood nearby, smiling ear to ear.

With hundreds of spectators and runners looking on, and Charlie Clarke clicking his camera all around them, Nick knelt down before Mattie right there in the middle of Columbus Drive.

Looking up at her, he asked, "Mathilde Jean Ross, will you marry me?"

Blinking back the tears, Mattie took a deep breath and replied just loud enough for the hundreds of spectators to hear, "Yes, Nicoli Giovanni Francesco DeRosa, I will marry you."

Laughing, Nick stood, his own eyes watering. Gently taking the bandaged fingers of her left hand in his, he pulled a reset and resized diamond ring from his pocket that he had threaded with a red, white, and blue Olympic medal ribbon and placed it over her head.

The crowd burst into applause.

Before she could even catch her breath, he locked his mouth onto hers in a kiss.

Then he lifted her into his arms and posed for a picture that ran on the *Gazette's* front page the very next day under a headline Lester himself had readied weeks before: "Comeback Kid Wins Marathon Mattie."

ABOUT THE AUTHOR

Barbara is an award-winning novelist and second-generation journalist. After spending a decade in maternity clothes, she has five boys to show for it and much fodder for her column, The Plate Spinner Chronicles, a long-running feature in the *Chicago Tribune*. A member of RWA's Windy City chapter, she still dreams of the day when her to-do list includes "Send NY Times book critic thank you note" and "Accept Godiva's request to be a taste-tester."

To learn more about Barbara Valentin, visit her online at:
http://www.barbaravalentin.com

Enjoyed this book? Pick up the next Assignment: Romance novel from Barbara Valentin!

Help Wanted

**an
Assignment: Romance
novel**

available May 14!

When Claire Nelson decided that her happily-ever-after lay not in marriage but in a spot on the New York Times bestseller list, she vowed never to tie the knot. But that was before she met Paul Mendez, handsome and charming enough to have her breaking said vow and marrying him shortly after college.

Almost fifteen years and four sons later, Claire is now a burned out breadwinner ready to ditch her quest for happily-ever-after, and Paul has traded his dream of chairing corporate board meetings for volunteering at PTA meetings as a stay-at-home dad. Feeling trapped in a demanding job, Claire's repeated attempts to get Paul to return to work fall flat. Contemplating divorce, she drafts a letter to the Plate Spinner, a popular advice columnist, asking for help. But when the reply contains an offer that may just put her bestselling author dreams back on track, Claire's only question is: will Paul be on board? Or does her charming husband make a surprise move of his own?

www.GemmaHallidayPublishing.com

48372635R00131

Made in the USA
Charleston, SC
02 November 2015